Praise for the Danvers Novels

"Enough bittersweet longing to pluck your heartstrings and enough heat to keep it interesting."
—*Kirkus Reviews*

"Wonderful . . . Landon's foray into contemporary romance has just the right amount of angst, sass, sexiness, humor, and, of course, romance."
—Fresh Fiction

"If you like the Cinderella-style story, this modern-day version is sure to be a hit."   —Once Upon a Twilight

D0040306

Room for *Two*

THE BREAKFAST IN BED SERIES

SYDNEY LANDON

JOVE
New York

A JOVE BOOK
Published by Berkley
An imprint of Penguin Random House LLC
375 Hudson Street, New York, New York 10014

Copyright © 2018 by Sydney Landon
Excerpt from *Keeping It Hot* copyright © 2017 by Sydney Landon
Penguin Random House supports copyright. Copyright fuels creativity, encourages diverse
voices, promotes free speech, and creates a vibrant culture. Thank you for buying an
authorized edition of this book and for complying with copyright laws by not reproducing,
scanning, or distributing any part of it in any form without permission. You are supporting
writers and allowing Penguin Random House to continue to publish books for every reader.

A JOVE BOOK and BERKLEY are registered trademarks and the B colophon
is a trademark of Penguin Random House LLC.

ISBN: 9780399587405

First Edition: February 2018

Printed in the United States of America
1 3 5 7 9 10 8 6 4 2

Man walking with document © 4x6/iStock photo
Woman on lounger © Kudia/Shutterstock
Pool and sun umbrella © gunnarAssmy/iStock photo
Water © wavebreakmedia/Shutterstock
Cover design by Colleen Reinhart
Book design by Laura K. Corless

For Alyssa

One

"What an asshole!" Dana Anders huffed in exasperation to her boss and best friend, Zoe Jackson. The fact that she was referring to Zoe's brother-in-law, Asher, didn't concern her in the least. If there was one rule in this world, it was that you always had your friend's back, even when it got tricky. "Since when is it acceptable to ask a woman if she shops in the teen plus-size section? He certainly knows how to multitask because he got in a dig at both my height and my weight."

"I swear, I don't know why he acts like that towards you." Zoe grimaced as they both watched Ash walk out of Zoe's Place. Dana had been the manager of the popular hotel coffee shop for several years now, and it was the best job that she'd ever had. She loved meeting all the new people that passed through the luxury Oceanix-Pensacola Resort as well as chatting with the regulars who came in daily. She was a people person, so the work suited her perfectly. At least it had until the moment when Asher decided to relocate from the Oceanix-Charleston to their Florida location. Dana normally got along with everyone—she had really never met anyone who didn't like her, so at first the animosity Asher leveled her way was puzzling. Then it finally began to piss her off. What had she ever done to the man to deserve his scorn? It was as if he'd decided within an instant of making her acquaintance that he didn't like her, and his attitude toward her had only gotten worse. But the most galling part of the entire situation was that although she gave as good as she received where he was concerned, she could admit, just to herself, that she was wildly attracted to the jerk. A humiliating fact she prayed he never discovered.

"Because he's compensating for his shortcomings by being a turd," she snapped. "I know the man is your brother-in-law, but I think you would have to agree with me on this one. He's never had one civilized word to say to me. What is his problem?" Dana inwardly winced when her question came out sounding more hurt than ticked off. The last thing she wanted getting back to Ash was that his behavior was hurting her. Well, that and the fact that she dreamed of him ripping her clothes off and taking her on the counter of the coffee shop. She suspected her boss would not approve of that particular fantasy either, although she was certain that Zoe and her husband, Dylan, had probably succumbed to it more than once. Speaking of Dylan, he was another Jackson brother with whom she hadn't particularly bonded. Although in their case, the verbal sparring was more like that of siblings, rather than the more insulting variety she participated in with his brother.

Dylan had thought that Dana was a bad influence on Zoe when Dylan and Zoe had finally started to date after years of platonic friendship. In the end, though, Dylan had married the woman he loved, and since the wedding he had mellowed a lot. Nevertheless, he still went through the motions of arguing with Dana just for fun. It was something they both enjoyed.

Zoe laid a hand on Dana's shoulder and squeezed it in commiseration. "I honestly don't know," she admitted. "I've asked Dylan about it more than once and he says that it's really out of character for Ash. He's normally very charming where the opposite sex is concerned, so we're both rather puzzled over it. Maybe I should talk to him," she began, before falling silent as Dana vigorously shook her head.

"No way. I won't let him have the satisfaction of thinking he's getting to me. Imagine how much that discovery would thrill him. You never give a bully that kind of power."

Zoe picked up the latte that Dana had made for her earlier and took a sip. "So what are you going to do then?" She gave her a look full of sympathy before adding, "I can tell that he's hurting your feelings. I've wanted to beat the crap out of him myself even though he's not saying that stuff to me."

Stiffening her spine, Dana brushed a hand down her black apron and tossed her head defiantly. "It's about time I started fighting fire with fire. If he can come into my place of business and insult me every day, then maybe I need to level the same treatment at him."

Zoe gave her a skeptical look before asking, "What exactly does that mean? You two already bicker when he's here. It's not as if you're just standing around taking it from him."

"True," Dana agreed, nodding, "but he gets the last word in because he is free to walk out the door whenever he wants. Since I'm always in the middle of my shift, I can't exactly follow behind him."

"You could signal me if I'm here so that I can take over for you," Zoe suggested helpfully. Dana thought to herself—not for the first time—that she'd hit the lottery in the boss department. Not many business owners would volunteer to cover for their employee so she could follow a customer out the door to continue an argument. Especially when she was now related by marriage to the other person. Zoe rocked, as a friend and as a boss.

Giving her first real smile of the day, Dana shook her head. "That's not necessary, but I absolutely love you for offering. No, what I had in mind was to give him a taste of his own medicine. He orders lunch and coffee from here almost daily. So from now on, I think I'll make that delivery myself instead of having one of the girls take care of it."

Dana saw the exact moment that the lightbulb went on above Zoe's head. Her friend's lips twitched before a loud giggle escaped. "That's rather brilliant, I have to admit. You're gonna bring the battle to his doorstep. Crap, I'd love to be around to see that the first time. He won't be expecting it."

"No, he won't." Dana offered an evil grin. "Of course, it'll only be a surprise once, but if I play my cards right, it'll make such a big impression that he'll think twice about opening his mouth to say anything to me other than a polite 'How are you today?'"

Cringing slightly, Zoe looked at Dana before saying, "I feel as if I should warn my husband out of loyalty.

I mean, it is his office that you're declaring war on."
When Dana narrowed her eyes at her friend, Zoe
laughed and held up one hand. "All right, my lips are
sealed. I'm sure Ash will tell him all about it after your
first delivery anyway. Plus, Dylan's brother seriously
needs to learn some manners."

They did a fist bump before getting back to work.
After that, the rest of the day passed by quickly as
usual, and when Dana left for home that afternoon, it
was one the few times since Asher Jackson had arrived
on the scene more than a year ago that she had pep in
her step. She had a war to wage tomorrow, and she
found that she was beyond excited to deliver some
justice to Ash along with his usual sandwich. Hell hath
no fury like a woman called "fat" by a man.

∽

When Asher Jackson's stomach growled yet again, he
glanced at his watch, wondering what was taking so
long for his food delivery. Since Zoe's Place was located in the same hotel, the service was usually very
fast. But it had already been almost an hour and
he was starving. He'd had a clingy one-night stand
the previous evening and he'd been determined not
to provide breakfast and mixed signals. When you
cooked for a woman, they made a lot of assumptions.
Usually he cleaned out the refrigerator before he went
out on the prowl. He didn't even keep cereal in his
cabinets. He'd made that mistake before and had a
woman eat that stuff dry when he'd told her he was
out of milk. Now he knew never to underestimate
a woman looking to make what was supposed to
be a brief sexual encounter into something more.

Truthfully, he discouraged women from staying over, but it had been so late by the time they'd made it to his place and the deed was done, that he'd just crashed instead of dealing with the awkward showing her the door routine.

Turned out he'd made a mistake by delaying that and giving them both a few hours of sleep. When he'd woken up, Betsy, Betty, or whatever her name was had been wandering around his apartment in one of his T-shirts while flipping through a family photo album. He'd had a creepy feeling that she was looking at his boyhood pictures and dreaming about what their future children would look like. She'd even motioned him over and quizzed him about his attractive female cousins featured in some of the pictures. He'd thought he was imagining the tension in her voice until he noticed her eye twitching. *Danger!* He'd been with his share of crazy chicks before and he knew the signs. So he'd made up something about an early meeting and literally dressed her before pushing her out the door. Afterward he'd found her name and number written in lipstick on his bathroom mirror with a big heart drawn around them. The same information had also been left duct-taped to his refrigerator door.

What he wanted to know was where in the hell had she gotten duct tape and what kind of person put that on top-of-the-line stainless steel? He'd barely gotten over that audacity when he'd returned to the bedroom to find more writing on the mirror in his closet and then later on his dining room window. Fuck, had she been raised in a barn? He was still trying to wipe the bright red stuff off when his housekeeper, Rosa, had arrived. She'd taken one look and connected the dots perfectly. She'd been with him less than a year, but the woman seemed to know everything and she damn sure wasn't shy about sharing her opinions with him.

"Pissed off another one, huh, Romeo? I hope this girl didn't cut holes in your expensive sheets or pee on your bath towels. That girl sure had a bladder on her. She nearly soaked through those extra-fluffy ones. Where do you find these women anyway? Have you considered taking out a personal ad? E-Harmony is supposed to run background checks, aren't they?" Without waiting for him to answer, she'd rolled her eyes and shook her head in disapproval. "No, that won't work. You need a service that runs an in-depth psych check. And probably not before you sleep with them. Because they're mostly normal at that point. But you do something during the hour or so that you let them stay to push them over the edge. If you ever decide to see one a second time, by some rare miracle, that's when the evaluation is needed." She had walked up to him with a bottle of Windex in her hand and pushed him to the side. "You do realize that crazy is just as contagious as a bad case of the flu, right? You keep dragging these nut jobs home and eventually I'm gonna walk in one day to find you sitting in the middle of the floor spinning a plate and clapping your hands together like that Sybil woman."

Rubbing his throbbing head, Ash had asked, "Who in the hell is Sybil?" He almost dreaded hearing the answer. He also wasn't brave enough to tell his rather intimidating housekeeper that if crazy was catching, he'd probably get it from her before anyone else.

She'd clucked her tongue as if he'd committed some grievous error. "That old movie where Sally Field had all of those personalities. That girl didn't know if she was a boy or a girl or what age she was. She was up, down, and all over the place."

Confused, Ash had asked, "What's that got to do with spinning plates? Have you been smoking your husband's medical marijuana again?"

Rosa poked her surprisingly bony finger into his side. "I know you were doing God knows what all night, but try to keep up. In the movie, Sybil sat on the floor while spinning a plate and clapping her hands. Bat-shit crazy, she was. That could be you one day if you aren't more selective about your women friends. Why can't you follow your brother's example and find a good girl like Zoe?"

Ash didn't bother to point out that she'd avoided his question about the marijuana. Rosa and her husband, Ted, reminded him of old-school hippies. He was almost certain there was some pot smoking happening at their house on a regular basis. He'd been around his share of weed, so he knew it wasn't weird perfume that Rosa reeked of occasionally. He didn't judge though. When she wasn't giving him hell, she made his life easier. Plus, he found he enjoyed these wacky conversations with her. She'd also shown more than one clinger to the door for him the next morning and that right there was more than enough to earn her a job for life. Hell, he'd make her employee of the month if there was anyone else for her to compete against. As it was, he paid her double the going rate for housekeeping and gave her generous benefits. Okay, so maybe she'd demanded all of that, but he'd given in quickly. She didn't need to know that he was a tad bit scared of her. "Zoe's one of a kind," he admitted truthfully. He was half in love with his brother's wife and wasn't shy about telling Dylan as much on a regular basis. Dylan just laughed it off because he had no worries where she was concerned. They were sickeningly in love with each other, and there was zero chance of either one of them ever straying.

"Yeah, you got that right," Rosa had agreed. "But surely she has some friends or maybe a sister. Someone who thinks that having good morals means waiting until the soup course before dropping their underwear."

Ash couldn't help it—he threw his head back and laughed. Damn, he loved the shit that came out of her mouth. If he could find a younger and hopefully more attractive version of his housekeeper, he'd damn well marry her. Considering the amount of stolen and damaged items that women had taken or destroyed through the years, he'd save a small fortune. Not to mention he'd sleep better knowing he wasn't going to take up a starring role in his own *Fatal Attraction* movie. Fuck, he had nightmares about psycho chicks standing over him with sharp objects while he slept. "I'm pretty sure that Zoe has already warned all of her friends about me, so I don't think there's any chance of that." The words had barely left his mouth when an image of Dana suddenly filled his mind. He squeezed his eyes shut, trying to block her out. The woman irritated the hell out of him on a daily basis, so it was beyond him why he spent so much time thinking about her. He'd never admit it, but a lot of the thoughts were regret over nasty things he'd said to her. Women loved him because he was full of compliments and charm. But around her, for some inexplicable reason, he turned into some school-yard bully. It was as if he was standing on the outside watching a stranger say all of that shit to her. But no matter how many times he promised himself that he'd do better, he never did. Within seconds of being in her company, he would unleash another volley of insults. The whole thing might have gotten old enough to put behind him by now if she didn't rise to the occasion so well. There were a few times that he thought he might have seen what looked like hurt in her eyes when they had gone a little too far, but it had vanished so quickly he'd convinced himself that he'd imagined it. Even his brother, who had a similar relationship with her, had pointed out more than once that he needed to back off before she either killed him or quit her job. If the latter happened, Zoe would make both Dylan's and Ash's lives a living hell.

Almost as if he'd conjured her from his thoughts, the object of his ire strolled into his office like she owned the place. He shook his head, thinking he was still in his apartment talking to Rosa that morning, but no . . . she was standing in front of his desk with her hands on her hips and a smug expression on her plump lips. *This ain't good*, he thought before gathering his wits and leveling a sarcastic smile her way. "You here to take me up on that offer to help you dress for your . . . size?" He'd made references to her lack of height and her stocky frame on his last round of taunts. Then offered to take her to Build-A-Bear for a new outfit. Yeah, it had been an asshole thing to say, but it was better than her discovering that she actually turned him on more than anyone had in years. He couldn't give her that kind of power. *When did I turn into such a drama queen?* He liked tall, leggy women with long, flowing locks. Not petite spitfires with short hair and a bad attitude. She was not his type at all and he'd never been with a woman like her . . . Well, there had been one woman, but that had ended badly years ago. They stared at each other for a long moment, and he felt sweat begin to gather on his brow when she showed no outward indication that his words had struck a nerve. Instead, she moved forward as if she didn't have a care in the world and placed a white bag carefully in front of him.

"Here's your lunch, Mr. Jackson. I'm sorry about the wait. The shop has been really busy this morning and we're short staffed. I added a few of those chocolate chip cookies that you like so much to make up for it."

What in the hell is her play here? Cookies? What a bitch! Okay, so maybe that last part was a bit irrational, but how dare she come up to his office—his sanctuary—and be all nice to him? That wasn't the unspoken dynamic that they'd agreed on. Being civil to each other had no place in their relationship. Dammit, he knew he was staring at her with a confused expression on his face. He needed to come up with a clever retort, but he was drawing a blank. The fact that she continued to smile at him sweetly wasn't making it any easier. *Think, man. Say something, anything.* "Um . . . thanks, Dana." Shit, he'd called her by her actual name and been courteous. He was really making a mess of the whole situation.

"Of course, Mr. Jackson." Then she further freaked him out by winking at him before adding, "There's plenty more cookies where those came from. I'll bring you some by soon." She turned for the door, giving him a perfect view of her delectable ass in the snug black slacks she was wearing. *I like big butts and I can not lie.* Then she busted him staring at her gorgeous backside when she looked over her shoulder suddenly. "Have a great day." With a twitch of her lips that let him know she'd caught him eyeing the goods, she left as quickly as she'd arrived. *What in the fuck just happened?* Ash slumped back into his chair feeling drained from the bizarre encounter. Truthfully, he'd have thought nothing of the exchange with one of the other ladies that usually delivered his food, but from Dana, it was off-the-charts weird. He had no idea what had changed, but he was uncomfortably aware that she'd somehow turned the tables on him. For if he wasn't mistaken, she'd declared war on him with—niceness. Who in the hell did something that awful? He eyed the bag on his desk as if it were a snake before grabbing it and tossing it in his trash can. There was no way he could risk eating that now. Okay, well, maybe the cookies were okay. He'd just get those out and have them for lunch. Then he'd do his best to figure out what had gone wrong. He needed to be prepared for the next attack. Hell, she'd probably do something horrifying like hug him, and that was simply unacceptable.

ॐ

Dana walked out of Ash's office and almost collided with Dylan's assistant, Lisa Merck. The other woman threw her hands up in the air as she asked, "What was that? I thought you were really going to give it to him. But you were so pleasant it made me gag."

Patting Lisa's shoulder, Dana winked before saying, "I came up with a better plan. He gets off on being a bully and arguing with me. I decided to take that option away and see how he handled it."

"And?" Lisa asked impatiently. "It sounded as if you are best friends now. Not that I was listening or anything. Just guessing."

Dana smirked, knowing damn well that Lisa had been eavesdropping. She'd practically fallen in the door when Dana had opened it. She didn't blame her though. She'd have done the same thing. "I had an epiphany seconds before I planned to go on the attack. Ash likes being an asshole to me. If I had gone in there with guns blazing, then he would have risen to the occasion. Sure, I may have gotten in a few verbal slaps, but as always, he'd have won the battle. Then I would have been forced to slink away once again with my tail tucked between my legs. But by being the exact opposite of what he was expecting, it threw him off his game. He was rattled and didn't have a clue as to how to respond, which is a first for him where I'm concerned." Bouncing on her heels in excitement, Dana added, "I was the one in control from beginning to end and he knew it."

Looking skeptical, Lisa asked, "So, what . . . you're going to be nice from now on? You know he'll be prepared for that next time. I don't think it'll work again."

Shaking her head, Dana said, "No, that's exactly what I won't do. I learned something today. Ash is used to people being predictable. And I've been playing right into his hands by doing the same thing every time. I toss out a few insults, then stomp off in a huff. So from now on, I have to keep him guessing. I want him so twisted up in the game that he doesn't know

which end is up. That's the only way to engage an
enemy like Ash and come out victorious. He needs to
be so rattled that he takes a deep breath before he
walks into the shop. I want him as uncertain as I've
felt every time he's around. I took his power today and
I'm keeping it. I'm no longer going to be pushed around
by Asher Jackson. The king has been dethroned and I
intend to make sure he stays that way."

Pursing her lips, Lisa looked thoughtful for a moment before nodding her head in approval. "I like it.
That's the beauty of men. They never expect a woman
to attack, especially when it's not physical. You gotta
love 'em, it's so easy to play mind games with them.
They take everything so literal. I have to admit, sometimes I do similar stuff to my poor husband when he's
made me mad. And even after all these years, he never
sees it coming. It almost takes the fun out of it when I
have to point it out to him. Men simply can't think
outside the box where we're concerned. They constantly underestimate us. Unless you're throwing a
physical punch, it sails right over their head."

Nodding, Dana grinned. "I personally hope that
never changes. I swear, I almost lost it when I saw the
look of utter confusion on Ash's face before I left. He
honestly had no clue what to do or say and the man
has never been at a loss for words around me before."
Sniffling dramatically, she added, "It was one of the
most beautiful moments of my life."

"Then you really need to get out more," Lisa
snorted. "But the man had it coming. I really have no
clue why he treats you that way. He's never said anything remotely insulting to me or any of the staff in
the office. Half of the women are in love with him. He's

practically the golden boy. Dylan comments on it all the time. His brother is the Casanova of the Oceanix. But the man turns into Satan when he sees you, which is just bizarre. And from what I've gathered, it's been that way from the beginning."

Dana's shoulders slumped as she admitted, "It has, and I'd give anything to understand it. Other than Dylan, I've never had this effect on a man. The difference with the brothers though is that Dylan and I both know it's a game that we enjoy. But with Ash, it's plain dislike. It's as if I offended him before we ever met, which is impossible. We'd never crossed paths until the day we first met in the coffee shop. The times that he'd visited the resort previously, we had no interaction. Hell, considering how Dylan looks, I was excited to meet his brother. And drool was practically running down the corners of my mouth when he walked into the shop. Then he looked at me as if I was dirt beneath his feet before turning and stalking away. That set the tone for our entire relationship. Well, actually I could have lived with the silent disdain, but when he opened his mouth on the next visit, I learned it was possible to despise a man who looks like sex on a stick."

Quirking a brow, Lisa asked, "So do you think it would be easier to deal with if he were ugly as opposed to hot?"

"Hell yeah," Dana hissed. "If he were some kind of troll, I wouldn't get tongue-tied when he launches a verbal grenade. I mean, he's telling me I have a haircut like a dude and I'm so caught up staring into those blue eyes that he has to repeat the insult a few times until it gets through. I've never let a man make me feel this self-conscious, dammit. Not bragging, but if they have a penis, then they usually act interested around me."

Snapping her fingers, Lisa said, "Maybe he's gay. That could be the answer to the whole mystery."

Shaking her head, Dana sighed, "No, I already thought of that. According to Zoe, who got the information directly from Dylan, Ash has plenty of bed buddies and they're all female. I have to accept that it's simply me that he loathes."

"Well, if it's any consolation, I think you're on to something with the whole niceness thing. If you can manage to continue doing it without puking, then you might be able to even the playing field."

Perking back up, Dana gave Lisa a high five and then hurried back toward the shop. When she got there, Zoe was sitting at a nearby table with her husband. Normally Dana would have walked over and traded a few barbs with him, but her heart wasn't in it today. So, instead, she waved in their direction and walked behind the counter to help out with the lunch crowd. Despite the activity around her, a certain dark-haired, blue-eyed jerk remained on her mind for the rest of the afternoon. She vowed that, no matter what, she'd find out why the man detested her so much. After all, she had plenty of time on her hands; the opposite side of her bed had been vacant so long there were practically tumbleweeds sitting atop the sheets. *I need to get laid,* she decided. *That's the only way I'll get him out of my head.*

Two

Dana carefully juggled a pizza in one hand and her keys in the other as she finally managed to get the door to her apartment open without dropping everything. After a long day, she hadn't been in the mood to cook so she'd opted for takeout instead. Of course, she had a hard time enjoying calorie-laden meals with Ash's pointed insults always fresh in her head. And for someone who loved food as much as she did, that seriously pissed her off. She knew she wasn't overweight. But at just a few inches over five feet, she had to be careful about her indulgences. As long as she exercised on a regular basis, she could enjoy her food in moderation without having to feel too deprived. She wasn't skinny by any means. She had curves and she'd learned to embrace them. This wasn't a one-size world. As long as you were healthy and comfortable in your own skin, that was all that mattered. She'd certainly never had a man complain before. Hell, self-confidence hadn't been something she'd had an issue with since high school when she'd been the victim of bullying by a group of mean girls. But Ash had brought all of those old fears back with some well-placed barbs. Damn him for that. It had taken her ages to build her self-esteem back after those difficult teenage years.

As close as she was to Zoe, even her friend didn't know about that time in her life. It was too humiliating to admit that she'd let that happen without sticking up for herself more. And with Ash, she appeared to be allowing the pattern to repeat. It seemed so different this time though. They were adults, for God's sake. From all indications, he was normally a nice, well-regarded man. Certainly not the type to indulge in such hateful behavior. Although his insults weren't as malicious as those of her former tormentors, they struck a tender nerve just the same. She'd been at a loss as to how to deal with it since the beginning. She knew that arguing with him wasn't the answer. It only made things worse when you lowered yourself to someone else's level, but she couldn't seem to find the high road. Add in the fact that she was attracted to him and it was just a freaking disaster. She felt like a hormonal mess more often than not now. Even on the days he didn't say anything biting to her, she was so tense from the anticipation that it was almost as bad. She was utterly confused by the fact that she wanted him regardless of how cruel he could be. He was the most confident man that she'd ever met and she was strangely drawn to him. She had always longed for a close-knit family like the Jacksons, and she grudgingly admired that Ash had uprooted his life in Charleston to move to Florida to help his brother out. That unselfish act had allowed Dylan and Zoe the time to finally have a life together that didn't revolve around the hotel. Ash might pretend it was purely a business decision, but everyone involved knew it was brotherly love and loyalty, pure and simple.

Opening the box of pizza, she took out a slice of the pepperoni-laden heaven and bit into it. The flavors exploded on her tongue and she rolled her eyes in bliss. Then she froze. What if Ash could see her now? She could only imagine the comments he'd make. And just like that, one of her favorite foods tasted like cardboard. She found she could barely swallow the one bite. *Shit!* She was angrier at herself than at him. She'd let him in her head, which meant that despite her earlier feelings of elation at turning the tables, he was still winning. Stiffening her shoulders, she picked up the abandoned piece and forced herself to finish it. She was not going to let this happen. She wouldn't turn into one of those stick figure women who survived on croutons and water to make a man happy. If it was the last thing she did, Asher Jackson would pay for the damage he'd inflicted on her self-confidence. She'd strike a blow for women everywhere who'd been made to feel like they didn't measure up to someone's standards. Maybe he thought he could get away with that shit because he was so damned hot, but he'd soon discover that he was wrong. Whereas her ultimate game had been a little muddled earlier, it was now crystal clear. She was going to make Ash fall for her, big butt and all. Women could be beautiful in all shapes and sizes, and it was high time someone made him realize it. Then she'd show him how it felt when someone made you feel as if you weren't good enough according to their ridiculous standards. She could only hope he wasn't so egotistical that he didn't feel the sting. Because he deserved to suffer.

Ash looked around the crowded local pub and felt absolutely nothing. There were scores of attractive women there, many of whom were looking his way with blatant appreciation, but he couldn't seem to bring himself to care about the female attention he'd drawn. As he sat on his barstool nursing his second beer of the evening, his thoughts constantly returned to the bizarre encounter in his office earlier that day.

Dana had gotten to him. She'd scored a direct hit and had done it in the most unusual way. He knew she didn't bear any kind feelings toward him. Being sweet to your enemy was the equivalent of taking fairy dust to a biker bar. It just simply wasn't done. But damn, it had been effective. If he'd felt guilty before about the way he had been treating her, he was drowning in it now. She'd made him fucking cookies and had remembered they were his favorite. He'd essentially called her a fat munchkin and she'd brought him to his knees with kindness. Why hadn't she attacked him as he did her? She always gave almost as good as she got, so this extreme change in behavior made no sense. You didn't reward a bully, but she had done exactly that. He wouldn't have been surprised to find a thank-you card in his bag of discarded food.

You're a fucking asshole. There was no escaping that fact. He was punishing a woman that he barely knew for the sins of another. He recognized that, but he couldn't seem to stop no matter how many times he vowed that he would. If he was any kind of a man, he would confess the whole thing to her and then beg to be forgiven. But he'd never been able to admit just how much damage Fiona had dealt him. More than his pride had taken a hit there. He didn't like acknowledging even to himself how scarred he still was by the whole failed relationship. It had been years and he was no closer to moving on and putting the past behind him than he had been. Instead, he'd been torturing Dana. Even Dylan, who enjoyed sparring with Dana in good fun, disapproved of Ash's behavior. When your brother couldn't defend your actions, things were bad. And Zoe had taken to sending him glaring looks of disapproval whenever he was at their place. He felt like shit on a shoe, yet he continued to commit the same offense almost every day. Maybe he needed to find some kind of support group before he alienated everyone around him.

Or you could take a page from Dana's book and try being pleasant for a change. Damn, that was a hard option to consider. He'd turned her into someone else in his head, a punching bag for his emotional wounds, and he didn't know how to undo it. He could simply avoid the shop during the hours she normally worked. But he found that as much as she infuriated him, he was also equally drawn to her in some unfathomable way. He could no more stay away from her than he could keep his big mouth shut. Which left things at an impasse.

When a hand landed on his thigh, he jerked so hard he splashed beer on his shirt and his jeans. "Shit," he grumbled. Then the hand was in his lap left before returning with a stack of napkins.

The as yet unidentified annoyance began wiping furiously at his crotch. "Sorry about that, Ashey. Let me take care of this wittle ol' accident for you."

Oh hell no. Please not Baby Talk Brittany. God, I know I deserve this, but please not her . . . Slowly turning his head to confirm his suspicion, Ash could barely contain his wince. Men always had women they regretted sleeping with, and Brittany was at the top of his list. Damn, that had been a mistake that continued to haunt him. Carefully shifting in his seat to get her away from his dick, he said, "I think I can handle it from here."

She rolled her bottom lip out in an elaborate pout that would have been impressive had it not been so irritating instead. "Ashey, I've been calling you. Have you been out of town or something?"

I believe you mean calling constantly, texting, and dropping by the office unannounced. Luckily, Lisa had had no problem showing her to the door each time. Of course, then he got the whole "men are pigs" look from her, but it was still better than having to do it himself. "I've been busy, Bethany." Yeah, he called her the wrong name on purpose, hoping she'd get the hint that she wasn't special. *You are an asshole.*

Unfortunately, Brittany didn't even appear to notice. Hell, he had a problem with names so that could have been the right one, for all he knew. If he'd thought her pout was impressive, she kicked her game up a notch by putting her middle finger between her lips and sucking on it while staring at him. *Does she have any idea the amount of germs there are in a bar?* "I've missed you, baby," she said as she finally took her hand away from her mouth. She moved to stand beside his barstool, then leaned over, putting her impressive cleavage in his face. He knew his way around a set of tits, and those puppies had screamed fake from the first time he'd met her. But being the nice guy he was, he didn't discriminate. Now they seemed way too big for her thin frame. He was actually afraid she'd over-balance and face-plant in his lap.

Then her tongue swiped up the side of his neck in a move that would do a golden retriever proud. *Ugh. Someone bring me a towel, some hand sanitizer, and maybe a bib for Brittany-Bethany.* "I—er . . . that's nice," he sputtered out as he leaned back as far as his chair would allow. "It was good seeing you again." But his hint fell on deaf ears. She was now damn close to inhaling his ear. Her tongue felt like it was going to come out the other side at any moment. She was also grinding into his waist and making some disturbing noises. Surely she wasn't getting off on this. "Um . . . what're you doing?"

Holy crap, she was growling at this point and using his earlobe like a chew toy. "Ashey, come out and pway with me."

If she thought this was exciting, she was way off the mark. His cock had practically packed up shop and was retreating inward. It'd been bad enough the first time they'd had sex. Then he'd made the mistake of repeating it once more. There was something alarming about a woman going down on you while talking like a toddler. He just couldn't get past it. Maybe she'd been taken off the bottle too early in life and it had created a shit storm of problems for her and every man in her path. Rosa would have a field day with this one. "Ashey needs to be going," he choked out as she continued to slobber on him. He could feel saliva beginning to ooze down his neck as she slurped at him noisily. He glanced around and noticed a group of what looked like college kids laughing hysterically. A couple of them had their cell phones out and pointed in his direction. There was no question that the footage would end up on YouTube. "Listen, Brittany, you really need to stop that," he said sternly. "You're soaking my shirt and I believe the bartender is close to calling animal control. You're up to date on all your shots, right?" he asked, only half joking. *I wonder if you can get a sexually transmitted disease in your ear.* If that was a possibility, then that sucker would be falling off shortly. She hadn't left an inch of it unmolested.

He was desperately trying to decide his next move when a man that he assumed was the manager walked up and cleared his throat loudly. "You two are causing something of a scene. Could you take this elsewhere?" Ash could feel his face flushing, which never happened. He wasn't a man easily embarrassed, but this was humiliating.

"I'd love to leave if I could get loose," he grumbled as he pointed to whatever the hell her name was. The manager's lips twitched as he tried to maintain his professionalism. "Go ahead and laugh," Ash added. "I would if this was happening to anyone else. Could you maybe give me a hand though when you're finished? I think she's in some kind of weird zone. She doesn't seem to be hearing any of this."

"I'm not allowed to touch customers, especially a, er . . . lady," the manager said, "but I'll have one of our female security members assess the situation."

Ash wanted to beg the man to stay. He wondered if Brittany was stoned because she gave no indication that she'd noticed any of the conversation going on around her. Instead, she continued to lick and suck on the side of his face like she was preparing to take a fucking bite. He'd just opened his mouth to attempt to reason with her again, when he caught sight of someone familiar. *And I thought this couldn't get worse. Please tell me it isn't her.* But even closing his eyes and quickly opening them again didn't change the fact that Dana was now only inches away and looking as if she was trying to keep from laughing her ass off. She was biting her lip as she stared at the woman clamped on to him.

"Hey, Dana, you come here often?" he asked, trying to sound casual.

Shrugging her shoulders, she said, "Occasionally." Nodding to Brittany, she added, "You need some help? Maybe the number of a good therapist? Were you weaned off the bottle too early as a child? A good pacifier might really be of help here." He gave her a helpless look, damned close to crying in desperation for an escape while all these people gawked at them. Then a miracle happened, and he wanted to fall to his knees in gratitude.

"Asher, what in the world is going on here?" Dana's voice rang out shrilly. "Who is this tramp and why is . . . Wait, is she licking your armpit?" Dana asked in disgust. "I can't believe you left me and our three kids at home for—this. I sent you out an hour ago to get some drops for little Asher and this is what you've been doing? Your son is so gassy he's about to take flight and you're in a bar? WHAT IS WRONG WITH YOU?"

As far as performances went, it was Oscar caliber. Even Brittany had stopped in her efforts to check him for deodorant and was staring at the petite dynamo before them. "Who is this, Ashey?" she asked as she popped a finger back into her mouth. The girl obviously had some issues. No wonder she did the baby talk—hell, she probably had a speech impediment if she walked around sucking her digits all the time.

Dana straightened to her full height, which was far less than Brittany's, but even Ash felt rather intimidated by her. "I'm Ashey's wife, that's who I am. And I'd better never catch you mauling my husband again. Now how about calling your parents and having them pick you up. Wait, do you need me to do it for you? Have they given you a phone yet?"

Ash had a hard time keeping his laughter at bay as Dana continued to toss questions at the other woman. Finally Brittany asked, "Why would I call my mom? I have a car outside."

Dana overenunciated her words as she said, "Oh. Great. I wasn't sure if you were old enough to drive. Plus, there was the whole 'licking a man in public like he's a teething ring' thing."

God help him, if he didn't get out of here soon, he was gonna lose it. In all the times he'd been swapping insults with Dana, he'd never realized how funny she was. Her body language alone was hysterical. With her hands now on her hips, she insulted Brittany in a way that flew right over the blonde's head. In that moment, he was strangely proud to have everyone nearby think that she was his wife. From the admiring glances being leveled her way, it appeared that quite a few other men were thinking something similar. A woman with a sense of humor as good as hers was a huge turn-on.

Brittany pulled on his arm, appearing confused. "So does this mean I should go, Ashey?" *After all that, she still needs to ask?*

Shrugging away from her, he nodded. "Yeah, I'd listen to my—wife if I were you." Hanging his head, he added, "I need to get home to all my kids. I'm a shitty father. You don't want to be mixed up with a guy like me." Dana's snort told him that she agreed with his last statement, but fortunately she didn't comment out loud.

Dana stepped forward and put a friendly arm around Brittany's waist. "Sweetie, do you need any help getting into your car seat? Oh sorry, I meant your seat belt. I know those suckers can be complicated. Are you sure I shouldn't call your mom for you? You know, too much hair dye or silicone can really have some long-term adverse effects. Do you often find yourself making poor decisions?"

Brittany twirled a strand of hair around one finger as she pondered the question. "Well, I did buy regular Coke instead of diet a few days ago." Glancing at her impressive chest, her eyes widened. "Do you really think these might be the cause? I also slept with my sister's boyfriend last year." Smacking her hand to her forehead, she grinned. "I knew it wasn't my fault. My sister said I was a whore, but it was out of my control, right?"

Asher saw Dana's eye twitch, but she held her composure together. "Um . . . sure, honey. Let's blame that one on lack of oxygen. Those pants you're wearing are so tight you're not getting enough air to that little brain of yours. Tell you what, why don't you buy some of those nice sweatpants they sell at Walmart? You know the ones with the elastic around the waist. You'd look adorable in the bright pink. Plus, you can get the complete set for like ten bucks. There's a twenty-four-hour store right down the street. You stop in there on your way home and take care of that. By this time next year, you could be almost normal."

Brittany jumped in place, clapping her hands. "Oh my God, thank you! I'll do that now. Bye, Ashey," she tossed over her shoulder as she took off toward the exit.

Shaking his head, Ash smirked at Dana. "That was the most surreal moment I've had in a while and that's saying something. I almost feel sorry for the people at Walmart. She'll need at least a dozen of them to help her find and buy that nightmare of an outfit you just conned her into."

Pushing past him, Dana ordered a glass of wine from the bartender before facing him once again. "You so owe me for that. By the way, does that stuff happen to you a lot? I mean, I'm not surprised that you go for the dumb blondes, but I'd have given you more credit than that. How much fun could she have been in bed? Wait . . . I'm guessing that whole suction thing is more interesting when it's not being used on your armpit. She could clearly suck rusted lug nuts off a passing pickup truck."

Asher had just stepped up to the bar and taken a drink of his now warm beer, which unfortunately he sucked up his nose and damn near choked on at Dana's matter-of-fact description of Brittany's talents. He felt her whack him on the back, perhaps harder than was necessary, but he couldn't really say that he blamed her. He certainly deserved a good ass kicking for all the shit he'd said to her lately. Even after all that, she'd still saved him from further public humiliation and the unpleasantness of getting away from Brittany.

"I really appreciate what you did," he said honestly, as soon as he had his laughter at her earlier statement under control.

"I'm guessing this kind of thing happens to you often," she replied ruefully.

He gave her a sheepish grin and a shrug. "I've had some issues. I seem to attract all of the crazy ones. Believe it or not, tonight was one of the most bizarre."

Dana raised a skeptical brow. "You mean women aren't trying to nurse from your neck and armpit on a regular basis? I've gotta say, that was disturbing. She was in some kind of trace. I'm surprised we were able to break her concentration that easily. I thought for sure it would take physical force to pry her loose."

Ash settled on a stool next to where Dana had taken a seat and signaled for a fresh beer. "I've only seen her a few times and it was a whole lot of baby talk on those occasions. This was something new. Maybe she's broadening her horizons."

"Or you drove her nuts," Dana pointed out. "You're not the easiest man to get along with, so she could have been desperate for another way to connect. I'm not saying this was it because, yeah, it was insane, but still I believe we can lay the blame squarely at your feet."

Raising his glass to hers, he grinned. "Touché. I deserved that. You know, you've missed your calling in life. You should have been an actress. Even I was buying into you being my wife. Hell, I still have the urge to run by the store for those gas drops for our kid that you mentioned. Guys would pay a fortune to have a woman handy to keep the Brittanys of the world at bay. Shit, I'd like to take you to some parties and business functions so I can relax on the nights I don't want to have someone make my life a living hell."

Dana paused with her glass of wine halfway to her mouth as she gave him an assessing look. He was both intrigued and a little scared that she appeared to be giving his offhand comment so much attention. Finally she asked, "So how much would something like that be worth to you?" Wrinkling her nose in a way that made his pride sting, she added, "I'm not talking anything physical here. But if you wanted me to run interference for you, what figure would seem appropriate?"

Despite his better judgment, Ash was intrigued. Hell, he felt like he was being both propositioned and slapped down all in one smooth move. What man wouldn't want more information about that? So he found himself asking, "Would that be a gig that you'd be interested in doing? You know, pretending to be my significant other on occasion when I asked? I don't think I could pass you off as my wife because a lot of the women know I'm not married. But fiancée or girlfriend might work."

He could almost have sworn he saw her shudder before she straightened her shoulders and said, "I'd do it for five hundred dollars an evening. If it was longer than that, we'd have to renegotiate ahead of time." He had no idea what he'd even been going to say, but as soon as he opened his mouth, she held her hand up. "Normally I'd laugh in your face. You've been such an asshole to me that I personally think you deserve to be eaten alive by the bimbos of the world. But—I just found out a few hours ago that the transmission is shot in my car, and rather than pour more money into it, I'd like to be able to afford a replacement. I was already considering a second job, and at least you'd mostly only need me in the evening hours, which would work perfectly with my daytime schedule."

He really should nip this whole idea in the bud before it got out of hand. What they were talking about was insane. Sure, he'd gotten frustrated dealing with the same old crap, but that was life, right? He'd lived in Florida for only a year, so he wasn't completely sure how he'd managed to gather such a collection of irritating and pissed-off women. To be fair, he hadn't actually had sex with all of them, but they seemed to be as bitter about being turned down as the ones that he'd never called again after the deed. Plus, he had visited the resort a good bit before he had relocated, so it wasn't as if he'd met them all since his move. Even he didn't move that fast. Looking Dana up and down, he couldn't resist a small dig. "You realize you'd have to dress better."

She stared at him with disdain before saying, "No problem as long as you're paying. I'm guessing you want me to wear the same type of clothing as your usual dates. Where are the teenagers shopping these days? One of those trendy stores in the mall where a tiny T-shirt costs fifty bucks? Wait—what about Baby Gap? Or is that too young even for you?"

Ash couldn't hold back his chuckle of amusement. Normally every word from her mouth irritated him, but that ire was curiously absent tonight. Strangely, he was enjoying himself more than he had in a while, which surely said bad things about his social life. His thoughts flashed back to his conversation with Rosa that morning, and it hit him that Dana was like a younger and hotter version of his housekeeper.

Neither of the women took any shit from him, and they were both brutally honest in their disdain of his casual dating lifestyle. And even though he knew it was a disaster in the making, he found himself ignoring her dig and holding out his hand. "You've got a deal, munchkin. And how about including some high heels in your shopping? It would be nice if you at least reached my waist."

Her nose turned up as she rolled her eyes and pointed to his crotch. "I'd think one of the requirements of your dates would be that they spend a lot of time around that area. Although things went terribly wrong earlier. She wasn't the brightest bulb, so maybe she thought your penis was located in your armpit. She certainly appeared to be hunting for something in there."

Again, he was unable to hold back a grin. He couldn't remember the last time he'd smiled this much. And most of it was at his expense. They both knew he didn't have much of a defense after Brittany's public spectacle. He could only imagine how much his sister-in-law Zoe was going to enjoy this, because Dana would certainly tell her. Maybe he should make her sign some kind of confidentiality agreement. There were bound to be more moments ahead that he wouldn't want his family to know about. "Let me assure you that Brittany does not represent the type of women I'm attracted to. It's a sad fact that sometimes you can't spot crazy until it's too late. Other than the baby talk, I had no clue she was that strange."

Dana giggled, which he thought sounded adorable. Hell, what was wrong with him? Too much stress? Since when had he indulged in sappy thoughts like that? *Five years ago and look how that ended up.* "So that's where the whole Ashey thing came from? Did she have a nickname for your pecker too? Maybe little Ashey? Wow, that's emasculating, isn't it?" In a perfect imitation of Brittany's voice, Dana said, "Can wittle Ashey come out and pway?" He groaned and lowered his head because that was exactly what she'd said that first night. Why in the world had there ever been a second time?

Reading him correctly, Dana began laughing so hard she was shaking. "Oh my God," she sputtered. "She actually said that to you and you were able to perform?" Then, lowering her voice, she whisper-shouted, "Well, unless it's true . . . Hey, no judgment here, they can't all be big or even average. It's not the size, but how it's used. She must have been okay with your petite member because she was mauling you right here for all to see. Actually this explains a lot about your hostile personality. You obviously get around, but I always assumed it was because you were a man-whore. When in actuality it could very well be that you're leaving a trail of unsatisfied women behind you and they're angry about your false advertising. Kind of like men who complain about us wearing padded bras."

Feeling his spine stiffen at her references to his cock, Ash had the urge to pull her out back and drop his pants. His dick was literally getting the short end of this one, and for a man, there wasn't much worse than those kinds of assumptions. "I'll have you know that there's nothing small about it and I've never had a woman that didn't scream . . . several times."

Dana cupped her chin, blinking those big blue eyes

at him. "Really? Are you sure it wasn't in horror? Like seeing one of those little wiggle worms on your floor. At first glance, you kinda think it's cute, but then you wonder what in the heck you're supposed to do with it."

Now exasperated, Ash's voice was louder than he'd intended when he snapped, "I'm packing a solid eight, sweetheart. Why do you think they keep coming back for more?"

The woman on his other side snorted before muttering something that sounded like "pig" under her breath. Dana studied her nails with a smirk on her lips. "I've heard that you should deduct three inches from the size that a man claims he is. It's nothing to be ashamed of. I'd say that's closer to the national average. It also makes sense about Brittany now. She's probably not good at math so convincing her you were a ten was easy."

Ash knew it was pointless to continue this insane debate. Plus, short of exposing himself, he couldn't prove her wrong. Why did it matter anyway? Sure, no guy wanted a woman to believe that he was less than stellar in that area, but this was Dana. He couldn't stand her. And he certainly had some payback coming to him for all the shit he'd said to her over the last year. With that in mind, for once he turned the other cheek. "Whatever helps you sleep at night, munchkin. Now if it's okay, can we get back to our business arrangement?"

"Of course, Ashey." She smiled sweetly. "What's my first assignment?"

"I'll be having dinner with my family on Friday night. Zoe and Dylan will also be there so that should make it more comfortable for you."

Looking confused, Dana said, "Wait—why would you waste money having me pretend to be your girlfriend in front of relatives? Won't they know it's a lie? Ugh, please tell me you haven't slept with one of them. That's low even for you."

Stung by her assumption, Ash frowned. "No, I haven't had sex with a family member, but thanks for the vote of confidence. The problem is my stepsister is a bit of a tramp. Every time I'm around, she says and does stuff that's not in the least sisterly. The whole evening will be hell because my mother is completely self-absorbed and my stepfather is a moneygrubbing asshole. Things would at least be more bearable if I could keep Claudia off me. That's where you'll come in. She's kind of a nasty piece of work too so don't expect her to be as easy to handle as our friend Brittany was."

Not looking the slightest bit intimidated, Dana scoffed. "Honey, I'm from the South. We know how to take out the trash when we need to, and I don't mind getting my hands dirty. As long as you aren't worried about me offending her. If you are, then let me know now."

Ash snorted and decided in that moment that Friday night was sounding pretty entertaining. "Hell no. I couldn't care less how you get the job done. She deserves anything you toss at her. We probably need to go with you being the girlfriend though since I haven't mentioned you before."

Nodding, Dana said, "Works for me. How will I need to dress?"

Ash laughed before pointing down to his jeans. "Charlotte—aka 'Mommie Dearest'—likes to pretend that she's a society queen so she'll want everyone more formally clothed. But Dylan and I don't like being told what to do, so we always go in the opposite direction. Wear your uniform from the coffee shop for all I care. It's up to you."

Getting to her feet, Dana gave him a salute before saying, "Alrighty then. Let me know the details and I'll do the rest. Oh, and I'd prefer cash if that isn't a problem. Otherwise I'd have to worry about you writing me a bad check just to be an ass." Without waiting for a reply, she turned and left, never once looking back at him. Which was a good thing, because his eyes were glued to the gentle sway of her hips and that plump ass that had his cock sitting up and taking notice.

What was it about her? How could she irritate the shit out of him one minute and turn him on the next without even trying? Strangely enough, he hadn't thought about her resemblance to his ex-girlfriend Fiona in the last hour. Instead, he'd reveled in swapping insults with her. *It's called foreplay, buddy.* No, surely that wasn't it. He had no intention of sleeping with Dana Anders. She might have a nice ass, but that was it.

This was strictly a business relationship. He'd use her to keep Claudia under control and buy himself a little peace. She was an employee and he didn't muddy those waters. Besides, knowing them, they'd be ready to kill each other again by tomorrow. And that was looking more and more like the best way to deal with her. People who hated each other didn't have sex.

Three

Zoe's eyes were as round as saucers when Dana finished telling her about the arrangement with Asher. "But you two hate each other. How in the world are you going to pretend to be in love? I can't believe you even managed to talk long enough to come up with this whole thing. Are you sure it was Ash? Maybe it was a guy that looked like him."

Dana snorted as she wiped down the counter in the shop. "I do actually know who the man is. Admittedly I was thrown a few times when he smiled. I had no idea he even had any teeth behind that snarl."

Zoe gave her a look full of concern before saying, "You know I would be happy to lend you some money. You don't have to do this."

Thinking yet again how lucky she was to have a friend like Zoe, Dana reached out and squeezed the other woman's hand. "I know, but I'd rather earn it. And weirdly enough, this sounds like fun. I've got a mouth on me so turning it loose on some bimbos and getting paid for it is my dream side job. I'll even have the opportunity to torture Ash some, which we both know he deserves." Throwing her hand up in the air, she did a fist bump with Zoe that had her friend giggling.

"I gotta admit, I'm intrigued. I'd love to be a fly on the wall when you two try this for the first time," Zoe said wistfully.

Wiggling her eyebrows, Dana said, "That's the best part. I'm going to be at dinner with his mother Friday night, and I understand that you and Dylan will be there as well. So, my dear, you've got a front-row seat to this one."

"Oh my God." Zoe rocked back on her feet. "I've been dreading that so much. Charlotte is so snooty and her husband acts like he's this big businessman, but he takes money from the Jacksons constantly." Shuddering, she added, "Then there's Claudia. She plasters herself all over Dylan and Ash as if she's not their stepsister. I swear, she'd sleep with them if they'd just say yes."

Dana nodded. "That's where I come in. Ash wants a night when he doesn't have to worry about getting attacked by the creepy stepsister. I'll pretend to be his girlfriend and take care of that hoochie. He's given me free rein to do or say whatever necessary to get her off him."

Zoe's squeal of delight had the customers in the nearby vicinity looking in their direction. Dana grinned as Zoe promptly clapped a hand over her mouth. "Whoops, I lost control there for a moment. But oh my God, this is too good to be true. Do you know how often I've dreamed of committing some kind of violence where she's concerned? It's not bad enough that she has to paw my husband. She's also a royal bitch to me. But she's smart enough to do it when Dylan isn't close enough to hear her. Then I feel as if I'm whining if I say something to him."

Snorting, Dana said, "Well then, this is your chance to get back at her. I'll do what I can to put her in her place. I swear, I can't stand women like that. For starters, you never attempt to pick up anyone at family functions. That's all kinds of low class. And stay away from men who are taken. There are enough single ones out there without fishing in someone else's pond. It's a basic rule of the sisterhood code."

Zoe added in a distasteful tone, "Especially if you're related to them. I mean, there may be no blood ties, but come on, I don't see a difference and neither does Dylan. She put a hand on his butt at Christmas, then claimed it was an accident when it was obvious that he was angry over it. I was ready to pull her bleached blond hair out over that. But even though he knows what she is, Dylan still has a hard time accepting that she's deliberately coming on to him. He'd rather bury his head in the sand and live in denial over it."

Nodding sympathetically, Dana said, "Well, luckily for you, Ash understands her perfectly and is tired of dealing with it. So let's put that tramp in her place." Eyeing her friend thoughtfully, she asked, "So what are you planning on wearing?"

Echoing Ash's sentiments, Zoe said, "Probably just jeans. Charlotte will have on something hideously expensive, but everyone else will be more casual."

Dana winked at Zoe as a thought took shape. "Not this time, honey. I'm assuming that Claudia wears some skintight jeans as well?" When Zoe nodded, the decision was made. "Then you and I are going in the opposite direction. I'm thinking dresses. It'll be the perfect way to make Claudia feel like an underdressed teenager. It's easier to put a woman in her place when she feels inferior to you."

"I don't know . . ." Zoe said doubtfully. "I think you're underestimating her. I can't imagine anything would shake her self-confidence, especially me."

"Oh, but you're wrong," Dana assured the other woman. "Plus, Ash has agreed to purchase any extra clothing that I need to play a part, so we'll be making a trip to the hotel boutique tomorrow. For this occasion we need to look sophisticated, yet sexy."

With a perplexed expression, Zoe asked, "And this is going to help us how?"

Dana said, "I can insult her all day, but if I seem as if I'm trying to compete with her, then she's just going to blow me off. I might get in a few good digs, but I'm not going to shake her confidence. After all, I assume she's younger and probably hot." Zoe's sour expression confirmed her assessment of their enemy. "So we do something that she isn't expecting. We make her feel like a kid. I did that very same thing to Ash's bimbo last night, and bless her heart, she was dumb as a box of rocks so I had to practically draw her a picture. But I don't think I'll need to do that with Claudia. I suspect she's shrewder than that."

"Bart's always bragging about her GPA and the fact that she's the president of her sorority," Zoe agreed.

As she rested her elbows on the bar, a clear picture of the enemy began to emerge in Dana's mind. Claudia sounded like everything she'd imagined and more. This girl would be a handful, but Dana was also more certain than ever that they needed to bring their

A-game. Thank God this wasn't a pool party. It would be hard to compete with a bikini. But a sexy dress with a push-up bra would work wonders. Now she just needed the right ammunition to get her friend in the game. Deliberately looking bored, she said idly, "Well, it's not going to be easy, and if you'd rather continue on as you have been, then I'll understand. You and I both know that Dylan will never take her up on what she's offering no matter how many times she gropes him. And if you're okay with her touching your man's dick, then I'll support you fully."

"His dick?" Zoe snapped, causing heads to turn once again.

"Um, you might want to keep it down. That group of old dudes at the table in the back are beginning to look excited. On the plus side, I'm almost certain they'll be back again tomorrow."

Zoe shot a quick look over her shoulder, then let out a mortified groan when one of the men in question winked in their direction. "Shit, they must have heard what I said. I bet this kind of thing never happens at the Starbucks down the street."

Wiggling her brows, Dana joked, "I don't suppose you'd consider sitting on one of their laps? They'd bring all their buddies back, guaranteed."

"Gross, no way. Now back to what you were saying. I'll do whatever you think we need to. Keep in mind that I'm still a newbie at all this, but I refuse to let Dylan continue to get felt up by her."

Tossing an arm around her friend, Dana gave her a reassuring side hug before saying, "You won't regret this. We'll put Miss Thing in her place and have some fun doing it."

Before Zoe could respond, one of the men who had heard Zoe's outburst walked up to the bar and dropped a twenty-dollar bill onto the counter. "Best coffee I've had in a while, ladies. The boys and I'll be back real soon." With a click of his tongue that had Dana biting back a grin, he and his cronies ambled out the door.

"Oh, shut up!" Zoe laughed. "And I'm keeping the whole tip. Apparently I earned it." They joked for the remaining hour until it was time to leave. When they parted ways in front of the shop, Dana couldn't help thinking what a difference twenty-four hours had made. Yesterday she'd been angry and dejected when she'd finished her shift, but thanks to the cease-fire with Ash, she was excited and impatient for Friday to come. And it had nothing at all to do with the weekend. She knew that it was insane to have feelings for someone who'd never been anything but nasty to her, but she couldn't seem to help herself. For a short time last night he'd shown the side of himself that he treated everyone else to. The Asher she always heard about from other people. He'd been funny, charming, and dammit, beyond sexy. How could she resist that? She had to wonder sometimes if it was that she wanted Ash or simply longed to be a part of his amazing family. She had thought herself long past the need to be accepted by others, but maybe that was another reason she desired what seemed unattainable. Or was it simply chemistry? Because her body came to life whenever he was near her, and no matter how often she tried to ignore that hum of attraction, it continued to blaze for Asher Jackson as if it had a mind of its own.

Four

"Are they for real?" Dana asked Zoe under her breath yet again. She was having a hard time believing that Ash and Dylan had come from the woman reclining on a pool lounger as if she were sitting on the throne beside Queen Elizabeth. Charlotte Jackson attempted to look regal but, instead, came off as stuck-up and constipated. And her husband was the complete opposite. He was loud, overbearing, and had a laugh that made the hairs on Dana's neck stand up. If he called her "sugar" one more time, she wouldn't be responsible for her actions. He needed a kick to the crotch in the worst way. Naturally his eyes had been glued to her cleavage the whole time they'd been there. He also ogled Zoe's ass when he thought no one was paying any attention. The tightening of his wife's overly Botoxed mouth told Dana that she hadn't missed that fact though.

"I'd like to say it gets better," Zoe murmured back. "But they're pretty much on their best behavior right now. Plus, the princess hasn't graced us with her presence yet. Maybe she's got other plans," she added hopefully.

Glancing down at her formfitting black sheath dress and spiky heels, which she'd charged to Ash at the hotel boutique, she whispered back, "I'm not returning this outfit if she doesn't show. We're freaking hot tonight." Zoe was wearing a soft green print sundress that was amazing against her tanned skin. They looked like they were complete opposites that cleaned up well. The dress Dana was wearing shaved ten pounds off her frame and she felt sexy and confident in it. Clothes might not make the woman, but they certainly gave a much-needed boost at times. The way that Ash's eyes had widened and his mouth had dropped earlier told her all that she needed to know. Unlike his disgusting stepfather, she enjoyed the way his gaze slid over her from time to time in obvious admiration. She had to give him credit as well—he hadn't lobbed an insult her way all evening. Of course, at this point she would have known he was full of it. Men can lie with their lips, but their eyes are another story. Most hadn't perfected that art form and Ash was no exception.

Before Zoe could reply, a voice called out, "Sorry I'm late, everyone. Traffic was a total bitch. I'm here now though."

"So it begins," Zoe hissed out as Dana's head slowly swiveled toward the new arrival.

"Holy silicone slut," she muttered as she took in the enemy of any normal woman in the world. Young, hot, blond, and oozing confidence. She hated Claudia on sight. She was the poster child of the mean girls who'd picked on Dana in high school for being less than perfect. When she rushed over to her father's chair and plopped down in his lap, she heard Zoe groan. "That's completely disturbing," she said, shaking her head. "Isn't she a little old for that?"

"Um, yeah, by about twenty years," Zoe agreed. "I know she does it just to keep the money wheels turning, but gross. Look at the way he's hugging her. It makes me want to take a shower."

Nodding in agreement, Dana said, "Honey, that's some serious 'spray me with Lysol' stuff there." Bart was making kissy faces at Claudia and literally bouncing her on his plump knee now. Charlotte looked like she had the desire to barf as she stared at the scene next to her. According to Zoe, Charlotte was the one with the money, so what in the world did she see in her husband? No wonder she still went by the Jackson surname. "Does this happen a lot?"

"Pretty much," Zoe sighed. "The first time I came for dinner, Claudia actually slid down the banister and into her father's arms. As if that wasn't bad enough, he twirled her around for what seemed like an hour. And she was wearing a short, flared skirt . . . and a thong. Since Dylan and I were standing in the foyer, we got treated to the sight of her ass on full display."

"Oh damn," Dana groaned. "I think I need to ask for more money. This is nothing like the simple whore infestation I was expecting. I mean, I already knew from you how Ash and Dylan's mother acted. But I've gotta say, girlfriend, you left out some of the other stuff."

"Sorry." Zoe grimaced. "I seriously try not to think about it unless absolutely necessary. Plus, after I found out you'd be coming tonight, there was no way I was going to risk you backing out."

Before Dana could reply, an amused male voice behind them said, "You two enjoying the show?"

Dana felt her body come to life as it always did around Ash. Even when he was being an asshole, she couldn't resist the pull she felt toward the handsome devil. If he only knew how many times he'd been the material for her solo hand sessions—if there was a God, he'd never discover that humiliating fact. Smirking, she whispered, "At what point does she give big brother a hug?"

"A hug?" Zoe hissed. "You mean a lap dance, right? I swear, she once straddled Ash's knee and—"

"Why don't we leave that painful memory in the past," Ash interrupted her wryly. "Contrary to what women might believe, all men don't actually get off on the twisted shit." When Dana turned her head to give him a disbelieving look, he amended, "With family members. Hell, even if she wasn't my stepsister, I still wouldn't be interested in her. She's not my type."

Now Zoe leveled a stare in her brother-in-law's direction and he scowled at them in return. "I realize that the whole Brittany thing might have damaged my credibility a tad, but I'm not into aggressive blondes with agendas bigger than my . . . well, you get my drift."

Reaching a hand back to pat his impressive chest, Dana gave him her best wide-eyed airhead look before saying, "Ah, honey, we know that. You just like 'em dumb. It's nothing to be ashamed of, everyone has a preference. Plus, I imagine it makes life easier when they don't do complicated things like think for themselves. I bet Brittany was perfectly content to let you order for her off the McDonald's Dollar Menu every time."

"They have a lot of options with those Happy Meals now." Zoe laughed. "I mean, really, should you have to choose between extra fries and fruit?"

Biting her lip to keep from laughing at Ash's pained expression, Dana said, "I'm fairly certain it's all about the toy for Brittany. From what I can recall, she's not eating more than maybe two fries for a meal."

The smile froze on Dana's face when she felt a hand land on her ass cheek and squeeze lightly. Then Ash's silky voice whispered in her ear, "I've got no complaints about where your food goes, sweetheart. And for the record, I've always been an ass man." Dana shuddered as his breath whispered against her neck before he stepped back and walked away.

She was still frozen in place when Zoe nudged her in the arm before fanning herself. "That was so hot even I was melting." Then, as if she was afraid that Dana had taken his words as another insult, she quickly added, "He wasn't being nasty this time. I was watching him as he was talking to you and he was so in the zone. There wasn't an ounce of anything other than admiration on his face."

"Er—what the hell is he up to?" Dana winced as her voice came out unusually high pitched. She took a moment to relax before turning fully to face her friend. "That's not the way our relationship works. Honestly, he can't go saying crazy stuff now after being a jerk all this time. How am I supposed to work under this kind of pressure? I'll be walking on eggshells wondering if he's going to do something insane like utter a sentence that isn't cruel or scathing. He's going to have to lock that shit down, you know what I'm saying?"

Zoe appeared utterly confused as she shrugged her shoulders. "Um—I guess. Sometimes men are bastards. I personally hate it when Dylan admires my body. It makes me feel so dirty. Ash has a lot of explaining to do."

There really was something to be said for the loyalty of a girlfriend, Dana thought. Even though it was obvious that she didn't really understand Dana's reasoning, Zoe was pulling on her boots and preparing to fight in the trenches with her. What she couldn't tell the other woman was that even though it hurt like hell at times, she could pull on her armor and mostly handle Ash when he was being a dick. But a sexy, complimentary Ash was altogether different. She was very much afraid she had nothing that would save her should he decide to turn his legendary charm in her direction.

She liked to keep her relationships strictly physical with no complicated emotional attachments, which was absurdly easy since most men seemed just fine with that. It had worked well for her through the years. The few times she'd come across a potential clinger, she'd ended it and moved on. Sex didn't need to be complicated and she wasn't looking for the gold ring at the end of the rainbow. People hurt you when you gave them too much power. As long as you kept the facade up and pretended to let their words bounce off you, then the pain was manageable.

She knew it resulted from the hell she'd suffered in her teenage years, but didn't everyone carry some kind of baggage from high school? Hell, your entire outlook on life, love, and relationships formed around then or at least hers had. Her lack of self-confidence had made it possible, but why split hairs? The end result was the same. And hadn't she learned that she could live a perfectly happy existence without romantic attachments? It wasn't as if she didn't develop feelings for people. She loved Zoe like a sister, and she was even kind of fond of Dylan, although she'd never let him know it. The last guy she'd been involved with, Paul, had managed to find a tiny piece of her heart. She wasn't a monster. She could appreciate a cute puppy, kitten, or even an occasional baby. She'd even gotten back together with Paul for a while after breaking up with him the first time, so she had given it more than a fair chance to grow into something serious, but it hadn't—at least not on her end. But what she didn't do was make herself vulnerable to a potential romantic partner. She'd already come dangerously close to doing that with Ash when she'd let some of his barbs find their mark. Now he was flirting with her? How did she handle that from a man who attracted her as no one else ever had?

Dana came abruptly out of her trance when Claudia suddenly appeared before her. She'd been so out of it she hadn't even noticed her approach. Game time. Confidence oozed from the younger woman in waves as she put one hand on her hip and cocked a questioning brow in Zoe's direction. Not bothering with a greeting, she simply asked, "Who's your friend? I thought this was a family dinner."

Without waiting for Zoe to speak, Dana drew herself up to her full height, which was still several inches below Claudia's, before giving the rude chit a blank look. "Oh, who're you?"

She could tell by the tightening of Claudia's mouth that she didn't like being dismissed. She felt like the star of the family and wanted to be treated as such. Well, too damn bad. "I'm Claudia," she sneered.

"Oh, you're the sister," Dana replied dismissively. Turning to Zoe to push the point home that Claudia wasn't important to her, she tossed over her shoulder, "I'm Dana, Ash's girlfriend."

"GIRLFRIEND?" the other woman practically shouted. Dana winked at Zoe and counted to ten before slowly turning to face the pain in the ass once again. "That's right." Then she pulled Claudia into a brief hug that drew a strangled gasp from Zoe. "Congratulations, sis, I heard you're graduating from high school soon." Patting Claudia's shoulder in false sympathy, she lowered her voice as she added, "You look a bit older than the standard eighteen though. Good for you. It doesn't matter how long it takes. I admire you for hanging in there after what must have been several years of failures." Donning her most concerned expression, which was damned hard, she asked, "So what happened? Was it a boy who got you all distracted? I know how you kids are at that age. I bet he turned your head with a bunch of pretty words and big promises and then broke your heart." By this point, Claudia's mouth was hanging open in shock and Dana was having a hard time keeping it together. Zoe had long since turned to the side, no doubt trying to collect herself. "But you hung in there. I know it must be embarrassing to be so much older than the others, but who cares? You had a dream of obtaining that diploma and you didn't let a little thing like that stop you. I'm sure your friends have *long* moved on to finish college and begin careers and that you must feel abandoned by some of them. Do they still talk to you?" Claudia's face was an alarming shade of red now as her jaw flapped up and down, but nothing came out. Dana figured she might as well take advantage of it and push a little harder before she found her voice. She dropped one hand and linked it with the boldly painted red nails that were hanging limply there. "I bet at least one of them is proud of you. If you decide to continue with your education, there's no shame in being over thirty when you obtain your degree. People are getting married and starting families later in life now. They'll just think you took some time off to find yourself before moving forward. You don't look a day over twenty-five, so you'll still fit in okay. I bet there'll be some at least as old if not older, right, Zoe?"

Zoe swung around as if she'd been shot. Dana had to give her credit for the quick gulp before she readily replied, "Oh, absolutely. My mom is going back to school right now and she says there are plenty of senior citizens doing it, so you'll actually look young to them."

"I am *not* in fucking high school!" Claudia suddenly bellowed as she pulled herself violently away from the two of them.

Gotcha, Dana thought to herself as all attention was suddenly fixed upon them. She wanted to rattle the other woman and she'd succeeded beautifully. Her chest was heaving and she appeared to struggle for her words. "Oh, honey, I'm sorry," Dana gushed out. "You didn't make it after all? I had no idea. I could have sworn someone mentioned your upcoming graduation. I didn't mean to hit on a painful subject. We all love you regardless, don't we, Zoe?"

"Er—sure we do." Her friend nodded quickly.

Claudia's fingers were clenching and releasing in a way that should have been alarming. Dana figured they might soon be wrapped around her neck if she didn't back off.

"Where did you come from?" Claudia snapped. "Asher doesn't have serious girlfriends." Dana could easily pick up on the note of jealousy in the younger woman's voice and knew that Ash hadn't been wrong to want to divert her attention. A crush was usually a harmless thing, but with someone like Claudia, it could turn into something else altogether.

"I wasn't aware you were the authority on me, little sister," Ash drawled silkily as he approached them. He stepped around Claudia and slid an arm around Dana as if it were the most natural thing in the world. "Now if you're finished acting like the teenager you claim not to be, I'm ready for dinner." He dropped a kiss onto Dana's neck and steered her toward the double doors leading back into the house. "You sure know how to poke the hornet's nest," he added under his breath. "This is the most fun I've had at one of these damn family dinners in a long time. You're worth every penny, munchkin." Rolling her eyes, Dana jabbed him in the side for the nickname he couldn't seem to let go. She was petite, not a freak. "Damn, you've got a bony elbow on you," he groused before returning to the previous subject. "I'm serious, what were you saying to the spoiled brat? She looked like she was going to have a seizure of some kind. Dylan and I were taking bets on how long it would take her to melt down."

"Who won?" Dana asked, glancing up at the devastatingly handsome man who had her tucked so closely against his body. *Sweet baby Jesus, he smells good.*

"Too close to call." Ash shrugged. "Plus, we got distracted and lost count when it happened. What did you say to get to her that badly? I mean, she's a nasty piece of business, but normally she's just smugly insulting. You actually had her stomping her foot—did you see that?"

Shaking her head, Dana said, "Even I wasn't brave enough to take my eyes off her long enough to look down. I heard Bart bragging about her finishing college soon. So I might have accidentally praised her for staying in high school despite her advanced age and graduating this year. I also tried my best to reassure her that she was never too old to better herself even if it took her until the age of twenty-five to make it through the twelfth grade."

In a move that had her swallowing her tongue, Ash roared with laughter. Dana could hear Dylan making a similar sound and figured that Zoe must be bringing him up to speed as well. "Oh, munchkin, you really struck gold. Claudia is far too conceited to have been rattled if you'd insulted something like her appearance. But her education, now that's a weakness. For all of his bragging, Bart has paid her way through school. I don't know if she's dumb or just fucking lazy, but she'd never have made it past the entrance exam without him opening his checkbook. And I know from the digs that Mother Dear has made that it was far from the first time. And that high school diploma you pounced on? She had to go to summer school and still ended up short on credits. I suspect there was some payoff there in the end as well. There's no way in hell that her transcripts got her into that fancy school, and her intellect sure as hell hasn't kept her there."

Dana felt a moment of discomfort at being the mean girl that she'd always despised, but she quickly brushed the thought aside. If she knew Claudia, the other woman would be coming after her with guns blazing. This wasn't the time to have doubts or back off. The blonde would eat her for dinner without a single regret. No, she was being paid to do a job and that was to save Ash from the unwanted advances of his stepsister. At least if Claudia was focused on her, then she wasn't likely to maul her brother at the dinner table. This was called taking one for the team and Ash had better damn well appreciate it.

Five

It was like having a front-row seat at a *Jerry Springer Show*, Ash thought to himself as he watched Claudia glare across the table at his fake girlfriend. When he'd asked Dana to accompany him so that he could enjoy a grope-free evening with the family, he hadn't expected the entertainment that would come along with her company. The feisty woman at his side pretending to be the love of his life was cool and poised under fire. She appeared to be clueless that Claudia was probably planning her death in some creative fashion. That's what made the whole thing work so well. He was certain that no one other than Dylan and Zoe would even suspect that this whole thing was an act. He couldn't swear to it, but his mother's lips had actually twitched at one point when Dana had asked Claudia what her favorite subject was in school. When his sister had remained silent, Dana had carefully and slowly enunciated her question, "WHAT. DO. YOU. LIKE. BEST? ART. MAYBE?" Her face had been perfectly sweet and innocent, showing not an ounce of deception. Dylan had choked on his wine, and Zoe had clapped him on the back before patting her own chest. Claudia had narrowed her eyes, but otherwise said nothing. Dana had given her a pitying look as if she felt sorry for her. Since then he figured they were all simply waiting for the next outburst and wondering when it was going to happen. Dylan had discreetly flashed five fingers a few minutes ago, indicating his bet, and Ash had acknowledged it and flashed both hands briefly. He'd been trying to keep Dana quiet since then for a while longer so he'd win. But when he felt something move against his leg, he figured the game might have shifted in a new direction.

Directly across the table from him, Claudia gave a smug smile that had his stomach clenching. Then what he now knew was her foot inched dangerously close to the family jewels as he attempted to shift away. *Damn, how long is her leg?* He couldn't seem to move backward fast enough to escape her touch. She'd just made contact with his cock when her chair went flying backward, landing with a loud clatter on the floor. There was a moment of dead silence before Bart jumped to his feet and rushed to his clearly dazed daughter's side. "Princess, what happened? Are you all right? Here, let Daddy pick you up."

Ash turned to Dylan, muttering, "What the fuck," under his breath. But instead of his brother, his eyes landed on Dana. She raised her wineglass to him in a silent salute before taking a small sip. All the while a smug smile played around her plump lips as she watched Claudia attempt to straighten her hair back into place. "I think I love you," Ash declared reverently, and he wasn't sure he was totally kidding in that moment. "What just happened?"

Dana appeared to glance over to make sure no one was following their conversation before she leaned close and whispered, "Your sister accidentally hit my leg while she was playing footsie with you. I simply waited for her to come within reach again, then I pushed. Granted, I may be a tad stronger than I thought. I was just trying to get her attention, not necessarily break her neck, but it got her off you either way, right?" Flexing a muscle in her arm, she added, "I think that new Zumba class is really paying off."

Ash couldn't help it—he started laughing, then tried to tone it down when his mother glared at him. "That was fucking amazing," he agreed under his breath.

Dylan, having apparently recovered by then, leaned across Zoe to ask, "Did you do that?" Shaking his head no, Ash nodded to Dana. He didn't miss the look of respect that crossed his brother's face. He knew that Dylan had carried a grudge for a while over Dana's interference when he was struggling to build a relationship with Zoe, but he'd gotten past it a while ago. They'd never be hugging buddies, but his brother liked the woman, even though they still argued out of longtime habit. Dylan didn't even pretend to misunderstand what had led up to their sister ending up on her ass on the floor. "Foot in lap?"

Grimacing, Ash said, "Yeah, same as usual. Instead, she miscalculated one of the times and ended up with Dana."

Zoe's shoulders were shaking as she tried to compose herself. Considering Claudia had pulled the same shit with Dylan before, Ash was sure Zoe was thrilled to see a little payback delivered. Claudia was a nasty piece of business, and they'd all had more than enough.

If Dana was brave enough to take her on, then Ash was happy to let her. Of course, he'd keep his eye on his sister. Dana had better never make the mistake of underestimating the other woman. Claudia wouldn't let this kind of embarrassment go. He was actually surprised that she wasn't making a huge scene right now and demanding Dana's head on a platter. But strangely enough, she'd yet to make any accusations. Maybe she knew it would require some explanation on her part as well and she preferred to play the innocent where her father was concerned. Ash was certain his mother saw through the act, but she was careful about picking her battles. Ash bit back a grin as Bart led a hobbling Claudia from the room, as if she'd just returned home from a war zone. "Come on, princess, Daddy will take care of you. I had no idea that there was a problem with that chair. We'll replace the whole set tomorrow. I can't have my baby getting hurt like that."

They'd barely left the room when his mother refilled her wineglass and let out a long-suffering sigh. "I swear, sometimes I wonder why I even bother. No matter how hard I try, these family dinners are horrid."

"Then why do you keep demanding we all attend?" Ash asked. "You have to know that we don't enjoy it." Dylan, who was always the more diplomatic of the pair of them, looked as if he was thinking of interrupting, but instead remained silent.

His mother took another sip from her expensive crystal goblet before saying, "If I didn't, I'd never see either of you. Do you have any idea how long it's been since I've seen your brothers?"

"Maybe you should have thought about that before you married Bart," Ash pointed out. He refused to let her heap guilt on him. She'd never been a mother figure to any of them, and playing the victim was a joke.

In an uncharacteristic display of emotion, she asked angrily, "What was I supposed to do after your father died, Asher, remain alone forever? You along with half of the country must be aware that while he was living, he chased everything in a skirt. Do you not feel as if I've served my time? Do you have any idea how mortifying it was to have women that you thought of as your friends sleeping with your husband? I went through a period where I was so depressed that I didn't leave the house for months. And do you think he cared? Your father only had two loves in his life, and that was the resorts and you kids. Everything else was expendable."

Ash stared at his mother in shock. Naturally he knew his father had been a womanizer, as the man had never made a secret of it. Ash had also never given much thought to how it affected his mother. Maybe that made him a cold bastard, but she'd always kept herself aloof and emotionally distant from them. Truthfully, he hadn't thought she really gave a damn as long as she lived in the luxurious style she was accustomed to and had a nanny handle the dirty work of child-rearing. Their father had always been the fun parent. He was crazy about them and would drop whatever he was doing if they needed him. It wasn't unusual for them to go days or even weeks without seeing their mother, but that was rare with their father. Shrugging, Ash said, "I don't recall it bothering you back then. You were a member of every country club in the state and spent more time there than you did at home with your family. Dad was usually the one we had dinner with in the evening. You were rarely around."

"That's the way he wanted it!" his mother snapped. "In the beginning I tried to be a traditional parent. I wanted to catch up with each of you at the end of the day. To ask about how you were doing in school, your friends, or even if you had a crush on someone special. Your father didn't want that though and he blocked me at every turn. He let me know quickly that my part in your upbringing ended the moment you left my body. He wanted heirs with a good pedigree and that was my role. When it had been fulfilled, he hired the best help that money could buy and told me to take up a hobby. He also let me know in no uncertain terms that if I didn't go along with the program, I could find somewhere else to live. So in order to at least stay close to you and your brothers, I learned to keep my mouth shut and take what moments I could get with you."

"I don't believe that," Dylan interjected, sounding uncertain. "Dad said you had no desire to attend our baseball games or anything else along those lines. He always seemed so sad over it. He said you just weren't the maternal type and he'd given up trying to change you."

A bitter laugh escaped her throat as their mother looked at first Dylan and then Ash. "I wanted nothing more than to be a real mother to you boys. Your father was always bigger than life; that's one of the things that I loved about him in the beginning. If he turned his attention toward you, then it was as if you'd experienced a sunrise for the very first time after a lifetime of darkness. That's how it was for me. I was raised by strict parents in a very sheltered household. I was working in the college library when I met your father. He was handsome, charming, and funny. I never stood a chance. My parents were thrilled because on paper he was the perfect match for me as I was for him. I was completely besotted, and when he asked me to marry him after dating for several months, I was over the moon. But our differences became apparent soon after we were married and I quickly realized that I'd never really known him at all. I was a family obligation that he needed to fulfill and you boys were the true joy that he got out of it. Unlike me, you were exactly what he wanted and he loved you completely and without reservations. The only problem was that he never saw a need for you to have a mother in your life. He wanted me to have no part in your upbringing; he was brutally clear on that."

Incredulous, Ash asked, "Are you trying to say he abused you physically?"

Waving a hand, his mother shook her head. "No, he never touched me in that way. His words and threats were enough. As I said, to be a part of your lives, I had to stay on the sidelines and not interfere. If I overstepped, then one of the staff was sure to let him know. He wanted the absolute best for each of you, and he didn't feel as if I had anything of value to offer to that end. He wanted strong sons and he felt that a mother would make you weak and clingy. I was a liability and he simply couldn't have that. As long as I knew my place, then he left me alone to come and go as I saw fit and he did the same. He was cordial and generous financially. He also made it clear that even though he sought out the company of other women, I was to remain true to our wedding vows. He didn't want the bad publicity that gossip would bring. He told me that when you boys were older, then he would release me from my obligations and I'd still be young enough to start over with someone who could give me what I wanted."

"So you stayed married to Dad for a set amount of time, then he gave you a divorce?" Dylan asked, now looking a little shell-shocked. Ash could relate. This was the longest personal conversation they'd ever had with their mother. She rarely spoke of their father and had certainly never volunteered the kind of information she was sharing with them today.

"That's right," she agreed. "I waited until the last of you boys had left home, then I asked your father to terminate the marriage. He had no problem with it. In fact, I think it was a relief to him to put that part of his life behind him."

"But you left him for Bart," Ash pointed out impatiently. He had no idea why she'd picked today to drop this bombshell, but since she'd started it, he wanted some answers to things he'd always been curious about. He knew his father had had girlfriends during his marriage; hell, he'd met several of them. But his father had always alluded to the fact that their mother did as well. As far as he and his brothers knew, it was an open marriage of convenience.

"Bart and I went to school together and had been friends since childhood. He's always been there for me, but there was never anything romantic between us while I was married to your father. That last year before our divorce, Bart's wife, Melanie, lost her battle with cancer and he was devastated. I was his shoulder to lean on as he'd always been mine. In the months ahead we decided that what we really longed for in our lives was companionship, so after my divorce we got married."

Ash was surprised when Dana spoke up. "Why would you leave what was basically one arranged marriage for another? Especially considering how the first one turned out? I'd have thought the next time you'd want to find love."

His mother's undignified snort had Ash smothering a grin. "I tried that and it didn't work out. There's something to be said for being with a man who knows you so well that there is no need for any type of pretenses. Which is what Bart and I have. I'm not saying that there aren't challenges at times, but isn't that true of any relationship?"

Before anything else could be said, Bart returned to the room minus Claudia. "Sorry about that," he said. "I had to make sure my little girl was all right before I left her alone. Charlotte, please contact the furniture company tomorrow and have them pick up this junk before anyone else gets hurt."

Ash didn't miss the slight roll of his mother's eyes before she replied, "Certainly, darling. I'll take care of that. How is Claudia doing? I hope she didn't hurt herself."

Bart still looked frazzled as he took a seat and gulped down half of his glass of wine. "I gave her an Ativan and put her to bed. You know she's very fragile."

Ash was pretty sure that he was the only one who heard Dana mutter, "Fragile, my ass." Although the look on his mother's face before she donned her blank mask said that she agreed with his fake girlfriend's assessment of her stepdaughter. To Ash, this seemed like a golden opportunity to make an early exit and he didn't intend to let it pass. He pushed his chair back and got to his feet before turning to Dana. "I believe you said something about opening the shop tomorrow. So if you're ready?"

"That's right, darling," she agreed easily as she stood to join him. "You always take such good care of me, muffin."

Ash heard Dylan snicker at the corny endearment, but he just grinned. Considering the amount of animosity that he'd had toward Dana for the better part of a year, he was certainly enjoying her company tonight. He almost hated to see it end because he kind of looked forward to seeing what she would do or say next. Oh well, he suspected there might be other pretend dates to look forward to. And strangely enough, he actually did anticipate them with enthusiasm. Putting his arm around her shoulders, he squeezed her against his side before planting a noisy kiss on her forehead. "Daddy knows exactly what his little munchkin likes."

Bart looked puzzled by the banter, while his mother shocked him yet again by bestowing what appeared to be a genuine smile upon them. Maybe she'd hit the hard liquor earlier in the evening. That would explain all of the oversharing she'd been doing. Possibly one too many of those Ativans that Bart had mentioned. "I'm so glad you could all come this evening," she said softly as she rose to join them. She took Dana's hands in hers and added, "It was a pleasure meeting you, dear. I hope to see you again soon."

"Um—of course." Dana stumbled on the words, clearly not expecting the warm good-bye from Ash's mother. Nodding in Bart's direction, she said, "I hope Claudia feels better."

Dylan and Zoe followed them out, and as the door shut behind them, Ash looked at his brother and said, "That was some *Twilight Zone* shit right there. What in the hell has Mommie Dearest been smoking?"

Shaking his head, Dylan said, "Dude, what was that? She even hugged us when we left. Do you remember the last time that happened? I sure don't. It kind of creeped me out."

"Honey," Zoe admonished softly. "She's your mother. And it sounded as if she wanted to make things right between you all. If what she said was true, then possibly you owe her the chance to reconnect."

"How are we supposed to know if it's a lie or not?" Ash pointed out. "I mean, Dad has been dead for years, so it's not as if he can defend himself. And why wait this long if she really wanted us to know the truth?"

Beside him, Dana shrugged. "Maybe you should ask her. I have a built-in bullshit detector and it didn't go off once during her speech. I don't think she was lying. As to the timing, maybe something happened recently that you're unaware of."

"Like mass quantities of alcohol," Ash added dryly. "Listen, I don't know about the rest of you, but I've had more than enough of the show for the evening. Let's get the hell out of Dodge before they figure out that we're still standing here." Saying a quick good-bye to his brother and Zoe, Ash put a hand on the small of Dana's back and steered her toward his BMW coupe, which was parked in the circular drive. He opened the door for her and waited until she was settled before walking around to the driver's side and getting in.

"You did well tonight," he acknowledged as he drove toward her apartment.

"Thanks," she replied softly. "I may have gone a tad overboard by shoving her backwards, but it kind of happened before I thought it out."

"No worries," he said, chuckling. "She had it coming. She'll be after you though. For your own good, I probably shouldn't take you to any more family dinners. I don't want to see you get hurt. She might play the poor little girl with her father, but I have no doubt that she's a vindictive little bitch."

"Ash, I can more than hold my own against women like her," Dana assured him. "She's far from the first mean girl that I've crossed paths with. And you hired me for a job. After seeing her in action, I understand why. Does she try to maul you at every event?"

Ash couldn't hide his shudder of revulsion. "Yeah, pretty much. She's never been that bad with Dylan, but she doesn't miss an opportunity where I'm concerned. I guess she knows I'm the bad seed of the family."

"That's ridiculous," Dana scoffed. "There's no possible justification for your sister putting the moves on you. If that's how you've rationalized it in your mind, then you're as screwed up as she is."

His head was beginning to throb as it always did after an evening with his family. And as grateful as he was to the woman sitting next to him for running interference, he found himself irritated by her comment. Who did she think she was? "Listen, honey, I could really do without the postmortem. You don't know anything about me. Although I would think the bastard that I've been to you the last year would give you some clue. I'm not a nice man. I go through women like you probably go through cookies. I'm the asshole that you're always accusing me of being. Don't delude yourself by believing I can be saved or that I'm mis- understood. The last thing I need is for you to develop some silly crush on me. We have a business arrange- ment and that's all it'll ever be. You've seen my type and you're not it."

Ash felt lower than dirt when he saw her wince out of the corner of his eye. Why had he said all of that shit? What was it about her that could turn his mood so damn quickly? One minute he was in awe of her and the next he wanted to destroy her. He was all over the place where she was concerned and had been since the first time he'd laid eyes on her. He'd never been this confused over a woman before, since it was usually pretty simple for him. He either wanted to fuck her or he didn't. But either way, he tried to be respectful to the opposite sex. Dana's voice was steady when she spoke, giving away nothing of what she was feeling.

"Oh, I'm quite aware of what you're attracted to. You don't discriminate, that's for certain. Intellect not only isn't a requirement, it's a negative where you're concerned. Tell me, did you have a bad experience once with a woman who could actually think for herself? Is that why you've lowered your expectations to rock bottom?"

She was closer to the truth than she might have expected with that question. Once he had been in love with a woman who was one step ahead of him the entire time. She'd been absolutely nothing at all like the Brittanys of the world that he'd gravitated toward since. Smart women had a lot of expectations that he had no intentions of meeting. They wanted things like love and commitment. The Brittanys of the world just wanted to have a good time. And that was something he could handle. "What's the matter, munchkin, you jealous because I haven't lowered them enough to include you? Was that why you sent Claudia sailing through the air? You jealous of her?"

Instead of being offended, Dana tossed her head back and started to laugh. It went on so long that the sound was grating on his nerves when she finally paused to catch her breath. "You're so full of yourself, Asher Jackson. You hired me for a job, and believe me, that's the only reason I got your stepsister away from you. Otherwise I'd have been happy to sit back and let her grope you. Maybe you're just upset that I interrupted her. Was she getting to the good part? For all I know, you two sneak upstairs and go at it like rabbits every time you have a family dinner."

"That's disgusting." He shuddered as he spoke. "I can assure you I've never willingly been touched by her, and I damn sure didn't go anywhere with her. I have some standards, you know. She's my sister, for fuck's sake."

"Sure, whatever you say, boss. I'm your employee so there's no need to explain or deny anything to me. It's a judgment-free zone here. You pay me, I do the job and keep my mouth shut. That is the way you want it, right?"

"Exactly," he sighed halfheartedly. He already regretted his outburst. Why did she constantly bring out the worst in him? He'd enjoyed her company immensely all evening, yet had to ruin it by acting like a dick in the end. She'd done nothing to warrant it, as usual. He just couldn't seem to help himself. "Listen," he began, "I may have gotten a little carried away."

"Ya think?" she asked dryly. "You haven't ever bothered to apologize before so why start now? You despise me. You've never made a secret out of that. It might make things easier if you were passingly civil while we're working, but I'll manage either way."

It stung more than he cared to admit that she thought he hated her. *Well, you've been so charming, how could she possibly believe otherwise?* Swallowing the lump in his throat, he managed to get out, "I'm sorry, Dana. I was out of line." *Damn, that hurt to admit.*

"I bet that sucked for you to have to say, didn't it?" She smirked. "You've said far worse to me and never choked out an apology. If you're worried about me quitting, don't be. I'm in it for the money. Although there's only so much I'll take from you before I go to Walmart and beg them to save me from working for you."

Ash found himself laughing again. If he could stop being an asshole, he might actually enjoy her company. Maybe they could get to a point where they could consider friendship. *That ain't all you'd like to do.* He did his best to block out the voice in his big head that was communicating directly with the little head in his pants. Both of them were constantly pointing out the fact that he was attracted to the woman that he insulted on a regular basis. He pulled up in front of her building and put the car in Park before extending a hand toward her. "How about another cease-fire? I'll do my best to keep my asinine comments to myself in the future."

Dana placed her soft hand in his, and Ash found his body responding to that small touch. "I'm sure you won't be able to hold out for long. Let's face it, I rub you the wrong way. We're oil and water and whatever else there is that doesn't mix. As long as you know that I'll continue to give as good as I get, we should be fine."

"I wouldn't expect anything less," Ash answered honestly. That was one thing he admired about her. She no longer took anything from him. And damn, she was creative with her insults. If he were a less confident man, he'd seriously have a complex by now. He'd admit that he'd checked out his dick a few times after some particularly cutting remarks about his size. Not that she had any firsthand knowledge, but a man couldn't help feeling paranoid about stuff like that. He reached for his billfold and counted out her payment for the night along with a generous tip because she'd more than earned it when she sent Claudia tumbling backward. "I'm hosting a business dinner at my apartment next Thursday evening. Will that work for you?"

She tucked the money into her purse without counting it and nodded. "Sure, that sounds good. Will Zoe and Dylan be there?"

"They will. I'm sure you'll decide to avail yourself of the hotel boutique again. How in the world did you manage to spend that much on a dress and shoes?"

Dana smoothed her hands down the formfitting black sheath she was wearing before asking, "Are you complaining about the end result? Did you perhaps want me to meet your family wearing jeans and flip-flops? I'd be glad to put something like that together for the next occasion. I believe I still have my old prom dress. It's a gorgeous shade of hot pink with lots of poufy lace. Plus, I had the heels dyed to match it. You could buy me a corsage and maybe get a matching tux for yourself."

Ash couldn't contain his grimace as he pictured them in the attire she was describing so vividly. He had no doubt that she'd show up exactly like that if he continued on. Hell, he didn't care about the money; he just enjoyed goading her about it. "Er—no, I have no desire to relive your high school years. Pick out whatever you like. Go ahead and get several outfits, both dressy and casual. Maybe I can get a volume discount. I'd go with some higher heels next time though. You still look like—"

"I hope you're not going to say your little sister," she interrupted dryly. "Considering tonight, it would seem wrong to be compared to Claudia. Other than her, you only have brothers, right?" When he nodded yes, her smile brightened. "Are any of them hot? With a better personality than you? What am I talking about, Dylan is already sunshine and puppies compared to you. Do you have a bad attitude because you're the ugly duckling in a family of hotties?" Slapping a hand on her thigh, she added, "I bet that's it! Wow, it must be rough. You know, usually the plain ones develop a sense of humor out of necessity, so what happened to you? Not only are you the least attractive, you're the surly one as well. That hardly seems fair."

Ash knew his mouth was hanging open. He'd never been labeled the unattractive brother before. To the contrary, women seemed to find him very handsome. "I'm not . . . You're wrong. Hey, where do you think you're going? I'm not finished talking here."

His awkward words fell on deaf ears as Dana

opened her door and slid from the car and onto the nearby sidewalk. "As you said earlier, I have an early day tomorrow, so good night." He called after her again, but she slammed the door in his face and never looked back.

"Son of a bitch," he muttered before shaking his head and pulling back out into the street. She'd done it again, dammit. She'd deftly turned the tables on him. Instead of irritation though, he found himself chuckling softly. *Well played, munchkin, well played.* For the first time in his life, he was actually looking forward to the upcoming business dinner. Thanks to his pretend girlfriend, his world had suddenly become a lot more interesting. And that thought also scared the hell out of him.

Six

T hat was freaking amazing," Zoe gushed to Dana the next day as they wiped down the tables in the coffee shop. "Dylan and I laughed all the way home. I kept seeing Claudia's legs in the air after her chair flew backwards. Do you have any idea how many times I've dreamed of her falling?"

Dana giggled at her friend's excitement. "I did feel bad about it for a while, but then I remembered how ugly she's been to you and how bitchy she was to me. I swear, women need to stick together, not try to destroy each other. I've never understood why some people feel the need to be so petty towards others. Life is not a competition and it takes more energy to be negative than it does to be positive."

Zoe held up her hand for a fist bump. "I completely agree. But competitive and superficial women like Claudia aren't happy unless they're tearing someone else down. That's what she gets off on. But maybe next time she'll think before she acts like that."

Dana's head was down as she cleaned a chair when she heard Zoe clear her voice loudly. Without bothering to look up, Dana continued ranting, "And the whole thing with her father was so weird. Did you see him practically carry her from the room? Their behavior is disturbing on so many levels. I can't believe Charlotte puts up with that." Once again Zoe made a strangled sound that finally got her attention. Glancing up, she saw her friend and employer nodding toward the door. Dana's eyes widened as she recognized Claudia and two other girls who appeared to be around the same age entering the coffee shop. She couldn't say that she hadn't been expecting something like this. Even Ash had warned her that Claudia would be after her. "Oh great," she sighed. "I'm guessing she isn't here to support her sister-in-law."

"Not bloody likely," Zoe groaned. "Why don't you go in the office and I'll get rid of her. I'm not going to let her make a scene in my shop or insult my best friend."

"I love you for that"—Dana smiled—"but I don't want to show any weakness near her. If I run now, she'll have the upper hand. I promise to take it outside if I get the urge to pull her bleached blond hair out."

Claudia had spotted them by that point and was strutting through the shop as if she owned the place. Confidence practically oozed from every pore as she and her friends laughed at some private joke. She came to a stop a few inches away from them with a sneer firmly affixed to her face as she took in Dana's work uniform. Without saying a word, she stepped around them and pulled out a chair from the table they'd just finished cleaning. Her minions followed suit, lowering their designer-clad asses gingerly onto the wood as if it were a snake that would bite them. "We'll have nonfat cappuccinos," Claudia demanded. Then she looked down at her expensive watch before adding, "And we're in a hurry."

Dana didn't expect any manners, but she was pissed that Claudia didn't bother to acknowledge Zoe. After all, they were family. Squeezing her friend's arm, she said, "I'll take care of it." She didn't want Zoe caught in the crosshairs of the war she'd started with the surly sister-in-law from hell. Laughter followed in her wake as she turned and walked toward the front of the shop with Zoe following closely behind. She clearly heard Claudia remark on her big ass, but again told herself to let the insults go. She refused to take the bait and make a scene here. That would play right into Claudia's hands and she wasn't giving her that satisfaction. "Ignore them," she whispered to Zoe as the other woman stiffened. "The sooner we get their damn coffee, the sooner they will leave." Dana took a deep breath and calmly arranged the cups on the counter. Within a few minutes, she had all three coffees ready. Zoe picked up one and Dana took the others. She plastered a pleasant smile on her face in preparation for delivering the order to a smug Claudia.

She'd barely set the last cup down when Claudia took a sip and promptly spit it on the front of Dana's shirt. "Oh my God," she hissed. "I told you nonfat. This is whole milk; I can taste the difference. Can't you hear properly?"

One of the clones with her gave a nasty laugh before saying, "What did you expect, she works here with Chloe, doesn't she? I told you we should have gone to Starbucks."

Dana could feel her face flush with anger. She didn't

give two shits if they insulted her, but she wouldn't let them do it to Zoe. Especially since she knew it was all directed at her. Leaning forward, she put both hands on the table and glared at the bitches sitting there. "Didn't your parents ever teach you kids any manners? Oh wait, I think we've already established that education was never your strong suit."

"You fucking cow," Claudia hissed. "You have no idea who you're dealing with. You might have Asher fooled, but I see right through you. You're nothing but a little gold digger who thinks she hit the lottery." A mocking laugh escaped her throat as she added, "Don't get any ideas. Ash sleeps with a different woman every week. You're nothing special. The novelty of slumming with you will wear off soon and he'll kick you to the curb like all the others. I have to admit, I've never known him to be into fat chicks before though. You may not make it as long as the slender ones."

Zoe was shaking with anger when she stepped forward and gently pushed Dana to the side. "You need to get out of my shop. And if I were you, I wouldn't ever come back here. I won't have you talking to my friend like that. I might have to put up with you at Charlotte's, but I own this shop and believe me when I say that you're not welcome here."

Dana felt her eyes sting at her friend's defense of her. She knew a war with Claudia would make things difficult for Zoe in many ways and she regretted putting her in this position. She should have thought it through before she'd agreed to accompany Ash last night. Business dinners were one thing, but causing problems between family members was something else entirely. The uppity little bitch might deserve to be knocked on her ass, but now Zoe would pay the price for Dana's interference. With that thought in mind, she swallowed her pride and turned to her friend. "It's okay, really. I've dealt with difficult customers before. I'll go make some more drinks for them and then I'll work in the kitchen for a while."

She had already turned to remove the offensive cappuccino when she felt a hand on her shoulder. Zoe was shaking her head as she stopped Dana. "Absolutely not. They're leaving. It wouldn't matter if you and I were personal friends or not. I'd never allow anyone to speak to an employee in that manner. I don't care that she's related to me. Well, actually, that makes her behavior even worse. Dylan would never stand for anyone to treat a member of his staff like that either. Since you are my best friend, I'm doubly pissed over it. Now please let me handle this." With that, she marched back to the table, where the three women still remained, and said in an icy voice, "It's time to show yourselves out or I'll have security remove you."

"This is my hotel," Claudia snapped. "If I want to stay, there's nothing you can do about it."

Zoe gave her sister-in-law a smile completely devoid of humor and calmly walked behind the counter and picked up the telephone. Within a few minutes, two security guards entered the shop. After speaking briefly with Zoe, they ushered a sputtering Claudia and her group of clones out the door. Dana heard Claudia screech, "Do you have any idea who I am?"

Dana watched Zoe carefully, waiting for the reality of what had just happened to sink in. But instead of looking rattled, her boss was calmly making what appeared to be a frappe while humming under her breath. "You want one?" she asked Dana as she nodded toward the blender. "It's caramel, your favorite."

Approaching her unusually calm friend, Dana asked hesitantly, "Are you all right?"

Zoe gave her a blank look in return before shrugging. "Sure, why wouldn't I be?"

"Um—because you just had your bitch of a sister-in-law tossed out of here on her ass. And something like that would normally freak you out. So this whole calm vibe you've got going on is a little creepy." Grabbing Zoe's nearby cup, Dana asked suspiciously, "Is there booze in this?"

Laughing, Zoe said, "No, but that's not a bad idea." Then she added, "Oh my God, did you see Claudia's face when those guys walked up to her table and told her she had to leave? I swear, I think I peed myself a little bit. And that horrible friend of hers, the redhead. Her name is Megan and she's just as bad as, if not worse than, Claudia. She's been to a couple of family dinners, and you should see the way she hangs all over Dylan and Asher. She doesn't give a damn if I'm there or not. Plus, she always purposely calls me by the wrong name to get under my skin."

Rolling her eyes, Dana said, "So she did say 'Chloe.' I thought I'd heard that wrong. I noticed the way she was egging Claudia on. The other one didn't say much. In fact, she appeared kind of embarrassed."

"I'm not sure who she is," Zoe replied. "It's usually just those two bitches. I've tried my best to be nice and keep the peace, but she crossed the line today, when she brought that crap in here. This is my business and you're my friend. I couldn't care less if Claudia hates my guts. She's nasty to me either way. I'm certainly not going to let her get away with that kind of behavior here. I'm sure she'll run home and play the innocent victim with her father and Charlotte, but big deal. I'll tell Dylan what happened tonight so that he'll be prepared, but there's no way he'd expect me to turn a blind eye to her antics. He's told me before not to take any shit from her."

"No one's ever defended me like that." Dana started to tear up as she said, "You have no idea what that meant to me, Zoe. I'm so sorry that I've put you in such an awkward position though. I should have known that it would come to this. Ash warned me she'd be gunning for me, but I was cocky enough to think I could handle her alone."

Zoe reached out and squeezed her hand. "You're more than my best friend; you're like a sister to me. You've always had my back and you know that I've got you covered as well. You'd wipe the floor with Claudia before you'd let her hurt me. So don't expect me to do anything less for you. We've both had our share of dealing with the mean people of the world. The great thing is that we have each other now."

"Damn straight," Dana whispered as she wiped the moisture from the corners of her eyes.

They'd been so distracted that they hadn't noticed anyone coming into the shop until an amused voice chimed in, "According to Mommie Dearest, you ladies have been busy today. Security? I have to admit, I'm pretty damn impressed. I could hear Bart yelling in the background about the humiliation his baby had suffered. I had a hard time not laughing."

"Oh shit," Dana groaned as she dropped her head. "I take full responsibility. Tell them Zoe was just defending her big-mouthed friend."

Ash pulled out a stool from the bar and lowered himself onto it. "Never show your enemies weakness, munchkin. You know better than that. And who gives two good fucks about Bart or his crazy daughter? Even my mother didn't sound as if she particularly gave a shit. She was going through the motions of protest for the sake of appearance."

Looking resigned, Zoe asked, "What did Dylan say about it?"

Ash grinned. "Well, he hasn't actually said much. He's been too busy laughing. Oh wait, there was some bragging about what a kick-ass woman he married."

Standing up straighter, Zoe said, "You know, I think I'll go say hello to him. Maybe see if he wants to catch an early dinner."

Dana gave her friend a light push when she hesitated. "I've got it covered here. Go do—er, I mean, see your man." That was all the encouragement she needed. With a wave over her shoulder, Zoe was gone, leaving Dana to deal with Ash on her own. "I appreciate you being nice for her benefit. And before you start in on me, I tried to handle Claudia without security having to cart her off. But Zoe wasn't in the mood to take any attitude from your stepsister today, and I can't say as I blame her. I don't know your sister well, but I've got to believe that she was at a whole other level of nasty while she was here."

Pointing to Dana's shirt, Ash asked, "Did she do that to you?"

Suddenly self-conscious about her stained clothing,

Dana turned away. "It's no big deal," she mumbled. "I guess I committed the horrible sin of using whole milk in her drink. I did offer to fix her another one."

Ash had a hand on her arm and he gently turned her back to face him before she could gather her composure. "Dana, I'm not planning on defending that bitch," he said kindly. "I wish you'd have called me when this was going on. She had no right to come in here and be cruel to you and Zoe. I'm sorry that I caused that to happen to you. I knew better. Hell, I even warned you, yet I didn't take any actual steps to protect you from her malice."

As usual, she was defenseless against a sweet Asher. She found herself flustered and tongue-tied. She was touched by the note of genuine concern in his voice. Finally she managed to croak out, "It's fine, Ash. I'm a big girl. I wasn't exactly prepared for Claudia to show up this soon, but I should have been. You paid me to help you out with a complicated situation and this comes along with it. If it makes you feel better, I don't think she'll come back in here. Zoe was a little scary today when she went off on her. Claudia might think twice before she tangles with her in the future."

"Dylan will take care of Zoe," Ash said dismissively. "It's you I'm concerned about. Even if we called off this whole charade, it probably wouldn't stop her from coming after you again. You got the best of her twice now and she's not likely to let that go."

"Ash, really, you don't have to worry about it. I won't let my guard down again, okay?"

"I'll start coming down here more during your shifts," Ash said. "Could you make me a copy of your schedule? I can even have some of my meetings down here. Plus, I should probably either walk you to your car or have one of the guys in security do it. We can talk about it after you get off work. Buzz my office and let me know when you're ready and I'll be down. We can have dinner at my apartment. My housekeeper usually leaves me something to heat up."

"I—you—what?" Dana stumbled over her words as she tried to make sense out of what Ash was saying. Had he just invited her to his place for dinner? Of course, she knew it wasn't a date, but he was voluntarily spending time with her—he was also going out of his way to protect her from Claudia even though she had assured him that she would be fine. Not that she needed it, but it felt really good to have a man worry about her. Oh, who was she kidding? It felt really good to have Ash worry about her. A week ago she'd have been surprised if he'd bothered to lift a finger to stop anyone, much less his stepsister, from knocking her down or pulling her hair out. But now there was no mistaking the fact that he was worried about her.

He sighed impatiently, putting a slight dent in her girlish fantasies of the white knight riding to her rescue before he said, "I said call me when you're closing." He grabbed a nearby order form and scrawled something on it before handing it to her. "That's my cell number. It's probably better to use it in case I'm away from my desk." Without another word, he turned and left.

Holy crap, what just happened? Could this day get any weirder? She'd had someone spit coffee on her shirt, Zoe had turned into a badass, and Ash had acted like a normal person instead of an asshole. Of the three, he was the biggest surprise.

Dana quickly finished cleaning up the coffee counter before going into the back of the shop to change into an extra shirt that she kept on hand for the rare evenings when she had somewhere else to go other than home. She ran a brush through her short hair and touched up her makeup before opting to text Ash instead of calling. She needed to try to keep things impersonal between them or she'd be following him around like the rest of those lovesick women were doing. The last thing she wanted to do was get into a fistfight with Claudia over his affections. No, she wouldn't lower herself to that level. He was simply being a gentleman because a member of his family wanted to kill her. Simple, right? *Keep it together. It's okay to look at his ass, but do not fall in love with the man. I repeat, do not fall in love with him.*

With a deep sigh, Dana turned off the lights and waited for Ash by the door. For added security she repeated every ugly thing he'd ever said to her and hoped that it would carry her through the evening. Because if it didn't, she was very much afraid that she'd do something drastic like beg him to have sex with her. After all, it had been far too long since she'd been with a man, and it was all Asher Jackson's damn fault. He was so damned hot that other men simply didn't stand out compared to him.

❧

Ash felt more than a little foolish now that the dust had settled and rational thought had returned. He had no idea why he had started acting like someone had appointed him as Dana's protector. Admittedly he felt slightly responsible for Claudia's actions since it was his nutjob stepsister who was now out to get her. But he could have left the situation in Dylan's hands. Instead, he'd charged downstairs like his ass was on fire. Dylan had been on his way to do the same thing, but Ash had literally mowed his brother down in his haste to check on Dana. Dylan had looked more than a little surprised, but for once had chosen not to comment other than to request that Ash ask Zoe to call him.

He ran a hand through his hair as he pondered his options. Why had he invited her to dinner? No, he'd demanded it. He should have worked out a plan while he was at the shop. There had been no need to extend this into the evening, yet he had. Maybe he'd take her to the resort restaurant instead. At least then there would be other people around. It would be far less intimate. Just another business dinner, right? She was technically his employee now. Yeah, that was exactly what he should do. Firmly resolved, he approached the shop and saw her standing in front waiting for him. She looked so damn small and vulnerable that it pulled at the heart he hadn't known could still be touched until that very moment. *Oh, I'm so fucked.*

Ash cleared his throat, struggling for composure right before he found himself asking, "Are you ready?" *Damn, she smells amazing.* He knew what he was supposed to do—really he did. So why was he opening the door to his penthouse apartment a few moments later and motioning her inside?

"You're home early, Romeo," said an amused voice that had him freezing in place. Rosa was still there? She was always gone by now. "Who's your friend?"

Turning to Dana, he said, "This is my housekeeper, Rosa. Rosa this is an, um—friend of mine, Dana."

Rosa approached them with a grin on her face. "I had a doctor's appointment today so I was late getting here." Shrugging her shoulders, she added, "I've never known you to bring a date home this early though. Is it because it's a school night?"

Ash was struggling with something he didn't feel often: embarrassment. He glared at Rosa, mentally willing her to shut up, when he was startled by the sound of Dana's laughter. Glancing over, he saw her shaking with laughter as she tried to catch her breath. "I love it," she managed to gasp out. "She's got your number, doesn't she?"

And just like that, both women were ganging up on him as a team. Rosa and Dana took turns tossing out comments about the type of women that he usually preferred. He strongly suspected he could have left the room without them noticing. "Honey, I'll never forget the day I opened the door and one of them stood there almost naked. She had on this tiny jacket, but it was hanging wide open. Let me tell you, she didn't even try to hide her goodies. She popped a bubble as big as my head, then asked if Asher was home. When I said no, she nodded and started to walk away. Every time she moved, you could see too much skin. I had to stop her and give her one of his shirts to wear home. He lives in a hotel after all. Didn't anyone notice her walking through the lobby? I swear, I could hear the marbles rattling around in her head when I explained to her that maybe it wasn't such a hot idea to be strolling around with so much of her business exposed. She had no idea what I was talking about, so I had to dumb it down for her."

"Oh my God"—Dana had to struggle to speak between giggles—"you should have been at the bar the other night with Brittany. I had to pretend to be Ash's wife so she'd stop sucking on his neck. She was even sniffing his armpits. The whole thing was disturbing. Even after I told her that he was my husband, she didn't see a problem. I thought I was going to have to pry her off him. Plus, she was calling him 'Ashey.' Everyone there was staring at them. Some of them had their phones out. I bet there's footage on YouTube by now. I seriously regret that I didn't record it."

"No shit." Rosa chuckled. "I'm glad he didn't bring that one home. Don't get me wrong, I've laughed more since I took this job than I have in my whole life, but it also makes me kinda sad at how low some women will sink for a man. Do parents not teach self-respect anymore? I know the boy here is a handsome devil, but for heaven's sake, men never buy the cow when you're tossing milk at them constantly. You know what I'm saying? If they learned how to play hard-to-get, maybe they wouldn't have to make so many walks of shame."

Shaking her head, Dana said dryly, "Between you and me, I don't believe there's a lot of thinking going on there. They're either not capable of it, or someone banged their brains out years ago."

Ash could feel his head beginning to ache as the two women continued to bond. Finally, when he couldn't take it anymore, he interrupted their bashing of his character to ask, "Do you think it would be possible to have dinner tonight? Why don't you two swap phone numbers and continue this another time? I, for one, am starving."

"He's always testy when he's hungry." Rosa sighed.

"I've got some lasagna in the refrigerator. Why don't I heat it and mix up a salad to go along with it?"

Relieved that he'd successfully distracted her, he said quickly, "That would be great, thanks."

"Rosa, you should stay and eat with us," Dana added.

He loved Rosa, but that was the last thing he wanted. He could easily picture them continuing to compare notes on his taste in women while he sat in the corner like a naughty schoolboy and hoped that the floor would open up and swallow him. He almost wept in gratitude when Rosa shook her head. "I wish I could, but Ted's waiting for me. Men are so helpless sometimes. After all these years, he still says he can't cook. I'd call bullshit on that, but the last time he attempted it, we had to call the fire department and remodel the kitchen. How you can set a room on fire making a bologna sandwich, I'll never know, but the place went up like an inferno. Now he either goes through a drive-thru or eats a bag of Doritos."

Ash's first thought was that old Ted might have left a joint burning nearby, but who was he to judge? He could use one right now himself. Maybe he should make friends with Rosa's husband if Dana was going to be around much. When the older woman walked away, he sank down into a nearby chair and looked over to see Dana giving him a knowing smile. "I really like her," she remarked. "I would have expected someone . . . different."

Rolling his eyes, he said wryly, "Trust me, I'm aware of your opinion of me. I'm sure you're thinking of a Playboy bunny, complete with the skimpy outfit and fuzzy tail. The only problem there is that she probably wouldn't cook or clean. And contrary to popular belief, I enjoy relaxing in my home. Not being chased around the coffee table."

All of a sudden Ash remembered something that had him smiling broadly. Dana gave him a suspicious look, shifting uncomfortably in her seat. "You know," he began, "if memory serves me correctly, we might have more in common than I thought. Because I seem to remember you dating a bit of fluff yourself. What was the musclehead's name that you were involved with? Unless I'm mistaken, he wasn't exactly a rocket scientist. Didn't he have a pretend date with Zoe to make Dylan jealous?"

Dana appeared to find her fingernails fascinating as she studied them instead of making eye contact. "I don't remember," she mumbled, clearly lying through her teeth.

"Oh, come now. Surely you know who I'm talking about." Ash pulled his cell phone from his pocket and hit a few buttons. "I'll just give Dylan a call. I'm sure he could help jog your memory."

"All right, dammit, it was Paul. Are you happy?" she snapped. "I'll have you know he's a successful business owner. Where is it written that you can't be intelligent if you're attractive?" she said defensively. "He's not even in the same league with Brittany."

Even if he hadn't known better, Dana's tone would have given her away. "Funny thing, one evening after he dropped you at work, we talked for a few minutes while he was waiting for his cab. I'm sure you remember that he blew the motor in his car by putting transmission fluid in the wrong place."

Dana's face was now bright red. "That's an honest mistake. It could happen to anyone."

"Mmm, yes. But would they cram paper towels in it next in an attempt to soak up the oil? Like poor Ted with the bologna sandwich, there was a fire and the car was a total loss. Which is a damn shame since it was a classic Firebird. I bet you looked good riding around in it."

"I hate you," Dana sulked. "You're just paying me back for telling Rosa about Brittany."

Shrugging, Ash said, "On the contrary—I'm pointing out that we've all had lapses in judgment. I've known you for a year and I don't recall you being involved in anything close to a serious relationship. Actually I don't remember seeing you with another guy after things ended with your boy toy."

"I've been busy. Not all of us need someone in our bed every single night, Ash. I happen to enjoy my own company."

Leaning forward, he asked, "Why can't you admit that we're more alike than you want to acknowledge? There's nothing wrong with not wanting a romantic hassle."

He was shocked when she appeared to ponder his words. "You're right. I'm not looking for anything serious, and the Pauls of the world expect no strings. When I broke up with him for the second time, he bumped me on the shoulder and told me to give him a call if I got horny. No tears, no drama, nada."

Ash couldn't help it; he laughed. "I've gotten a similar reaction before. Well, except for the clingers who have passed through my life. But most women I encounter are content with a good meal and an even better dessert."

When Dana licked her lips, Ash felt his cock jump to attention. He shifted in his chair, hoping she wouldn't notice. "I've forgotten how that feels, it's been so long. Plus, Paul had . . . performance issues. Steroids may help build muscle, but they can seriously derail your performance in the bedroom. After the first few times, I stopped taking it personally. He did make up for it with his . . . other talents."

Grinning wolfishly, Ash leaned forward and whispered, "Honey, a real man doesn't need a plan B. My equipment has never failed me and it's been tested by some weird shit. Baby Talk Brittany for one." Shuddering involuntarily, he added, "Imagine that voice asking little Ashey to come out and pway. I'm not gonna lie, I had to focus on the task at hand that night. I'd never been less in the mood."

"I bet so." Dana grimaced. "I once dated a guy that named my body parts, then talked to them, as if they were real people, while we were having sex. It was so confusing I found myself looking around to see if someone had joined us. Needless to say, I ended that one soon after the first night we spent together." She leaned her head back, resting it on the sofa. "Are there any normal men left out there?"

"Sure." Ash nodded. "But they all come bearing diamond rings, minivans, and a crap load of kids. Oh, and did I mention a serious lack of imagination between the sheets?"

"The ones who want to settle down aren't the only dudes who are boring in bed," Dana pointed out. "Actually I've found it to mostly be the rule and not the exception. Why do you think I've been content to be dateless for this long? I can get myself off faster than anyone I've ever been with. Plus, there's no awkward conversation afterward or stroking of an overinflated male ego."

Ash let his eyes wander down Dana's curvy body thinking it was a damn shame she had to resort to her hand or a vibrator to take care of her needs. For a real man, that was inexcusable. It didn't matter if you got yours or not; it was your job to make sure the woman came first, literally. "Baby, I could make your eyes roll back in your head and make you scream loud enough to be heard in the next state. Your problem is that you've been with a bunch of pussies instead of a real man."

Her mouth opened and closed so many times that he thought she might be choking. He was getting concerned when she finally said in a shrill voice, "Um—you might be right."

Before he could reply, Rosa walked back into the room and saved him from possibly propositioning the woman who'd had an undeniable knack for getting under his skin from the moment he laid eyes on her. "Everything's all set out in the kitchen. I'm going to head home now. You two kids enjoy yourselves." Looking at Dana, she added, "How about not peeing on any of the towels if he makes you mad."

Dana snickered, having heard the whole story earlier from his big-mouthed housekeeper. "You got it."

They said a warm good-bye to each other as if they'd been friends for years and then it was just the two of them. Ash got to his feet and motioned toward the kitchen. "Let's eat." He waited for Dana to precede him, then almost walked into a wall staring at her ass. *Damn. Get it together, man.* He pulled a chair out for her, then took his own seat. She picked up her plate and added a generous portion of the fragrant lasagna and salad. She then surprised him by picking up a piece of garlic bread. In his experience, women didn't eat in front of a man, which he hated. There was nothing worse than going to a restaurant and having a date watch you enjoy your meal while she moved her food from one side of her plate to the other. So he sincerely meant it as a compliment when he said, "It's nice to see a woman with an appetite."

She froze with her fork on the way to her mouth. "You're always telling me I'm too big for my height so you shouldn't be shocked that I'm stuffing my face. Let me guess, it turns you off when chicks eat. Do you want me to take it into the other room? Maybe tie a napkin around my neck so I don't drip anything on my shirt."

Now he was the one with his mouth left hanging open. He'd meant no offense, but he could understand why she'd jump to that conclusion. It was yet another reminder that he'd been a colossal asshole to her for months—and dammit, he regretted it. She was in no way overweight. Hell, even if she had been, it was none of his business. Women were beautiful creatures no matter what size they were, and the clear fact that he'd made her feel less than attractive gave him a sick feeling. He'd been nothing short of a bully to someone who'd done nothing to deserve it. "I'm sorry," he said quietly. "You're absolutely gorgeous and I've been a real prick to you. There's nothing I can say in my defense because it doesn't matter why I behaved that way.

And I wasn't insulting you about the food. I truthfully find it refreshing that you eat like a normal person instead of pretending that you're not hungry, even though I know that act is bullshit."

Dana watched him thoughtfully for what seemed like an hour but was probably less than a minute. Then she shrugged and ate a few bites before replying. "Thanks for the apology; I appreciate it. And I shouldn't have been so defensive. My weight has been a touchy point for me on and off so I assumed the worst. Plus, given our history, it seemed as if the comment would be negative instead of positive."

"I get that," he replied before pausing to enjoy some of his own meal. "I meant what I said by the way. You're beautiful and you have a figure that would make any man drool. I hope that I'm not the cause of your body-image issues because you should have none. I'm ashamed to admit that I just picked on the one insecurity that I know most women struggle with. It had nothing to do with me thinking you were overweight, because you're not."

He shifted uncomfortably, not used to sharing this type of honesty with someone. He was absurdly grateful when she joked, "Wow, you seem almost human. Damn, I bet that whole confession hurt." Looking him over, she asked, "Are you breaking out into hives yet? If you have any suspicious rashes, you could probably attribute them to nerves this time and skip the STD check."

Unable to stop himself, he chuckled at her audacity. He wasn't used to anyone other than his brothers and Rosa speaking to him like that. Well, aside from Lisa, Dylan's assistant. She took a lot of pleasure in busting his balls. "I can assure you I've never even had a scare in that area. I believe in wrapping it up."

Dana raised her glass of water and tapped it against the one he had picked up. "Good boy. You wouldn't want that sucker to fall off. Think of all the airheads in Florida who would mourn the loss. Although you could probably convince most of them that it was divine intervention rather than a disease."

"You should know that I have dated intelligent women as well. I realize that meeting Brittany would make you question that, but not all of my dates have been crazy. In fact, I recently escorted Erin, who's a public defender, to a charity function."

Raising her brows, Dana commented, "I'm impressed. Were you needing some free legal advice? Maybe on a pesky and embarrassing paternity issue? Is there a little Ashey running around out there? That would be tragic to inflict upon the world. But look on the bright side, you could buy both your kid and your date a Happy Meal for less than ten bucks."

Shaking his head, Ash tossed a piece of his bread at her. "Cut me some slack. I have no offspring and I've already told you that my dates don't usually eat. Now the playground at McDonald's is a different story. Brittany had her last birthday party there. She just loves the slide."

"Oh brother," Dana murmured under her breath. "I know that's a joke, but I can easily picture it. It's sad that Claudia would be a step up for you. Well, if it wasn't for the whole relative thing and all. Bart might not like his baby going out with you. I mean, whose lap would she sit on at family functions, his or yours? That could get confusing."

"Don't even go there," Ash groaned. "But while I attempt to scrub that image from my head, we should talk about her. Specifically how to keep you out of her crosshairs. She might have barely made it through school, but she's an expert when it comes to being a bitch. The fact that she pulled that shit in the shop today should tell you something. She's not afraid to attack you. Now that she's had the added humiliation of being carted out of the hotel in front of her buddies, she'll be out for blood. Probably both yours and Zoe's."

Dana put her fork down and gave him a serious look. "That's what I'm afraid of. I don't want her to mess with Zoe. Maybe if I drew more attention to myself, then it would distract her. You'll take me to dinner again and I'll—"

"Dammit, did you hear nothing I said?" he snapped. "You need to lay low and let this blow over. In the meantime, I'll go over and have a serious talk with both her and Bart. She might be his little princess, but he also loves the lifestyle that this hotel affords him. I'm sure he could be persuaded to deal with his daughter if it were threatened."

"Don't you think that'll just make it worse?" she asked. "It's obvious that she's very close to her father, so that might not be the best approach to take."

"Then let her come after me for it." He shrugged. "I couldn't care less. What's she going to do, make my life a living hell? I think that ship has already sailed. I can handle her shit, but you shouldn't have to. Dylan will raise holy hell if she messes with Zoe again as well. I'm sure he's already planning a visit to talk about that very thing. As much as I hate it, she's a member of the family to some degree, and as such, it's our job to deal with her. It's my fault you were at the family dinner in the first place."

"It was me who kicked her chair over," Dana pointed out. "You weren't exactly counting on that. And I'm not one of your damsel-in-distress-type dates that needs saving. I've dealt with my share of vindictive girls like Claudia. I would have taught her a lesson the moment she showed up here, but I was trying to get rid of her before Zoe could get involved. In the end it didn't work out. I didn't know Zoe would pick that particular moment to go all Rambo on her."

"Be that as it may, I'm still responsible for you coming into contact with her at all. Therefore, I'll handle it. In the meantime, you don't have to worry about her coming back to the coffee shop. Between Dylan and security, she wouldn't dare."

"Ash," she said quietly, "I don't want to cause a problem for you with your mom. It sounded the other night as if things might be changing there for you. How long will that last if you make an enemy of her husband?"

He shocked them both by laying a hand atop hers. "I've been dealing with Bart since they got married. My mother isn't stupid, nor is she blind to the type of man that he is. She won't take sides in this and there's no love lost between her and Claudia. In fact, I figure she'll get a lot of pleasure out of me putting Claudia in her place."

Dana still didn't look convinced. Almost as if she wasn't aware of doing it, she turned her hand over. Before he knew it, their fingers were linked together and his first inclination was to pull away. He wasn't the type for intimate gestures, and this hand-holding suddenly felt very intimate. But it also felt unsettlingly good, which was scary as hell. But hadn't he started the whole thing by touching her first? "You know them better than I do," she conceded. "My method hasn't exactly been a success thus far, so if you think you can do better, be my guest."

Clearing his throat, Ash nodded. He was both relieved and disappointed when she broke away from his hold. As if by mutual, unspoken agreement, they didn't mention Claudia again as they finished dinner. The conversation flowed with surprising ease, and Ash found that he enjoyed himself immensely in her company. Once they'd finished, they loaded their plates in the dishwasher and Dana teased him about actually knowing which buttons to push to operate it. "I've been a bachelor for a long time," he said, grinning. "Plus, Rosa gets pissed when I don't make an effort to clean up the small stuff. I try to keep her happy because she scares me when she's angry."

"I'm sure she does." Dana nodded in agreement as she wiped down the table. When they were finished tidying up the kitchen, he found himself reluctant to say good-bye to her. But short of asking her to stay, he couldn't come up with a reason to prolong their evening. And she seemed to be of a similar mind as she picked up her purse and walked toward the door. "Thanks for everything. I had better get going, I have to get up early in the morning."

Ash picked up his door card before saying, "I'll see you to your car. It's gotten late and you shouldn't be in the parking garage alone." She shrugged her shoulders and stepped out into the hallway, waiting for him there. He locked up and hit the button for the elevator. "I had a nice time tonight."

I need to stop saying things that could make her think this was a date. I sound like a nervous schoolboy hoping to score a kiss.

"Er—me too," she replied, appearing startled by his statement. "I like your apartment. It's got a great view of the ocean."

"Yeah, it's okay. I'd rather have a house though. Considering I live in the hotel, it's as if I never leave work. That means my staff doesn't think twice about calling me over every little thing since they know I'm so close by."

They remained quiet for the short elevator ride down to the lobby. Ash then found himself once again staring at her phenomenal ass as he followed behind her to the parking garage. He slid his hands into the pockets of his pants and shifted from one foot to the other as she stopped beside her car. She turned, giving him what looked like a nervous smile. "So I'll see you tomorrow, I'm sure. I mean, not that I expect to or anything. But you normally come by for coffee. Well, unless you have it delivered, which you sometimes do. So I might see you and I might not." She continued rambling for another few seconds before coming to an abrupt stop. "Crap, that was painful." Releasing a loud breath, she added, "You should probably go back to insulting me. I don't know how to deal with this nicer version of you. It kinda freaks me out and makes me more awkward than usual."

Ash found himself relaxing enough to laugh. "Damn, me too. I can't remember the last time I was this uptight around a woman. You're right, we did handle it better when there were ugly words flying back and forth between us. Now it's as if I'm meeting you for the first time and have absolutely no game at all."

Quirking a brow, she asked, "Why would you need that? Ahhh, are you trying to hit on me, Ash? If you're flirting, the moves could use a little work."

Lazily reaching out, he tapped her shoulder. "Oh, you didn't just say that. I'll have you know that you're only saying that because I haven't unleashed my charm on you yet. Those panties would be dropping if I had."

She giggled as she opened the door to her car and slid in the seat. He assumed she was going to leave without responding until she rolled her window down. "Hey, Ash?" He quirked a brow and she winked before saying, "I'm not wearing any underwear so there's no danger of that happening tonight." With a wicked smile, she started her car and left him standing there with his mouth hung open and his dick saluting.

"Well, hell," he murmured as he turned to retrace his steps. This had been an interesting evening, to say the least. And he'd come out of it certain of one thing. He might have spent the better part of a year in denial about his attraction to Dana, but there was no longer any lying to himself. He wanted her—badly. Unfortunately he knew that was a fucking disaster in the making. Not only did she work at the resort, but she was also best friends with his sister-in-law. His casual approach to sex could certainly get messy with Dana. But he had the impression that she had a similar approach to dating . . . if he was direct about what he wanted and she was interested, then where was the problem? Even as he tried to rationalize it, he had a sense of foreboding. No, he needed to keep things strictly business between them. There were plenty of other women out there without ties to his family. No need to fish so close to home. She wasn't even his type. End of discussion. If all of that were true, he had to wonder why he didn't feel more confident in his ability to stay away from her.

Because you've been infatuated with her for months. You just can't admit it.

And there was the whole problem.

Seven

He's driving me crazy," Dana admitted to Zoe as they walked through the local shopping mall. It was a rare day where they'd both managed to schedule a few hours off at the same time and they were making the most of them with a leisurely lunch followed by some window-shopping at a few of their favorite stores. "He's being too nice. There are times when he slips up and the old Ash makes an appearance, but it doesn't happen that often."

Giving her a confused look, Zoe asked, "How's that a bad thing? You hated the man when he was being an ass. Now you want that version of him back?"

Running a hand through her hair, Dana sighed. "I don't know. I'm just not sure how to deal with him anymore. He's far too irresistible like this. He even flirts with me, which is both amazing and scary as hell."

"Oh God, don't sleep with him," Zoe hissed. "You know how he treats women. I mean, don't get me wrong, I'm sure he's good at what he does, but then he tosses them aside until he gets an itch again. Plus, you're so not his usual type. You actually have a brain."

"Don't you think I know all of that?" Dana muttered. "I'm not going to be another Brittany. But that doesn't mean I don't have the urge to let him do me. I bet he's amazing in bed. I mean, we're both adults and all. We could bang it out of our systems and then move on. Nobody needs to get hurt here. As long as I was up front about things, why would it have to be a big deal?"

Zoe dropped her head in her hands. "That sounds like something he would say. Wait—you two haven't discussed this, have you? You're not, like, already planning to get it on, right?"

"No—God, no, there's been no conversation about anything like that. I'm just tossing it out there as an option. He might not even be at all interested in sleeping with me. I'm probably a pity flirt for him. Sometimes I think hot guys can't help but do that. They walk around letting their sexiness touch everyone in its path."

Dana had been expecting outright laughter from Zoe over her last statement so she was surprised when instead her friend nodded. "That's true. I used to think the same thing about Dylan. I believe I even complained about it a few times. He would pass women and they were pulled into his gravitational field. I don't know if it's the cologne or something else, but whatever it is, women make complete fools out of themselves over it."

"I so don't want to do that," Dana pouted. "But he's wearing me down. I'm either going to have to sleep with him or beg him to return to his previous asshole behavior. Because there's no way we can be friends without me letting him in my pants. There's too much sexual tension between us. Heck, in another week, I'll be begging him to sleep with me. I've had to change the batteries in my vibrator twice since he turned over this new leaf and it hasn't even been a week. I'm horny all the time. And it's his fault because I haven't been with anyone else since I broke up with Paul, and truthfully I haven't felt the urge until recently."

Zoe pulled her down onto a nearby bench before saying, "Okay, so maybe you just need to get laid. Blow the dust off your little black book and make a date or a booty call. I bet Paul would be happy to take care of that for you. Then afterwards you can enjoy the new, nicer Ash without getting naked. Perfect, right?"

"Oh, come on," Dana groaned. "You've seen Paul. There's no contest between him and Ash. Plus, sometimes Paul has an equipment malfunction that leaves matters . . . unsatisfied. I can't bring him back into my life and give him false hope. A night of subpar sex is hardly worth that. But Ash, on the other hand . . . you know you'd get yours with a man like that. He could give me a night of mind-blowing sex, then the itch would be scratched. Afterwards we could return to this fake boyfriend-girlfriend thing and I'd be much more relaxed and able to perform my duties better. Even if he were lousy in the sack, I could take comfort in the fact that I'd been missing out on nothing and that I never wanted to do it again. Either is a win-win, right?"

Zoe wrinkled her nose, looking disgruntled but resigned. "I want to go on record as saying this is a very bad idea. You should never eat where you shit."

Laughing, Dana pointed out, "I believe you mean you never shit where you eat."

"Shit is shit." Zoe snorted. "And you know where I'm going with this. If things go bad between you two, then everyone around you suffers for it. What if you fall for him? There's no way that ends well. Ash doesn't do relationships. He might mean well with you, but he'd end up breaking your heart. Then you'd have to see him at the hotel every day. And probably with a bimbo or two trailing after him. Do you really want to subject yourself to that? I love Ash. He's a great brother-in-law, but I can say that because I've never dated him. That's a completely different matter."

"I know," Dana groaned. "Believe me, you're not telling me anything I haven't already told myself a dozen times. I should stay far away from him. But then there's that crazy voice in my head that says I'll never get past him until I get it out of my system. And in my experience, the only way to do that is to end the mystery and satisfy my curiosity. If he's great in the sack, then I'll have a good memory out of it. If he's lousy, then I'll get a laugh. But if I do nothing, I'm always going to wonder what he would be like. Plus, I've never believed in lust at first sight, but there's some insane chemistry between us. Sparks fly when we're together and he feels it too. He was actually nervous last night when I was leaving his apartment. It was like the awkward end to a first date. We said all of these polite things while we tried not to stare at each other."

"Wow." Zoe whistled. "I didn't think Ash ever suffered from anything as common as nerves. He's too smooth for his own good. But then again, he's had a different reaction to you from the beginning. I guess it would stand to reason if he stopped the nastiness, he would struggle with the nice part. Maybe what they say is true—when boys are mean to you, it's because they like you. That would certainly explain a lot where he's concerned. Because everyone who knows him has been baffled by his asshole attitude towards you."

Holding her hand up, Dana shook her head. "Don't even go there. I'm not going to get into this fantasy world where Ash has a crush on me and we're soul-mates. You're all hearts and flowers, but I'm not. I'm tequila and sweaty sex. Not champagne and white weddings. I'm not going to ride off into the sunset with Mr. Wrong, nor am I trying to change him. If we decide to do the deed, then it'll be a one-time thing that we both want. Afterwards it'll be business as usual."

"I don't know . . ." Zoe said doubtfully. "I believe I thought something equally insane where Dylan was concerned. Admittedly I was in love with him. But still I was willing to take whatever he was capable of giving me as long as I had some part of him. It wasn't long before I figured out that I wanted the whole package. I'm just lucky that he did too. But I can't see the same happening with Ash. And I don't want my best friend getting hurt."

Throwing an arm around Zoe's shoulders, Dana said, with more confidence than she felt, "I'll be fine. Don't worry about me. Right now we just need to focus on this business dinner where I'll be playing the girl-friend role again. You'll be there, right?"

"Yep, I will. Dylan said that Rhett was supposed to be visiting soon. Too bad he won't be here for the party. I don't think you've met him before."

Licking her lips to make Zoe laugh, Dana asked, "What's up with all these hot Jackson brothers? I mean, talk about a blessed gene pool. Are there any ugly ones?"

Zoe gave her a dreamy smile in return. "Nope, there's not. I swear, it isn't fair to the rest of the men out there. Who would stand a chance against them? I've made the mistake of joking about it to Dylan and he gets kind of jealous. I'm afraid he's going to catch me checking them out. I love the man, but come on, it's hard not to look at that kind of eye candy."

"Honey, believe me, I get it. Last night, Ash almost caught me looking at his crotch. I swear, I saw the outline going down his leg. That sucker must be huge. No wonder the Brittanys of the world keep coming back for more. I'm surprised the poor girl wasn't bow-legged. Or at least walking around holding her back."

"Really?" Zoe grinned. "No—wait, I didn't need to know that. Now my eyes will automatically go there the next time I see him and I'll really be in trouble." Lowering her voice, she whispered, "Like how far down are we talking here?"

When Dana placed her hand down her thigh, Zoe's eyes widened. "No way. Dylan's a big boy, but if what you're saying is true, Ash is a freak of nature. Was he hard?"

Dana gaped at her normally shy friend. Marrying Dylan had certainly brought her out of her shell. Their conversations had never been this graphic before and Dana loved the change. "I said I looked, not that I touched. We'd just finished dinner, so I'm kind of doubting he was. Unless he really got off on the lasagna. Plus, after Rosa and I spent so much time insulting his past dates, I'd think his pecker would have retreated inwards if anything."

Pursing her lips, Zoe admitted, "That's pretty impressive then. Good grief, imagine how big that sucker must be in all its full glory. You're a brave woman for even considering it. I'd put my hand over my crotch and run like hell." Then slapping her hand over her mouth, she added, "Oh shit, you know he's probably into anal. There's no way things would go back to normal after something like that. I swear, if you decide to sleep with him, you better make it known beforehand that you consider that strictly an exit. I don't want to see you sitting on one of those plastic donut cushions at the shop because my brother-in-law messed you up for life. Workers comp doesn't cover stuff like that."

By the time Zoe finished her tirade, Dana was leaning against a potted plant holding her sides. She was laughing so hard that tears coursed down her cheeks. "You—nut," she managed to gasp out. "He's not . . . putting that . . . monster there. And when did you become the expert on that, my friend? Have you and Dylan been taking a walk on the backside?"

"Of course not!" Zoe huffed.

Her friend's pink cheeks had Dana laughing harder. "Thou dost protest a bit too much. Come on, this is me you're talking to. If you and big D have been getting freaky, you can tell me. This is a judgment-free zone." Truthfully Dana was kind of impressed that her formerly repressed friend and longtime virgin was apparently experimenting with something that a lot of women weren't comfortable doing. To Dana, it was all about trust. If you had a partner who you knew would make it good for you, then why not?

"It was just a finger," Zoe whispered. "I haven't been brave enough to go beyond that, and Dylan would never pressure me. I'm not sure if it'll ever happen, but I enjoyed what we did."

"That's all that counts," Dana assured her. "If you both like it, then that's all that matters. There's no right or wrong in the bedroom between consenting adults. If you want to explore something new, then go for it. Dylan will always take care of you. If it's something you don't want, then all you need to do is talk to him about it. You two were friends long before you were lovers, so communication shouldn't be an issue."

"It's kind of embarrassing." Zoe shrugged. "At first I had a hard time communicating with him about stuff like that, but it's gotten easier. And he always asks me first about it when we try new things."

"You've got yourself a good man." Dana smiled, wondering why she felt a pang in her heart at her friend's good fortune. She'd never wanted a relationship like that. She didn't need a guy to take care of her. Or to worry about her needs. She was far from the virgin that Zoe had been until she'd slept with Dylan. Naturally he would be concerned about his wife seeing as he was her first and only. But Dana was a more experienced woman. Sure, there'd been a real lack of good sex in her life, especially recently. But the possibility was out there. She just had to find it.

She knew that Ash would give her more than she could handle, but despite her assurances to the contrary, she wasn't sure how she'd deal with the possible aftermath. Would she be able to bear seeing Ash with another woman soon after sleeping with him? She'd always made certain not to have sex with a guy at work. And even though they didn't technically have the same employer, she would still see him every day.

When Zoe nudged her in the shoulder and pointed toward a nearby store, Dana pushed her thoughts of Ash aside. She didn't have to make a decision today. Besides, he probably wasn't even interested in her like that.

⁓

Ash felt like a schoolboy about to be scolded by his father. It was apparent from the glare that Dylan was leveling upon him that a lecture was imminent, and he didn't have to wait long. "You absolutely can't fuck Dana," Dylan snapped. "You know she's Zoe's best friend. Do you realize that anything you do to her will come back to bite me in the ass? My wife will be pissed if it ends badly, and we both know that it will. You've had a woman piss on your towels, for God's sake. What could you possibly have done for that to happen?"

Ash shrugged before he answered. "I believe I called her by the wrong name. Or maybe I told her to leave without asking her name . . . or her number. Hell, I don't really remember. The mornings after sometimes start to blur together."

Dylan shot him an incredulous look before he asked, "You've had more than one woman pee on your stuff? Fuck, tell me they didn't do anything else."

Ash couldn't help laughing at his brother's disgusted expression. "To my knowledge, they never wiped their ass. I'm smart enough to throw my toothbrush away every time. I've seen enough chick flicks to know they always stick those in the toilet and put them back."

Dylan slumped back in the chair in front of Ash's

desk, shaking his head. "I can honestly say I've never given that any thought. And I've certainly had my share of one-night stands." His brother looked a little green around the gills when he added, "Damn, that would explain some questions I've had before. I actually caught one girl with my toothbrush in her hand, but she put it back quickly saying she'd accidentally picked it up."

"Dude," Ash scoffed. "Tell me you didn't use it after that. She'd just put that sucker somewhere, count on it." Ash was afraid his brother was going to barf at any moment.

"I didn't have any reason to think she was lying. Who does that?"

"A woman you fuck and then blow off," Ash replied. "They don't call them 'women scorned' for nothing. See, men think very straightforward, but women are diabolical. They'll do evil shit to you that you'd never think about. They don't want to be straight up about it. They'd rather be at a bar that night laughing to their girlfriends about the wreck they left behind in your apartment. That's why I don't drink after I've had someone over or eat a meal they've prepared. Basically don't put anything in your mouth that they've had in their hands. If I get a bottle of water out of the refrigerator and the seal's been broken, then that sucker is going in the trash. I'd never have thought of checking the linen closet, but after pee girl, I've since learned to put the expensive stuff away and leave only the cheap hand towels out. Those can just be thrown away."

"Holy hell," Dylan marveled. "There's no telling what I've ingested through the years. I knew some of my dates were disgruntled when I didn't ask them out a second time, but I didn't give it a lot of thought. Hell, no wonder that woman Erica and her friends looked so amused when I ran into them a few months back. She was so fucking pissed when I failed to ask for her number that she tossed her shoes at my head. Then I see her in a restaurant while I'm at a business dinner and she's laughing her head off."

"Man, you totally got screwed." Ash nodded. "She got your ass back somehow and you'll never know what she did. I swear, women should be in charge of planning and fighting all wars because they'd never need guns. If the enemy was male, they could outthink him in the blink of an eye. The dude would be begging for mercy."

"No kidding." Dylan shivered. "I'd have been happy never knowing what they're capable of. Now back to our previous conversation about Dana. Tell me you aren't thinking about going there. There's no shortage of females in Florida. So why would you consider looking this close to your home base? You know better than to muddy the waters. Didn't you learn anything from Fiona?"

Ash froze in shock. It was an unspoken rule that no one mentioned that name to him, especially his own brothers. Dylan's apologetic look let him know that it hadn't been planned. Keeping his voice steady, he said, "That was different and you know it. To begin with, I was a lot younger and considerably dumber. I still believed in the whole soulmate bullshit. I've since learned better. When and if I sleep with Dana, it will be a mutual decision about nothing but sex. I think you're concerned for nothing. She's a lot more like me than you all seem to realize. She doesn't do serious relationships either."

Dylan shook his head. "She dated that asshole Paul for quite a while. I remember her being pretty giddy when they got back together. It didn't look like just a physical thing. I'm not sure where you're getting your information, but possibly you should check your source."

"You do realize that you can actually date someone and not fall in love or have any desire to get married, right?" Ash pointed out. "I've actually gone out with the same woman more than once before. If there's a good physical connection and no expectations, then there's no reason that things can't continue for a while. You did the same thing back in your dating days. Hell, if not for Zoe, you'd still be doing it."

"True," Dylan conceded. "I know you're both adults and I can't tell you what to do. But be careful. She's a pain in my ass, but I don't want to see Dana get hurt. Nor do I want some big awkward scene around here. I won't even mention the fact that she could probably kick both our asses if she was pissed off."

"I'll take that under advisement." Ash laughed. "Oh, yeah, I wanted to let you know I'm going to talk to Bart and his demon seed tonight. I'm not letting Claudia get away with that shit she pulled in Zoe's shop. She spit her coffee out all over Dana like she was ten years old."

"Yeah, I heard all about it," Dylan snapped. "It's fucking ridiculous. I was planning to have a word with her myself even though, from the sound of it, my wife more than handled things."

"Can you imagine Claudia getting kicked out by security?" Ash chuckled. "I don't know about you, but that's one piece of footage that I can't wait to watch. I think I'll fix some popcorn tonight and make an event out of it."

"Already beat you to it," Dylan smirked. "It was even better than you could imagine. She was flailing around like she was having some type of attack. I could practically hear her shrieking at the poor guys. Needless to say, I've already given them a raise. They never hesitated when Zoe called them. Anyone else might have panicked at escorting a family member out. I'll forward the video to you. That is—if you can fit it in around those chick flicks you mentioned watching. Don't think I missed that. Since when are you into those? I guess you read those Nicholas Sparks books that Zoe loves so much. I mean, I can see a little *Fifty Shades* because a lot of men are intrigued by those movies, but seriously, bro, aren't there enough violent action flicks out there to keep you entertained? Only married guys are excused for doing stuff like that."

Sheepishly, Ash admitted, "Rosa has those on a lot for what she calls 'background noise.' She gets kind of pissed when I turn them off. So I might have seen a few minutes here and there."

Raising a brow, Dylan stated, "You're scared of her." Holding up a hand, he added, "Not that I blame you. She intimidates me too. The last time I was at your apartment, I used the bathroom. When I opened the door, she was standing right there almost nose to nose with me. She demanded to know if I made a mess of the floor."

Ash couldn't help it; he started laughing. "She's rather obsessed with urine. I think she was more traumatized than she'd care to admit over the whole pee on the towels thing. She claims she has trained her husband to wipe his dick instead of shaking it off. She said she wasn't put on this earth to have piss standing around the toilet. I can't bring myself to go sissy for her, but I make damn sure to clean up after myself. It's not worth the grief I catch if I don't."

"I ran like hell that day." Dylan shuddered. "I was afraid she'd find something and stick my face in it."

"I can tell you, it wouldn't be pretty." Ash shook his head. "But if you and Zoe ever need any help around the house, you should think about hiring her to clean your place. She'd have you potty trained in no time at all. I'll have a lot of free time on my hands after all since you're telling me I have to stay away from Dana. I can just do my own cleaning so my dear brother can benefit from it."

Dylan got quickly to his feet. "You're a grown man, do whatever the hell you want. Just keep Rosa away from me. I don't need to stress over the situation with Dana anyway because if you screw up, my wife will hand your ass to you." With those words, Dylan walked back out of his office. Ash took a quick look at his watch and decided there was no time like the present to have a talk with the family. Might as well get that ass chapping out of the way so that he could focus on more pleasant matters—like Dana. He might be making a huge mistake, but it never hurt to test the waters. She might not even be interested. After all, he'd gone out of his way to make sure she hated his guts.

It didn't really matter to him either way. He could find someone else, no big deal. The fact that he'd resorted to lying to himself should have been a red flag, but instead, he swept it aside and tried to convince himself that he was still firmly in control.

Eight

Ash fought the urge to roll his eyes when Bart answered the door wearing a pink polo shirt and bright green shorts. No doubt he'd spent the day on a golf course somewhere. Working never seemed to be a priority for him. Even when he was asking for money to finance his next get-rich-quick scheme, he never actually put much effort into it. Ash and his brothers could probably have retired years ago if not for supporting their mother and her second family. "Just the person I want to see," Ash said tightly.

He generally tried to avoid the other man, so even Bart appeared surprised by his statement. "You do?" the other man asked warily. "What can I do for you, Asher?"

Ignoring his question, Ash walked around him and into the foyer. "Let's talk in the living room. Is Claudia home? I'd like for her to join us as well since this concerns her." Ash took a seat in one of the wingback chairs and Bart perched on the nearby couch.

"No, she's not here," Bart huffed. "She's still upset over what happened at your damned hotel. I sent her shopping with her friends to relax. Do you have any idea how much she's been through lately? There was the fall at dinner, then she was mauled by your security guards. I've a good mind to sue the resort for that," he blustered.

Ash counted to ten, trying to rein in his temper. Finally when he was somewhat in control, he said, "Isn't that a bit like biting the hand that feeds you? I'm sure you realize that we own the Oceanix. So you'd actually be filing legal papers against your stepsons. The same ones who provide you with this house that you're living in and the money in your pocket. Should I go on?"

Bart's face paled as he picked up on the steely inflection in Ash's voice. The man might be many things, but he wasn't a complete idiot. He knew well that he was on a train heading for derailment if he didn't backtrack fast. "Um—I meant no offense to you personally, Ash. I'm just saying that the whole thing was unnecessary. Claudia was simply asking for another coffee when the first one was prepared incorrectly. I have no idea why Dylan's wife took such offense to that. Hasn't she heard that the customer is always right? I'm surprised she has any business at all. I realize that your girlfriend works there as well and you're trying to defend her, but don't you think that they took things a little too far? Since when do you toss family out for a thing like that?"

Ash got to his feet, towering over the other man. He'd had about as much of this shit as he could handle. As usual, Claudia had spun her own brand of reality. He had no idea whether his mother had bothered to correct the misinformation or if Bart ignored everyone but his daughter. Probably a little of both. Bart gulped when Ash glared down at him. "Claudia and her friends were being bitches as usual. She didn't simply send her drink back, she spit it all over Dana, then called her a fucking cow. When Zoe asked them to leave, Claudia refused and continued to show her poor manners. So she got what she deserved. I'd have instructed any of my employees to do the same thing. We don't treat people like second-class citizens regardless of what family connections we have."

Dana had just skimmed over the incident with Claudia, but Zoe had relayed it to Dylan, who'd filled Ash in as well. And he'd never felt like a bigger hypocrite than he did at that very moment. *What about all the things you said to Dana over the past year?* He pushed that thought aside in order to deal with Bart, but his gut churned with guilt. Apparently Zoe should have called security and had his ass carted out. He might not have spit on her, but he'd verbally abused her for a year. Fuck, he should be on his hands and knees begging her forgiveness, not trying to get into her pants. *I'm such a bastard.*

"I—er, that is, are you sure? Claudia didn't mention any of that," Bart mumbled.

Ash could tell by the expression on the other man's face that he believed him. He might try to pretend like his little princess was an angel, but he wasn't completely blind to what she was capable of. Ash didn't bother to answer the question; instead, he said, "Talk to her and see that she understands that she's to stay away from the resort and the coffee shop. Also, I don't want her anywhere near Dana unless it's a family meal and I'm present. Is that clear?"

"Sure, sure, Asher," Bart replied quickly. "I'll take care of it when she gets home. I'm sure it's all some misunderstanding, but we'll get it straightened out."

Ash headed toward the door before turning back. "If there are any further 'misunderstandings,' I'll have to ponder the family finances long and hard. I've been thinking about putting everyone on a budget for a while, but I simply haven't had the heart to do it."

Bart picked up on the threat to his livelihood immediately. "No need to waste time with that," he said weakly. "Consider it handled, Asher."

Ash flipped around on his heel and hurried out before he could throttle the older man. Despite what his mother had said the other night, he still couldn't understand her staying with Bart all of these years. No amount of love or the need for companionship could force him to remain with someone like that. He was more convinced than ever that relationships were bullshit. What more did a person need in life besides great sex? Anything beyond that wasn't for him. Maybe Dylan was right and it might be best to avoid taking things any further with Dana. She needed to remain firmly in the fake girlfriend category, where there was no room for confusion on either of their parts.

༄

When someone tapped her on the shoulder, Dana swung around, then gaped in surprise as her ex-boyfriend, Paul, stared back at her. Before she could open her mouth to ask what he was doing there, he'd pulled her into an enthusiastic hug. "Hey, baby doll, you look amazing. I sure have missed you."

Paul had been the closest thing to a long-term relationship Dana had ever had. Mainly because there had been no pressure there. He was very involved in running his gym, which meant he didn't have a lot of free time to smother her. If the sex had been better, she might have stuck it out longer. *And if Ash hadn't come along.* "Hey, Paul. It's good to see you again. How've you been?"

He had always answered questions as if they pertained to his gym and not to him personally—and this time was no exception. "Things are going great with Ript. Membership is up twenty-five percent. I've had to hire a few more personal trainers and I've been able to purchase extra equipment. You should come by and check things out. You know there's never any charge for you."

"Aw, thanks. That's really sweet." Dana smiled. Paul was a nice guy. It wasn't his fault that they simply had nothing at all in common. He was a serious health-food nut who scrutinized every bite he put in his mouth. Although he'd never criticized her, she'd still felt as if he noticed what she ate and wanted to comment on it at times. It wasn't a welcome feeling to someone who struggled with body-image issues. "What are you doing at the Oceanix? I thought this place was too prickish for you." Paul had never been comfortable around the crowd that frequented the upscale resort and had often commented on how he could never work in this type of atmosphere. To Dana, people were people. Money didn't have that much to do with it. You could be just as much of an asshole when you were poor. She was certain that Claudia would still act the same way even if she didn't live a privileged life.

He shifted on his feet, looking uncomfortable and out of place in his muscle shirt and spandex shorts. He was certainly a walking advertisement for the gym that he owned. She had to admit that she was temporarily distracted by the huge muscles flexing in his arms. There was no denying that he was nice to look at. "I came by to see you. I thought maybe we could have some coffee and catch up. I've kinda missed just having someone to talk to. When we broke up, I lost one of my best friends as well as my girl."

Looking at his downcast head, Dana felt like a heartless bitch. She'd never given much thought to how Paul had taken her ending their relationship. He hadn't seemed terribly torn up over it. But even she had to admit that she'd missed having the sort of companionship they had shared while they were dating. Especially after Zoe had started spending so much time with Dylan. Dana didn't really have anyone else in her life that she hung out with on a regular basis. That had never been an issue when she'd been more active in her love life, but in the last year, that had seriously run dry. *Thanks to Ash.* "I'm sorry," she murmured sincerely. "You never said anything. I assumed you'd moved on. I know you stay pretty busy, so I didn't think you'd miss having me around. I figured it might actually be one less thing to juggle."

He looked up at her in shock. "Are you kidding? I was crazy about you. I haven't been out with another woman since you ended things. I mean, there are a few at the gym who have asked me out, but they're not you. And believe it or not, it takes me a while to get comfortable with someone new."

Now that he'd mentioned it, she did remember him

being awkward at first. She felt even worse now about how she had ended things. She should have made the effort to check on him. Instead, she'd walked away like she always did when it was over and hadn't given it that much thought. She'd already broken her rules by staying with him longer than she normally did. And now she could see that it had been a mistake. He'd formed an attachment to her, and dammit, she'd hurt him. Something she tried her best never to do. "Paul—why didn't you say anything? I thought you were okay with the way we ended things. If I'd known . . ."

He gave her a sad smile before shrugging his shoulders. "You'd already checked out a while before you actually made it official. I couldn't ask you to stay. I knew I'd been on borrowed time for months. The reason I didn't seem upset was because I was expecting it. That's not to say it didn't suck all the same, but there was no element of surprise. If you remember, I did ask if we could remain friends and you agreed. But when I called you a few times and left messages, you never responded. I figured you wanted to cut all ties. You were never interested in taking things to the next level. You practically broke out into hives when I mentioned living together. If I'd have done something insane like pop the question, I figure you would have been on the first plane out of the country within an hour."

Holy crap, I deserve to have the scarlet letter on my chest. I'm a horrible excuse for a person. Sighing, Dana put a hand on his arm. "I'd apologize again, but it wouldn't be enough. Paul, you deserved better than you got from me. If it helps, it was never about you. You're pretty much my longest relationship ever. I just have a ton of baggage from my earlier years that has given me a rather twisted view of people. It's no excuse and I can't believe you were even interested in seeing me again."

Looking sheepish, he said, "Good friends are hard to find. If you have time to take a break, I'd like to buy you that drink now. We can talk about what an idiot you were for letting a catch like me get away."

Dana couldn't help herself; she giggled at his humor. Most of her attempts at jokes had flown right over his head. He took everything too literally. Another big difference between them. She couldn't help thinking of Ash. He might be an ass at times, but he seemed to get her. "Give me a few minutes," she replied before pointing toward a table in the back. "Still black coffee with Splenda?" He nodded, looking pleased that she remembered.

She was behind the counter fixing a latte for herself when Zoe walked in. She looked around, then her eyes widened as she spotted Paul. "Oh my God," she hissed as she reached Dana. "What's he doing here? Are you two together again? I thought you said he couldn't—you know."

"Shhh," Dana hissed, "he's going to hear you. I've been horrible enough to the poor man without him knowing I told you about his pecker issues. Do you realize what that could do to the guy? He already has confidence problems with women. He might never get that flag up the pole again. I mean, not that it was hanging high much anyway, but at least it happened sometimes."

Zoe giggled, before sneaking a quick look over her shoulder. "Dylan had to stop by his office to pick up some papers so I told him I was going to wait here. Boy, I'm glad I did now. Tell me everything. I thought you two hadn't talked since you dumped him."

"We hadn't. He showed up here a little while ago and said he'd missed me. Shocked the hell out of me. Then he proceeded to make me feel like an ass for not being a better friend to him." Holding up a hand when Zoe opened her mouth, Dana added, "Don't bother to defend me—I deserved it. I'm just not used to staying in touch when the sexual side of the relationship is over. Normally I'm not with anyone long enough to become buddies, but this time I slipped up."

"I see," Zoe said carefully. "You're feeling guilty. I don't want to add to it, but I did think it was a tad odd that you cut all ties with him after you guys had been going out for that long. I mean, you never had a big, ugly fight, nor was there any cheating going on. Usually that's the big reason you don't see someone anymore. I thought maybe there was more that I wasn't aware of."

"No, not really," Dana murmured. "Paul is a good person. Things had just run their course. Actually they had a while before that; even he was aware of the fact. But I didn't get restless until—"

Dana snapped her mouth shut, aware that she'd almost blurted out more than she'd intended to. But Zoe was too astute to have missed it and immediately picked up on her slip. "I believe that was right about the time that Ash moved here, wasn't it? Was that the reason behind your decision to be free again?"

Picking up a nearby towel, Dana began wiping the already spotless counter down. "Um, of course not. I don't even remember how long he's lived in Pensacola.

It was a mere coincidence, that's all. Plus, you know that we've spent most of the time he's been here arguing with each other. The man hates me."

Zoe rolled her eyes. "You know what they say, there's a thin line between love and hate. Or with you two, 'lust' may be a better word. The air practically sizzles with energy when you're in the same room. I swear, there were times I expected to see you two rip your clothes off and go for it right here. The fact that I know you're toying with the idea of having sex with him only confirms that for me. So with that thought in mind, what do you plan to do with Paul? Doesn't that complicate things slightly?"

Dana glanced toward where her ex-boyfriend was patiently waiting and shrugged. "He just misses our friendship. There's nothing else to it."

"Don't be naive," Zoe scolded lightly. "A man doesn't make the first move after being dumped because he wants a buddy. That might be his excuse to get his foot back in the door, but I'm betting he's hoping for more. You need to be careful about encouraging him. You don't want to risk hurting his feelings again."

"That's all I need," Dana groaned. "I feel bad enough already. I really hope he isn't thinking that we can go back to the way we were. That's not happening."

"Hey, ladies." The seductive voice from behind them sent a shiver down Dana's spine. They both whirled around to find Ash standing there looking good enough to eat. Did the man never have a bad hair day? Sure, Paul had most women drooling, but to Dana, there was simply no contest. Ash was hot, sweaty nights of amazingly dirty sex, while Paul was steroids and protein shakes. Each had his strong points, but she was more attracted to Ash than she'd ever been to anyone else. If she was a romantic, she'd say his soul called out to hers. She almost giggled out loud as she imagined Ash cringing should she ever utter those words.

"It's a little late in the day for your usual coffee, isn't it?" she asked.

He slid onto one of the barstools in front of them and propped his head on one hand. A lock of dark hair fell across his forehead, and Dana fought the urge to reach out and push it away. He looked tired, which brought out a tenderness in her that she hadn't known existed. She wanted to find out what was wrong and make it better. *You need to lock that down right now. He's not the type that needs saving.* "I just got back from having a chat with Bart."

Forgetting all of her uncharacteristic thoughts, she moved closer and asked, "How'd that go? Was Claudia there?"

Shaking his head, he said, "No, she wasn't. She was shopping to deal with all of her recent stress. So it was just Bart and me. Luckily it wasn't a long conversation. He got the point and my threats pretty quickly. He's promised to speak to his daughter and make certain that she understands the repercussions should she have another error in judgment where either you or Zoe is concerned."

"Good for you," Zoe sighed. "That couldn't have been pleasant, but I appreciate you going to bat for us. Dylan wanted to go over there and raise holy hell. I asked him to at least wait a few days until he'd cooled off."

"I don't think that helps much," Ash said dryly.

"There's something about Bart and Claudia that can push your buttons regardless of how relaxed you think you are. Hell, I'm not even including our mother in that. She's an expert in that area herself, but she seems to make herself scarce when she knows the shit is going to hit the fan. She doesn't like her stepdaughter regardless of how good a show she puts on for Bart's benefit."

"Thank you," Dana said softly. "It'll be nice not to have to look over my shoulder. Being spit on once was enough for a while."

"Hey, babe, are you about ready for our coffee date?" Dana froze as Paul appeared next to Ash. Zoe suddenly looked very interested in her phone as she tried not to stare at the scene playing out in front of her.

"I—um—er," was Dana's incoherent reply as Ash slowly swiveled to look at Paul.

Zoe's manners picked that moment to kick in as she blurted out, "Oh, Ash, this is Dana's boyfriend, um, I mean ex-boyfriend, Paul. Well, actually I think they're friends again now. Sort of reconnecting after not speaking for a year. I believe they were going to catch up. You know, talk about old times and such."

Dana could only gape as her best friend continued to stick her foot in her mouth and ramble on. *I'm so going to kill her.* Finally, Dana decided to intervene before Zoe started talking about Paul's erectile dysfunction and God knows what else. "Paul, this is Asher Jackson. He's Zoe's brother-in-law as well as a friend of mine. Ash, this is Paul Ward. He and I dated at one time."

What happened next had Dana's mouth dropping

open. Ash got to his feet and leaned over the counter. Before she knew what was going on, he'd put one hand behind her head and pulled her closer to his chest before dropping his mouth onto hers. *Sweet Jesus, he's using tongue*, Dana thought dreamily as Ash plundered her mouth. She feared she was moaning like a turned-on porn star as he leisurely explored every inch of her mouth before finally releasing her. When she stumbled backward, he made a quick grab for her. "You okay, baby?"

Once again she sounded like an idiot as she managed only to say, "I—what—you."

Ash kept one arm around her while extending a hand to Paul. "I believe what Dana was trying to say is that I'm Ash—her boyfriend. We haven't been dating for long and you know how independent our girl here is. She doesn't like to put labels on relationships, am I right?"

Paul had gone a bit pale by this point, but managed to shake Ash's hand while saying, "That does sound like her. We were together for a long time, but she never wanted to have anything serious. I would have married her in a minute if she'd been interested."

Ash gave her an affectionate look that had her heart threatening to beat out of her chest. *It's not real.* "Paul—really," she protested before Ash cut her off.

"Munchkin, you know you have a tiny problem with commitment." He gave the other man a pained expression before adding, "We're working on some of those self-help exercises to curb her tendency to flee from anyone who shows her affection." Ash appeared so sincere that even Dana found herself riveted. "It's been tough, I'm not going to lie. The moment I saw her,

I just knew that we were soulmates, but when I made the mistake of saying that, well . . . she laughed in my face. I've gotta say, man, it nearly broke my heart. I mean, look at our girl. She's a freaking beauty, but she has no idea what she brings to the table. She has so much to offer as a potential life partner, but she won't let anyone love her."

Oh, dear God, are those tears in his eyes? Ash was turning in an Oscar-winning performance, and both Zoe and Paul were giving him looks full of sympathy. She could see Paul being taken by the act, but what was wrong with her best friend? This was her brother-in-law after all. She knew the man had done half the women in the state of Florida. She reached her foot out and nudged Zoe's leg, effectively pulling her from her Asher-induced trance. "Now, Ash." Dana fluttered her lashes at her fake boyfriend. "Honey bunch, you know why I have all these commitment issues." Ash raised a brow as if he sensed something big was coming. Dana turned to Paul and summoned up some damp eyes of her own. "I was all ready to take the plunge, Paul. I was convinced that I had the real deal with Ash. Bu—but one night I came home early from work and . . ."

"What happened?" Zoe asked impatiently. Apparently her friend was still in some kind of dream world. How had she forgotten the whole thing was entirely bullshit?

"You remember, Zoe. I cried on your shoulder all night over it. I found Ash in the bed with—"

"That other man!" Zoe shouted out, causing the couple nearby to stare at them. Good grief, they really had to work on her inside voice. And what the hell?

Ash stiffened as he stared at Zoe in shock. "I think your memory needs some serious work, my dear sister-in-law. I can assure you that Dana has never found me in the sack with a dude."

Dana wanted to go with it, really she did. But since Ash had made this mess, she might as well use it to send Paul the message that they could only be friends. Her having a serious boyfriend would accomplish that. So as much as she hated letting Ash off the hook, she found herself saying, "Oh no, Zoe, I said she *looked* like a man. I mean, she towered over Ash. She practically tossed him across the room when he told her to leave. I was afraid she was going to body slam both of us. I did think it was a guy at first—but it wasn't."

Snapping her fingers, Zoe nodded quickly. "That's right. I got that all mixed up. She was the one with her wallet on a chain and those shit-kicker boots. I think he was terrified to turn her down. He was probably petite compared to her."

Dana nodded, doing her best to look sad. "We've really been having to work on our relationship since then. But I'm doing better, right, pookie? Plus, those sex addict classes you're attending have really helped. I was so proud of this guy for admitting that he had a problem. That's the first step, you know. That he would do that for me was such a major breakthrough for us. It was even his idea for us to abstain from intimate relations until he was better. He didn't want me to feel as if he wanted me only for that. So now we're using all our free time in the evening to do fun couple things. Like last night we took a pottery class. Tonight it's the book club. He's even taking one on quilting. He's already made the most amazing bedspread for me."

Dana could barely hold her laughter back as Paul cringed and looked away from Ash. Apparently, her fake boyfriend had just lost serious man points thanks to her. Ash himself appeared vastly amused. She knew why when he piped up, saying, "Doodlebug, we'd do anything for each other. I mean, you know my tendencies, and since we're both exploring each other's worlds, I have to say that I'm so blown away that you'd agree to give swinging a try. It's so important to my recovery to have a supportive partner. As long as it's something we're doing together, my therapist feels that it's okay."

Damn, he's good. Dana felt her face flush as Paul turned and gaped at her. "Well . . ." she began, stalling for time. How was she supposed to respond to that? Even Zoe appeared to have been taken in by their lies once again. How could she be married to a Jackson and still be so gullible? Finally inspiration struck and Dana fluttered her eyelashes at Ash before giving Paul a huge smile. "That's right, muffin. Now we just need to decide on a couple to experiment with. Paul, do you think that's something you might be interested in? I'm sure there's someone at the gym who could round out our foursome. Ash isn't particular at all when it comes to that, so anyone would do."

Inwardly wincing at Paul's dismayed expression, Dana thought that she might have taken things a bit too far. The only comfort she had was that Ash no longer looked happy. In fact, she'd say "pissed" was a more accurate description. If she didn't know better, she'd say he was jealous of Paul. The fact that he'd come into the shop and immediately staked his claim on her was further proof of that. Now if she only knew why. It wasn't as if they were really involved. There had been what she'd call sexual tension between them recently, but they'd never made a single move to act on it. So what game was he playing? Brushing up on his acting skills for the upcoming business dinner maybe? "Pumpkin," he bit out, "remember that I agreed to try medication before we moved on adding other people to the mix. And it's always better to go a little further from home for these things. I'm sure Paul isn't interested in joining the party. But it's nice to know where your thoughts are."

Zoe was studying the pattern in the floor as if it were the most fascinating thing that she'd ever seen. While Paul gulped hard so many times Dana wondered if he'd swallowed his tongue. She was seconds away from thumping him on the back when he opened his mouth and said, "I—if you do decide to—you know, do what you were saying. Could you call me first? I've never tried anything like that but—I've always wanted to. And since we already know each other, Dana, it might be fun." Paul's face was as red as a tomato when he finished his awkward declaration.

Dana glared at Ash, who was giving Paul the same type of stare. Dammit, he'd started this whole mess. Not only hadn't she let down Paul gently, but she'd all but promised the man a threesome. Even though she might not be able to do anything about Paul now, she could damn sure get under Ash's skin. Giving her ex-boyfriend a brilliant smile, she touched his arm, letting her fingers trail over the bulging biceps. "Well, of course, honey. You'll definitely be at the top of my list. Now, I do still have your correct phone number, right? You haven't changed it on me, have you?" Even she wanted to cringe when she let out one of the fake giggles that she hated to hear women do in front of a guy.

Paul practically wrenched his arm out of the socket as he frantically dug into his back pocket and pulled his wallet out. "I switched networks not too long ago. Here's one of my cards with the correct information on it. Hey, are you on Facebook? We could instant message. You can even do the live video thing."

No way in hell. "Oh, sorry, honey," she pouted. "You know how I feel about social media. Plus, Ash doesn't like for me to reconnect with many of my old male friends. He's so possessive, aren't you, lamb chop?"

"You know me, sweet cheeks," he ground out. "I don't like to share my toys with anyone. It's always been somewhat of a problem for me."

Dana reached out to cup his cheek, rubbing a thumb over his lower lip. "I know, sparky. But you do realize a threesome would be me and another man, right?"

"Thanks so much for pointing that out, love," he all but snarled. Someone wasn't happy.

Dana was absurdly grateful when Zoe cleared her throat and pointed toward a group of women coming in the door. "I hate to break this up, but we've got the ladies from the tennis club arriving. They always swing by for coffee before going home. Although I'm sure they'd be riveted by this conversation, as I certainly am."

"Me too," Paul chirped. "But I should get back to the gym. Sorry we couldn't have that coffee, but I'll be in touch. If anything, um, changes before then, give me a call. I'll make sure I'm available."

"Sure thing, sugar." Dana winked as he walked away. She noticed the way the new arrivals turned to gape at him as he strolled past. Much like Ash, Paul had never lacked for feminine attention. That's where the similarities ended though as far as Dana was concerned.

Ash got to his feet and stomped out without saying another word to either of them.

"What's his problem?" Dana hissed under her breath as the first customer approached to place her order.

"He's jealous," Zoe murmured knowingly. "He was all fine and dandy until Paul made that crazy offer and you flirted with him. I swear, I could see steam rising from Ash's ears from that point forward. And just now, he was livid. He didn't even bother to say good-bye."

Shrugging, Dana said, "Seems like the old Ash to me. That's pretty much the treatment I've gotten for the last year. Maybe the nice part of his personality has worn off and the surly one has returned. That might be safer for me."

"That's not it at all," Zoe insisted, after they'd taken all the orders. "This was different. And he kissed you. I mean, with tongue, right? That wasn't faked for anyone's benefit. You were both into it."

"That was for Paul," Dana pointed out.

"But why bother?" Zoe insisted. "It served no purpose at all. There was nothing to be gained. He wanted to warn Paul off. And it gave him the opportunity to do something he's been wanting to do. Dylan's not going to believe it. This is so not Ash."

"I think you're making far too much of it," Dana insisted, although she felt a tiny flutter of hope at Zoe's words. It was true that they had both been carried away when their lips had touched for the first time.

She knew she wasn't the only one who had felt it. Ash had moaned at one point. You didn't do that unless you were lost in the moment. Was it possible that he might want her as badly as she wanted him? And was she brave enough to act on it? She didn't want to make the first move and have him rebuff her. That would be beyond humiliating. Maybe she should play it by ear and see how he acted at the upcoming business dinner. If he was an asshole, then she'd give up and move on. But if the spark was there, then she was more than ready to fan the flames. One way or the other, she needed to get the man out of her system. And she feared the only thing that was going to do that was to hit the sheets with him. Hell, she wasn't picky—the couch or a nearby wall would do just as well. Out of respect for Rosa, she'd refrain from peeing on his towels if he disappointed her.

"If you say so." Zoe shrugged.

They worked side by side to fill the rest of the orders. Dana was grateful for the distraction because without it she feared that she'd make the mistake of buying into what Zoe had said. And if she ever let herself believe that Ash felt more for her than he did, she wasn't sure she'd be able to stop herself from falling head over heels in love with a man who was a self-professed player.

Nine

"Good luck with him tonight," Rosa said as she ushered Dana into Ash's home. "He's been even grouchier than usual this week. I swear, I don't care what the experts say, men get PMS just like women do."

Dana laughed as she followed Rosa into the kitchen. "Are you handling the food for the party? I'm not much of a cook, but show me what needs done and I'll attempt to help out. It would probably be better for everyone if I manned the microwave or handled the drinks."

Rosa snorted. "Honey, the boy always hires one of those fancy catering companies for stuff like this. He's afraid of what I'd say to the guests if they complained about my cooking. Plus, I sure as heck wouldn't be doing all of the cleanup afterwards. Some people are pigs. Although those are usually just the women that he sleeps with and makes angry."

"Where is he anyway?" Dana asked casually, hoping that Rosa hadn't picked up on the fact that she'd been anxiously waiting for Ash to make an appear-

ance. She hadn't seen him since he'd stalked out of the shop several days earlier. He'd texted her that morning letting her know what time to arrive today, but that had been it. She hadn't been expecting him to add some smiley emoticons, but he could have at least asked how she'd been.

"He's dressing. He was late getting home from work, so he's probably still in the shower."

Don't think about him naked, Dana silently reprimanded herself. She had the desire to go offer her assistance to help him wash those hard-to-reach areas, but she managed to control herself. Instead, she ran her hands nervously down the red sheath dress she was wearing. It was a bold color, but she knew she looked good in it. And tonight she could use all the confidence that she could get. If Ash was still being a jerk, then the possibility she'd stressed over all week would be a moot point. But if the sparks were flying, then her outfit might give her the boost she needed to close the deal—or the bedroom door—and have a night with the man she hadn't been able to get out of her head. At that moment the doorbell sounded and the next several minutes were a blur of activity while the caterers arrived and began to set up. Rosa bossed them around, letting them know that all hell would break loose if they messed up anything. They were respectful and obviously used to dealing with demanding clients. Dana moved to get out of their way and found herself wandering around Ash's apartment. She washed her hands in a nearby bathroom before continuing on down the hallway. The place was huge and elegantly furnished. She saw two spare bedrooms before stopping in her tracks. A nearby door opened and Ash stood there clad only in a towel that left little to the imagination. "Sweet Jesus," she whispered shakily.

He smirked as he looked her up and down. "I like the dress," he said in a voice that rolled over her like warm honey. "I assume it came from the hotel boutique. Remind me to congratulate them on their excellent taste."

"I—er, thanks," she managed to get out. "I'm glad you approve since you paid for it."

"You look good enough to eat," he purred as his eyes continued to devour her. "I'll be the envy of every man here tonight having a girlfriend this gorgeous."

Dana felt her core tighten. He was seducing her without a single touch. She was ready to toss herself on whatever surface she could find and beg him to do dirty things to her body. It was apparent that he'd gotten past whatever had pissed him off so much in the shop earlier in the week. And Dana didn't know whether to be happy or sad over that fact. She had no defense against the man before her and he knew it. "Maybe you're just hungry," she replied, forcing herself to look away from him.

He stepped closer until she felt his firm outline against her stomach. He was hard—that much was obvious—and he wasn't bothering to hide it. "Oh, you're right about that. I'm starving." She gulped for air, but still couldn't manage a full breath. Then he put his hand on her arm and pulled her into what she now knew was his bedroom before shutting the door behind them. "I think I need an appetizer to tide me over until later." That was the only warning she got before his mouth came down onto hers and his tongue slid inside. She felt his hands on her ass, urging her closer,

as they feasted hungrily upon each other. "You're fucking delicious," he moaned as his lips slid down the
curve of her neck while he kneaded her butt through
her dress.

Dana wanted to scream in frustration when a loud
noise had them both jumping apart. "Whatever you're
doing in there needs to be put on pause," Rosa yelled
out. "Unless you want your brother and his wife to
join you. Because this is the only place they haven't
looked. I had to resort to locking them outside on the
balcony." Dana could hear the faint sound of someone
knocking in the distance.

Ash cursed under his breath before dropping his
hands away from her. Dana knew how he felt because
she wasn't ready for this to end either, but the timing
was terrible. The other guests would begin showing
up at any moment. She felt his stare burning into the
top of her head, but she refused to look up. She needed
a moment to gather her composure first. "I'll, um—go
rescue them," she muttered before turning to make
her escape.

Before she gotten far, he grabbed her arm and whispered in her ear, "We'll pick this up later." She nodded
probably a bit too enthusiastically and then opened
the door to face an amused Rosa.

"The boy need some help getting dressed?" the
older woman asked in a voice dripping with amusement.

"Oh, hush." Dana rolled her eyes. "I'm sure you
know the drill. You've worked for him long enough."

"True," Rosa drawled as they made their way
toward the other end of the apartment. "But he doesn't
usually have women in there during the daylight

hours. I thought for a while they must all be vampires until I figured out they were mostly whores."

Dana burst out laughing at the sarcastic humor. His housekeeper reminded her a lot of herself. She'd never been one to sugarcoat anything, which didn't always make her the most popular person. Dana could see Dylan banging on the glass panels ahead of them so she hurried in that direction and opened the door. Dylan led Zoe back inside before turning to glare at Rosa. "Care to tell me what all of that was about? You obviously knew my brother wasn't out there."

Rosa didn't look perturbed in the least at Dylan's ire. Instead, she stared back at him blankly before saying, "I'm just an old lady. Sometimes I'm forgetful. I was sure I saw him go that way earlier, but I must have been mistaken. Besides, it's a nice evening outside and you had a view overlooking the ocean. A smart man would have taken advantage of it and had a romantic moment with his lady."

Zoe giggled softly as she elbowed her husband. "I guess she told you, didn't she, babe? If you hadn't been so determined to murder Rosa, we could have fooled around."

Dana was surprised to see Dylan shuffle from one foot to the other, appearing almost embarrassed. "I'll remember that the next time," he muttered before pulling his wife close. "In my defense, I didn't know what in the hell was going on though. I thought maybe one of Ash's crazy women was on the loose. You have no idea the kind of shit they do."

"Trust me, we've been informed." Dana smirked. "It's the stuff comedies are written about. Rosa kindly filled me in and I passed it along to my best friend soon after."

"What's the huddle about?" Ash asked, looking wary, as he joined the group. He seemed to sense that he was the topic of conversation, as usual.

"You don't want to know," Dylan advised. The doorbell sounded before Ash could question them further, and in what seemed like just moments, the apartment was near full to bursting with men wearing suits and women wearing expensive dresses. Dana would have certainly felt out of place in anything from her own closet, so she was glad Ash had generously supplied another outfit from the resort shop.

"I hate these things," Zoe whispered in her ear as they stood on the edge of the crowd, sipping wine and gossiping. "See that blonde over there with her fingernails on Dylan's sleeve?"

Dana zeroed in on the woman in question and felt an immediate dislike for the ultrathin waif who oozed sex appeal. "Yeah, I see her. I think you need to go over there and stake your claim."

Zoe shrugged, not appearing jealous. "I'm not worried. He can't stand her. Apparently, she's on husband number four, who happens to be a wealthy investor. He's also old enough to be her grandfather. Dylan thinks they have an arrangement that she can sleep with anyone she wants to as long as she's discreet, which she isn't. So she paws all over anything in pants like some kind of bitch in heat."

Dana smiled as Dylan pulled free of the other woman's hold and walked away. Then the amusement fled when the bimbo moved on to Ash and literally rubbed herself against his side. "I may need to teach this woman some manners," she ground out. "After all, it's what I'm getting paid for." Throwing her shoulders back, she stalked over to her fake boyfriend's side and gave him a besotted smile. "Hey, baby, who's your friend?"

Ash didn't miss a beat as he lowered his head and brushed a brief kiss across her lips. "Hey, sweetheart. I was just wondering where you'd gotten to. This is Monica Annin. Monica, this is my girlfriend, Dana."

Dana put one arm around Ash's waist before giving Monica a polite nod. "Nice to meet you. Is your husband with you tonight?"

"He's here somewhere," Monica said indifferently. "All he wants to talk about is business—so boring. At least Ash understands that there's more to life than that."

I'm going to choke this slut, Dana inwardly fumed. There was no way she could miss Monica's meaning. She'd either already slept with Ash or she damn well wanted to. "Honey, could you help me with something in the kitchen, please?" Dana asked as she pulled him away from the other woman and out of the room. "Please tell me you haven't sunk low enough to do her," she muttered as she literally dragged him through the doorway.

"Fuck no," Ash hissed. "I'm not going to be the next notch on her bedpost. Believe it or not, I do have some self-control. She disgusts me."

Raising a brow, Dana said, "Well, after Brittany, I had to ask. I can hardly do my job if I don't know everything. If you want me to make myself scarce while you hook up with someone, then you have to give me a sign." Dana seriously hoped that her voice didn't betray how jealous she felt. The last thing she wanted to do was stand idly by while he was with someone else. Just the thought of it made her feel a surge of nausea mixed with violent tendencies.

Ash glanced around the busy room filled with guests and catering staff before pulling her into what appeared to be the pantry. In the pitch-dark surroundings, he pushed her against a nearby wall and lowered his body against hers. "I couldn't give a fuck about anyone else here. I can't get your taste or the feel of your ass out of my head. I want to bend you over right now and sink so deeply inside of you that I don't know where I end and you begin. As soon as this party is over, that's exactly what I want to be doing. You'll be screaming my name, while I think of every way possible to make you come until you beg for mercy. And then I'll do it all over again."

She felt him kiss the side of her neck before he added, "And that's all you need to know right now. Any questions?"

"Yes—er, no. I have no idea," Dana whispered shakily.

He chuckled, before somehow managing to find her nose in the dark and tapping it with a gentle finger. "I'm glad we got that cleared up. The goal for the rest of the night is to get these damned people out of here as quickly as possible. Got it?"

She nodded dumbly. She doubted he could see her, but it was better than croaking out more gibberish. Her body was still going crazy with desire, and it was taking everything she had not to plaster herself against him and beg him not to make her wait any longer.

Only the thought that she'd be little better than Monica made her fight harder for control. He took her hand and linked their fingers together before ushering her back into the bright lights of the kitchen. She hoped she didn't look as shell-shocked as she felt. Rosa appeared from out of nowhere with her hands on her hips. "What is it with you two tonight? I swear, every time the boy goes missing, you're stuck to him. You better not have done anything in there that I'll have to clean up because I was just coming to say that I am leaving."

Dana knew her face had to be as red as her dress. But Ash didn't seem in the least uncomfortable. "I assume you've covered everything with the caterers?"

"Of course," Rosa grumbled. "They know exactly what needs to be done. I also told them there'd be a big tip if they got out of here fast." Winking at Ash, she added, "I figured you'd appreciate that."

"You're a rock star," he praised.

"Damn straight," she deadpanned. "See you tomorrow." Then turning to Dana, she added, "Make sure he wears a condom. There's a case of them in his bedroom closet." With that parting advice, she was gone.

Dana dropped her head before murmuring, "I can't believe she said that. Is it written on my forehead or something? How in the world does she know?"

Ash leaned closer. "It could be because your nipples look so fucking sexy sticking out like that. Or else . . . she's really good at reading people."

Horrified, Dana clamped her hands over her traitorous breasts, which were indeed standing at attention. "Dammit! I'm going to have to ice these things before I go back out there."

Ash put an arm around her shoulders and pulled her into his side. "Nope, I'm afraid not. You look perfect for the part, sweetheart. Everyone will know my girlfriend and I have been making out. Well, unless you'd rather Monica believe that I'm available. In which case, then by all means hide out in the kitchen."

"Point taken," she snapped before straightening her shoulders. "Let's go."

After that, they worked the room at each other's side for the rest of the evening. He seemed to constantly find an excuse to touch some part of her body, which keep her in a heightened state of constant arousal. She was so turned on by the time Dylan and Zoe, the last remaining guests, finally left that she could hardly stand it. Which was why when Ash looked at her, she closed the distance between them and began ripping at the buttons of his dress shirt. He growled low in his throat as he tossed his suit jacket on the floor. Impatient with her fumbling fingers, she yanked on each side of the material of his shirt and buttons went flying in all directions. He turned her around and lowered the zipper of her dress, before pushing it down her body, where it pooled at her feet. She had no idea how they made it to the bedroom, but soon they were standing there in only their underwear as their hands and tongues tangled wildly. "So fucking sexy," Ash whispered to her as he zeroed in once again on her ample behind. "I swear, I've had so many dirty thoughts about your ass."

She wasn't sure what she'd been expecting, but her breath hissed out when he smacked one cheek, causing it to sting. "Ouch," she cried. "Do you mind being a little more gentle?"

When he repeated the move on the other side, she had to admit that it felt surprisingly good. Her clit throbbed and moisture pooled between her thighs. Without wasting any time, he picked her up and carried her until she felt a smooth surface against her back. "This first time is gonna be hard and fast. I trust that works for you."

"Oh, yeah." She gestured impatiently for him to continue.

He laughed softly, then pushed her panties to the side and she felt him impossibly large against her opening. Apparently, he'd managed to remove his underwear somewhere along the way and put on a condom. How in the world had he done that in such a short amount of time?

"Ash—I want you right now," she demanded, then almost screamed at the overpowering sensations when he slid deep inside her. She wound her legs around his waist, then moaned as they frantically raced toward the finish. She'd never been one to come from intercourse alone so she was shocked to feel her orgasm building. Then it washed over her in wave after wave of bliss. She cried out, grinding against him to prolong her pleasure. "Oh my God," she chanted over and over when she didn't think she could take any more. "Mercy, please, I may die right here otherwise." She was almost relieved when he shuddered and found his own release. In true Asher Jackson fashion, he shouted out a few obscenities instead of words of affection.

He rested his head against her neck as he struggled to catch his breath. Finally he managed to say, "That was amazing, but embarrassingly short."

Dana giggled, always appreciative of his sense of humor. It lightened what could have been an awkward moment. He'd mentioned them doing several things earlier, but still she hated being in the position to wonder if she should pick up her clothes and leave or wait around and see what he said. She'd never really had to deal with this kind of thing before since she was usually more like Ash in sexual encounters. She let loose an exaggerated yawn. "Maybe you're not as good as you thought. These poor women might keep coming back because you're leaving them unsatisfied. Have you ever thought of that?"

"Really?" he asked her lazily.

"Yep." She bit her lip to keep from laughing at the injured male ego he wasn't quite managing to hide. Patting his chest, she added, "It's nothing to be embarrassed about. Not every guy can go the distance. It's easy to get overexcited and lose control. You could try thinking about sports and anything else that would distract you. I bet if you practiced more, you could work up to the five-minute mark."

"I'll see what I can do." He nodded. "Since you had to suffer so much, how about I bury my face between your legs and make it up to you? Would that help?"

"Only if you insist," she huffed out. He slid his still-hard cock out of her and threw her over his shoulder. "What're you doing?" she squealed as he walked toward what she thought was the bathroom. "Put me down," she insisted. She really didn't want her ass in the air for him to scrutinize, but he ignored her demands. Instead, he reached out to turn on the shower. Then he stepped into the glass enclosure with her still in his arms. She'd almost given up hope of him releasing her when he put her gently onto her feet before reaching for a bottle of body wash. He poured a handful into his palm and began washing her. "Ash, I can do that," she croaked out, but he acted as if he hadn't heard her.

When he reached the apex of her thighs, he simply said, "Open." She automatically complied, then moaned as his slippery fingers moved over her still sensitive clit. Then his hand moved farther back to her ass and she quivered. She'd never tried that and she didn't intend for the first time to be in a shower with Ash, but damn, his touch there was arousing. She was close to coming once again and was disappointed when he continued up her body and away from where she wanted him the most. He circled her nipples next—in response, they immediately stiffened to hard peaks—before saying gruffly, "Turn around." He cleaned her back with quick efficiency, then made fast work out of doing the same to himself. She would have loved to return the favor, but he was already rinsing himself. "Lean against the wall," he instructed, and she didn't even think about arguing; she simply turned around again and did as he asked. Then he dropped to his knees and pulled one of her legs over his shoulder. "Hold on to me, Dana."

That was all of the warning she had before his mouth was buried in her wet heat and his tongue started driving her insane. Her clit throbbed when he sucked it before sliding his tongue back inside her. "Ash!" She cried out his name, digging her fingers into his hair. The man would probably be bald tomorrow, but she was too far gone to care. He added one finger, then another. Soon he was pushing into her hard and fast, while he nipped at her clit with his teeth. "Oh my—damn, more!" she hissed as she spiraled toward her release. "Harder," she groaned, needing just a little more pressure to come. When he pinched her clit, she exploded. Black spots danced in her vision as she shuddered. "Ash—Asher."

Afterward she was so limp, she was barely aware of him helping her from the shower and drying her off with a towel. She sighed in pure bliss a few minutes later when her body met something soft and she burrowed down into it. After a few minutes, she opened one eye, looking up at him. He had his huge dick in one hand, stroking it from root to tip. "I've been dreaming about those lips, baby."

Suddenly her fatigue was gone and desire returned. If she'd been the subject of his fantasies, then she wanted to show him that the real thing was more than he could ever imagine. So she forced herself from the warm cloud she'd been lying on and went down onto her knees in front of him. He'd turned on one of the bedside lamps, so she could see the gleam of approval in his eyes as she glanced up at him before moving his hand out of the way and replacing it with her own. She gripped him firmly, impressed by his sheer size. She couldn't believe that had been inside her not long ago. She licked up his shaft, circling the head before wrapping her tongue around the tip. He groaned low in his throat as she continued to tease him. When he least expected it, she took him deep in a single move that had him bellowing out loud. She applied suction and pumped her hand and mouth in the same tempo. He put a hand on the back of her head, guiding her until they worked as one unit, each completely focused on his pleasure. He was so deep he was touching the back of her throat. She struggled not to gag before managing to relax enough to give him all that he wanted. When he pulled almost all the way out, she let her teeth drag against the sensitive underside of his cock and he shuddered as he came in her mouth. She licked and sucked him dry until he moved back from her. She dusted her hands off and got to her feet. "My work here is done," she joked. In truth, she felt as if she needed to retreat. This was Asher Jackson. He wouldn't want her to stay and she wasn't going to stick around for him to give her some trite line about having enjoyed their time together.

Dana had everything all worked out in her head, so she was shocked when his hand landed on her elbow. "Where in the hell do you think you're going?"

She shrugged uncertainly. "It's late and I'm tired. I'm going home. You should be happy that I'm not peeing on your towels or the floor."

"That joke is seriously getting old," he grumbled. "You'll sleep here," he said as he pointed to the bed.

Now she was just plain confused. "But—why? Don't you usually want your women to leave rather than spend the night? If you think because I'm your fake girlfriend that you're obligated to be nice, then don't sweat it. I mean, I've already been on the receiving end of your rude side so it's really not a big deal." She crossed the room, looking for her dress.

"For fuck's sake, Dana," he snapped. "I don't want you to go, all right? Must you make me into an asshole when I'm actually trying not to be one? I fully expected that you would stay. Can you please let me be a decent guy for once? I'm trying here, but you're making it damned difficult."

She could only gape at him. He was sincere; that much was apparent. He ran an agitated hand through his hair as if awaiting her reaction to his words. She knew she should take off. No good would come of this. But he was putting himself out there, and dammit, she didn't want to be the one to rebuff his attempts. So despite her inner voice screaming for her to run like the wind, she walked back to where he stood and nodded. "I swear, you're going to have to deal with Rosa in the morning," she warned. "Do you have an extra toothbrush?"

They stood next to each other at the double sinks and it was so domestic that it was almost surreal. She ushered him out the door while she used the restroom, then he took a turn before joining her in the bed. She was curled on her side, already drowsy, when he pulled her into his arms. For a moment she froze, unused to the intimate feeling of sleeping in a man's arms. It wasn't that she'd never shared a bed with anyone before, but she usually much preferred to have her own space. And she'd certainly never figured Ash for the cuddling type.

She still couldn't believe that he'd all but insisted that she stay for the night. This added a whole level of uncertainty to their encounter that she wasn't ready to deal with. Sex wasn't supposed to be so complicated, but if she wasn't careful, things with Ash could get that way fast. She hardly expected him to declare his undying love for her while begging for her hand in marriage. Quite the opposite really. It might be her doing something crazy if she didn't watch out. Even when he was being an ass to her, she was still more drawn to him than she'd ever been to anyone else. She didn't stand a chance against this kinder version of him. More than anything, she needed to keep things light and make a clean escape in the morning. She wouldn't give him the power to hurt her.

This was just another one-night stand. Nothing at all to be worried about, right? Except as she drifted off to sleep, she knew she was lying to herself because Ash was far more than that. He was the man she'd fallen in love with even when he'd been at his most insulting. She'd hated the mean girls for so very long, but she'd given her heart to a mean boy almost a year earlier. She'd seen pieces of the man he truly was in how he treated his brothers and the resort employees. A few months after Ash had moved to Florida, Dana had been taking a walk out by the resort pool to stretch her legs. There had been a small boy near the poolside crying to his mother about not being able to swim as the other kids could. His mother had ignored him as she conversed with her friends. The child's shoulders had drooped when he'd turned away. Dana had been shocked to see Ash rise from a nearby lounge chair and approach the child. He'd squatted to his knees and began explaining the basics of swimming. He'd then asked the mother if it was okay to take the boy into the pool for a lesson. Dana's break had been almost over and she'd been forced to leave, but she'd taken the same route a few more times that week and had seen Ash once more giving instruction to the child. And a part of her had fallen hopelessly for him then and there.

"Is Dana still asleep?" Rosa asked, then continued on without waiting for an answer. "You know, when I told you to find a nice girl, I didn't expect you to do it so fast or so close to home," Rosa remarked dryly as she put a plate of pancakes in front of him.

"Yes, she's sleeping and what's the occasion?" Ash asked, looking at his breakfast suspiciously. Normally he was lucky to score a bowl of fruit from her in the kitchen. She might cook dinner and leave it for him to heat later, but she didn't provide him with any other meals. He'd never really cared since he usually picked up coffee and a muffin from Zoe's on the way to the office. He'd didn't want to admit it, but that had become his regular morning routine mainly because Dana normally opened the shop. He had found he got off on the adrenaline that arguing with her gave him.

"I don't think Dana is one of your usual anorexic bimbos, so I figured she'd appreciate something more substantial than a glass of water. Although I do remember one of them inhaling everything in the refrigerator before barfing it all over the bathroom. I swear, boy, you certainly don't discriminate, do you? You've slept with every kind of crazy there is."

"In her defense, Mindy—or maybe it was Mandy— said she had some kind of stomach bug," Ash pointed out before taking a bite of his food.

"Oh, naturally." Rosa chuckled. "The first thing you do when you're nauseous is to eat a leftover bowl of roast beef and a pound of mashed potatoes. Then stick your finger down your throat ten minutes later. I could hear her through the door cursing herself about the five pounds she was going to gain and how that couldn't happen since she had a swimsuit shoot the next day."

"Oh, yeah, I forgot about that." He shrugged. "I'm pretty sure she did the same thing after dinner as well. I should have insisted we go to her place. But after the whole dog thing, I couldn't risk it."

Rosa poured herself a cup of coffee before taking the seat across from him. "I don't think you told me about that. I could use a laugh this morning, so let's hear it."

Ash knew he was only giving her more ammunition to use against him, but he'd come to enjoy their chats. She probably knew him better than almost anyone else aside from his brothers. "Right after I moved here, I met up with this woman in a bar. I ended up going back to her apartment. I'd had a long flight that day so I fell asleep, which was a mistake. When I woke up the next morning, her dog was sitting on my legs. The damned thing was a Rottweiler and his teeth were only inches from the family jewels. She was nowhere to be found and he was growling and snarling like he was going to fucking kill me. Every time I moved so much as an inch, he'd snap at me. The damn thing was also drooling by the bucket load. So there I am butt naked with slobber on my crotch and a beast that was dying to yank off every protruding part of my body. I was trying to figure out how much damage he could do by the time I called 911 when she finally came back carrying a couple of cups of coffee. She thought it was adorable that her dog—who was named Cupcake— had made friends with me. When I got her to call the thing off, I put on my pants, grabbed the rest of my stuff, and ran like hell. That was the last time I stayed anywhere other than home. Which, as you know, has created its own problems. But I haven't been mauled by a four-legged beast."

Ash heard laughter coming from behind them and turned to find an amused Dana standing there. He swallowed deeply for composure as he noticed the fact that she was wearing one of his T-shirts. Since he was a lot taller than she was, it hung to well past her knees. She looked so freaking sexy that he wanted nothing more than to throw her down onto the table and have her for breakfast instead. "That was another classic encounter," she joked before saying good morning to Rosa without an ounce of discomfort. She waved the other woman away and fixed her own plate as well as a cup of coffee, then settled down next to him. "Good morning, dear," she said easily as she took a bite and moaned in bliss. "Oh my God, these are scrumptious, Rosa." She surprised him by patting his stomach. "How in the world do you keep that six-pack? If I had this every day, my ass wouldn't fit through the door."

"This was all for your benefit—she doesn't normally put this much effort into me. Apparently you rank higher."

Ash's dick jumped to attention when she closed her eyes to take another bite and groaned again. "I think I love you, Rosa. This is like crack and that makes you my dealer. I'll be following you around and begging for another fix. I swear, if you do toilets as well, I'll marry you today."

"Hey, I've already proposed to her on numerous occasions and she says she can't leave Ted. So forget it. I've called first dibs. If you want the food, you'll have to get it here."

Rosa grabbed her chest before saying dramatically, "Well, I never thought I'd see the day. Asher Jackson actually wanting a woman to come back again. Usually he's in here hiding and begging me to go show them to the door. I deserve hazard pay for the amount of times I've been in the trenches. Some of them were downright scary too. You never know when they're gonna go off and starting throwing shit. I can handle the tears, but flying shoes are dangerous. Especially those spiky ones. We had to plaster a hole in the wall a few months ago after one woman tossed her shoe so hard the heel went about three inches in and she couldn't get it back out. Talk about pissed. She kept raging about how much the damned things cost, when it was her that threw the fit and the Jimmy Who's."

"I think that's 'Jimmy Choos.'" Dana giggled. "Although I've never been able to afford them myself, but I've seen enough movies to know the name."

Rosa shook her head. "All I know is that she looked pretty crazy when she insisted on putting the one left on and limping out the door. I have no idea how she made it home that way. I offered to get her a pair of socks to wear, but she wouldn't hear of it. Said she wasn't going through the hotel like that. But I figured she would have attracted fewer stares in socks than she must have with all the hobbling she was doing."

Dana looked at Ash and clucked her tongue. "You really do a number on these poor souls, don't you? Were you cowering while all of this was going on?"

Not feeling an ounce of embarrassment, he said,

"Hell yeah. I figure they'll think twice about messing with a poor old lady. But I'd be a different story."

Rosa reached out and swatted his shoulder. "Watch it, kid. Next time I'll let you clean up your own mess and you know you don't want that."

Ash elbowed Dana. "You heard that, right? If you go all bat shit, Rosa's not going to like it. She'll tell everyone far and near about your antics. You'll be the talk of the hotel if you don't behave."

Dana looked surprised, but simply said, "I'll keep that in mind." She took the last bite off her plate, then stood to load it in the dishwasher. Rosa looked at her approvingly as she cleaned up after both herself and then Ash. "I need to head home so I can get ready for work. I only have about an hour until my shift."

Ash didn't like the thought of her hurrying through the Florida traffic. "Why didn't you bring something with you to wear?"

She darted a glance at Rosa as she lowered her voice. "I didn't exactly plan to stay over. I have an extra shirt at work, but I don't have any pants."

After pulling out his cell phone from his pants pocket, Ash said, "Why don't you run down to the boutique and pick up a pair? I'll call and let them know you're coming."

She rolled her eyes. "I'm not spending a couple hundred bucks because I'm too lazy to drive across town. It's really not a big deal. But I need to get going or I'll be late."

Ash stood and crossed to her. He lowered his head and said softly, "They know to put anything you buy on my account. Do you want me to walk you down?"

Dana looked exasperated now as she blew out a

breath. "I'm not letting you buy me clothes because I didn't come prepared for the walk of shame. You're making this into more than it is. It's not as if I live in Cuba or something. But Zoe isn't going to be happy if the shop doesn't open on time because I was arguing with her stubborn brother-in-law. Now if you'll please let me by, I can leave."

The woman absolutely drove him nuts. He didn't understand why there was a problem. "I bought the dress you wore last night, so it's not as if this is a first. Just go get a damn pair of slacks and stop being so pigheaded."

He saw Rosa shake her head at him before she glanced over at Dana. He knew he was making a mess of this but he wasn't used to this kind of objection. He'd never had anyone refuse to shop on his dime. It was practically unheard of. Even his own mother took great pleasure in charging her purchases to either him or his brothers. Suddenly he was studying Dana like he would some kind of science experiment. He hadn't been aware that there were even people like her in the world other than maybe Rosa. She reached one arm out and poked him in the chest with her bony finger. "Listen, buddy, the wardrobe was for the job. I'm not one of your bimbos who wants something from you. You don't need to flash your platinum card or call one of your hoochie outlets to clothe me. I might not have expensive designer things, but my Walmart slacks get me by just fine. Now if you'll please move your ass, I have somewhere to be."

Ash had opened his mouth to argue when Rosa cleared her throat loudly. "You best throw in the towel on this one, boy. It's only gonna get worse if you keep going. And I'm thinking you might want this one to come back again." Since it was now two against one, he did what any intelligent man would do—he shut his mouth and retreated. Any thoughts he'd had about morning sex or at least a kiss were gone as the petite blonde he'd shared a bed with the previous night stalked past him and slammed out the door. "That didn't go so well." Rosa stated the obvious. "You had it wrapped up until you wouldn't take no for an answer. Dana is a normal girl. You can't treat her like a booty call."

A booty call? Ash cringed at his housekeeper's ghetto terminology. What had she been watching on television lately? Probably some crazy reality show. "Why am I the bad guy for simply trying to make her life easier this morning? It wasn't as if I offered to buy her a damned Porsche or some trampy lingerie. I asked her to stay over last night, so naturally I felt responsible that she wasn't prepared this morning. I was simply attempting to be considerate. But you two ganged up and turned it into an asshole move."

"Cool your jets," Rosa scoffed. "I knew where you were coming from, but she didn't. And that one is carrying around some past baggage. I didn't say you were wrong, I was trying to keep you from making a mistake where she's concerned. I like her and you appear to as well. So instead of throwing a hissy fit, you should be thanking me for putting a stop to your downward spiral. You didn't notice it, but that ship had sailed and was damn near about to run ashore while you argued with the captain."

Ash scratched his head as he stared at her in confusion. "Do I even want to know what that means? Can't anyone around here just say what they're thinking instead of making it so complicated?"

She slapped his arm as she walked over to the sink and began to clean up the remaining dishes. "Let me put this in terms you can relate to. You were fucking up and I saved your ass. She can't be bought like a tramp of the month. I have a feeling you've made a mess of things with her at various times so you don't have a lot of credibility to fall back on. If she does carry scars from past relationships, you're gonna make her as nervous as an eighteen-year-old virgin going to prom with the high school quarterback."

And I actually thought this conversation couldn't get weirder. Has she been smoking Ted's weed again? Maybe she'll share if I beg. "Since you and Ted have been together forever, I doubt you remember much about those pesky innocent years," he joked and was pleased when she cracked a smile. "If I'm understanding you, then you're saying I should try a different approach with Dana. I mean, if I want to see her again. Which is kind of absurd because you and I both know that I don't do repeats often. It's been a huge mistake every time I've attempted it. Hell, she was seconds away from putting a hole in either my head or the wall before she left. It's best that we both cut our losses and move on."

"What's this about her doing a job for you? Is she working in that fancy office of yours? Heck, I might be interested in applying for a position if you're supplying a wardrobe. You don't even replace my shirts when I get Clorox on them."

He rarely kept anything from Rosa and he didn't see the point now. She might be an employee, but she was also more like a mother to him than his own. "I hired her to be my fake girlfriend. She needed money for a new car and I wanted to enjoy a few social occasions where I didn't get pawed all night. She accompanied me to dinner at my mother's last week and ended up making an enemy of Claudia when she kicked her chair backwards and dumped her ass out onto the floor. Then they had a whole ugly scene where Claudia and her cronies came into the coffee shop and Claudia spit coffee on Dana. Zoe had security kick them out, which pissed off the parental unit, well, Bart at least. I think my mother rather enjoyed it. So I had to threaten Bart to get his daughter to back off. And last night Dana was here because she was pretending once again to be the woman in my life. It certainly helped keep that clinger Monica off me for the evening, so I'd say it was a success."

Rosa stared at him in disbelief. Then she threw her head back and started laughing. "That explains a lot," she finally managed to wheeze out. "I couldn't figure out why it seemed as if you suddenly had a real relationship for the first time since I've known you. And Dana is so different than any other woman you've ever dated. I thought you'd either smartened up or she'd lowered her standards. So this makes more sense. The world as I knew it seemed to have gone mad there for a while."

"Gee, thanks so much," he muttered dryly. "You really never worry about offending me, do you? You better be glad I'm not overly sensitive."

"Oh, stop whining." She rolled her eyes. "So I guess that you two hit it off and that's why you were sucking face earlier last evening and then she stayed over."

"I've been attracted to her for a while," he admitted. "But there was also something about her that rubbed me the wrong way. For the better part of a year I've insulted her almost daily. And I'm not talking about your garden-variety snide comments. No, it was full-on mean stuff. Even I couldn't believe some of the shit that came out of my mouth around her. I'm surprised she hasn't hit me with her car by now. But that night at the bar when she saved me from neck-sucking Brittany, we came to a mutual understanding. She needed money and I'd had enough embarrassing scenes. I also saw that I'd been wrong about her all this time. I was punishing her for someone else's sins. And no, I'm not getting into that," he added quickly when Rosa attempted to interrupt him. "Dana and I are a lot alike in regard to our views on relationships so it seemed like the perfect solution for both of us."

"But it's gotten complicated because you actually like this one?" Rosa clearly wasn't giving up on her interrogation yet.

Ash shifted on his feet, not comfortable thinking along those lines. "She's become a good friend," he admitted hesitantly. "We also get along well most of the time. But that's all there is to it. That's all it'll ever be, so don't go trying to turn Dana and me into one of those romance novels you leave lying around my house."

Rosa acted like she didn't hear him. "You could send her flowers. From the sounds of it, you owe her. Even the hardest heart melts over roses."

"You've officially lost it," he said in disgust. He hadn't done anything like that since Fiona and look at how unsuccessful that relationship had been.

"Maybe you don't know it yet, but you've met your match. I already see changes in you. You can deny it all you want, but she's gotten under your skin. I said the same thing to Dylan about Zoe, and I was right."

"My brother is a different story," he argued. "He was ready to settle down. I'm not wired that way. So save all your self-help talk for someone who needs it. Now I've got to get to the office." He walked down the hallway to his bedroom trying to block out her words. She didn't know what she was talking about. Ten years from now he'd still be doing what he did best: avoiding messy attachments and hysterics. He was lucky that this time he'd slept with someone who felt exactly the same way. He didn't have to worry about Dana getting the wrong idea. And as long as they were on the same page, why not enjoy the perks that came along with their business relationship? The next time he wouldn't offer to buy her any clothes though. After all, a smart man always learned from his mistakes.

Ten

You want to get a drink tonight and discuss some
of the events over the next few weeks that I'd like
you to attend?

Dana frowned as she looked down at the text message from Ash. Obviously her meltdown that morning
hadn't changed anything in their business arrangement. She'd planned to end it after he'd pissed her off
that morning but pride goeth before the fall and she
needed the extra money that being his girlfriend
brought in. But the sex . . . that shouldn't happen again.
It made things messy, and other than Paul, she tried
not to double-dip. Knowing Ash, he wouldn't be interested in a repeat anyway. Surely the incident with
Brittany had taught him a lesson. So what if he'd been
the best that she'd ever had? God willing, he'd never
discover that. The man was conceited enough as it was.

He'd definitely surprised her last night with the
whole cuddling thing. And he'd remained wrapped
around her all night. Maybe that was something he did
with all of his women. It might explain why they were

so confused and pissed the next morning when he tossed them out. That kind of intimacy could lead to expectations. Half of them were probably picking out their china patterns while they were using his toothbrush. Even she'd been a little off her game when she'd woken up plastered to his chest. She thought she might have felt him drop a kiss onto the top of her head at one point. She'd say he was naturally affectionate, but in her experience with him, that certainly wasn't the case. She didn't consider being called "fat" a term of endearment. Possibly he reserved stuff like that for her alone though.

The only clear answer here was that they should never cross that line again. She didn't intend to be one of his floozies. She'd wanted to take his head off that morning for offering to buy her pants. It seemed that already he was losing respect for her and flaunting his wealth. She might not have much in this world, but she had self-respect. Life had taught her the hard way that you could never depend on anyone because people would always let you down.

Zoe was one of the very few people that she trusted. Thanks to her high school experience with bullies, she knew that help was rarely offered without an ulterior motive. Ash had simply been trying in his own way to pay her for sex, which was completely demeaning. It also was a way for him to let himself off the hook. Payment for services rendered.

She'd made a mistake by letting their relationship cross over from a business arrangement into something more personal, and she'd remedy that immediately. So she quickly tapped out a reply that he should meet her at the bar down the street, and she hit Send. He probably expected to have a drink at the hotel, but she felt neutral turf gave them equal power. And she'd wear her work uniform. No sense in Ash thinking she was dressing for him. Come to think of it, she wouldn't bother to brush her hair either. He'd get the natural version of Dana. That should send him running for the hills. He'd never been her biggest fan, and it was time to remind him of that fact. So with new determination, she locked up the shop and walked out to her car. It felt good to be back in control. He'd find that unlike most of the women he dated, she was totally immune to his charm. She had this, right? No problem.

༄

Was that Dana heading his way or a homeless person? Ash couldn't help wondering if he had mistaken someone else for her when a vaguely familiar blond woman stopped next to his table. Her disheveled appearance included a stained shirt, hair that stood up in places, and pants covered in what looked to be flour. She even had smudges on her cheek as if she'd rubbed a dirty hand across her face countless times. So much for the smoking hot woman in the red dress from the previous night. "Hi. Did you come straight from work?" he asked with a smile plastered onto his face.

"Oh no, I had time to go home and relax first," she said brightly. "I'm glad you texted. I could really use another payday, ca-ching!" She said the last part so loudly that several people at nearby tables turned to stare at them.

"Did you also have a few drinks while you were there?" Ash asked uncertainly. He thought he'd seen every side of Dana by now, but this was certainly a new one. She reminded him of the mean lunch lady he'd had in elementary school who tortured them if they opted for junk food over whatever the kitchen was serving. She usually looked as if she was wearing most of the meal on her outfit each day. She also tended to yell since it was rumored she was half deaf.

"Nope." She shrugged before flopping down into a chair opposite him and crossing her legs like a guy. She picked up a menu and it was then he noticed that she was chewing gum. She blew a bubble that covered most of her face and then popped it so loudly that it sounded like a gunshot. "So what's good in this joint?"

"How should I know?" he asked dryly. "You're the one who picked it. I assumed you'd been here before."

"I have," she said, nodding, "but I usually just drink my dinner, if ya know what I mean." Before Ash could reply, their waitress showed up and he wanted to slink down in his seat and beg for divine intervention. Because naturally on the evening that Dana was acting stranger than usual, their server was someone that he'd slept with before. He hoped like hell she didn't recognize him because he couldn't remember her name. He was facing a situation that could get awkward in a hurry.

He kept his head down, studying the menu. "What'll you have, Dana?"

"Hmmm, how about an order of hot wings? That sound good to you, Asher?" He wanted to cringe when she used his name.

"Ash! I thought that was you. Where ya been, baby? I was just telling Marla that we should give you a call. We both had a blast that night after the concert. I thought you were moving back to South Carolina. Are you just here visiting someone?"

Dana extended a hand to the other woman before she started speaking in a gushing tone. "You must be one of Ash's girls. It's great to meet you. I'm Dana, his sister." He could only gape at her in shock as she continued to spin out a false story. "Ash, I can't believe you didn't let this lovely woman know that you live here now. What an oversight on your part." She then proceeded to take a pen from her purse and write something on a napkin before handing it to her newfound friend. "This is Ash's number in case you don't already have it. Give him a call sometime. He's been doing nothing but sitting at home because his last girlfriend has a scorching case of the crabs. But don't you worry, Ash has been tested and there's no sign of those suckers on him."

Ash was trying to decide if he wanted to laugh at her creativity or kill her when another voice joined in. "Damn, why didn't you tell me, bro? I can't believe I had to hear all about this in a bar from our . . . sister?" Ash turned to see his brother Rhett smirking down at him. He'd completely forgotten that he'd told him to join them if his flight got in early.

"Yeah, it was news to me as well," he muttered as the server scurried away.

Instead of looking embarrassed, Dana seemed thrilled by the new addition to their table, which didn't sit that well with Ash for some strange reason. "And who's this?" She batted her eyes at Rhett.

"Dana, this is my brother Rhett. He's in town for a few days, but he's based at the Miami resort."

Rhett gave Dana a smile that had Ash glowering at him. Then he made it even worse by taking the seat closest to her, instead of next to Ash. Not that he cared.

He didn't have any claims to her, nor did he want to have any serious claims on a woman. What did it matter if his brother was on the prowl? "I've heard my brothers mention you." Rhett offered her a grin. "It's good to put such a beautiful face with the name."

"Oh, I can only imagine what they've had to say." Dana huffed out a sexy laugh. "I'm not exactly on either of their Christmas card lists. But I have to admit that Zoe was right. There isn't an ugly Jackson among you, is there?"

"Now you're just trying to make me feel good." Rhett chuckled. "I've always considered myself the mutt of the crowd." Pointing to Ash, he added, "I'm not in the same league with this handsome devil here."

"He is pretty." Dana shrugged. "But he knows it, which takes serious points away. So unless you've slept your way through the entire state, you're still ahead of him."

"I wouldn't say the whole state," Rhett mused, "but I'll confess I've made the rounds in Miami. All work and no play, you know." Then he put his hand over his heart and Ash thought he might barf when he said, "Now if I had the pleasure of seeing you each day, I'd have mended my ways long ago."

Ash knew he should find the whole thing laughable. There was Dana looking as if she hadn't taken a bath or brushed her hair in a week, but dammit, she still looked hot sitting there making goo-goo eyes at his brother. And rather than being turned off by her unkempt appearance, Rhett was openly admiring her curvy frame and beautiful features. "Well, I'll say one thing for you," she purred, "you've certainly got the manners. The other two have their moments, but they're assholes more often than not. Ash over there has spent the better part of the last year calling me as many versions of fat as he could come up with. And Dylan is constantly telling me to get on my broom and fly home."

Rhett looked faintly shocked when he glanced over at Ash. They might not have been raised by your typical strict or affectionate parents, but they certainly knew you didn't speak to women in that manner. Rhett had always looked up to him, so Ash found himself wanting to make excuses when there really were none. He'd been a dick plain and simple. "I can't speak for Dylan, but I have apologized," he offered with his gaze trained on Dana. "I realize that it'll never be enough, but not a day goes by that I don't regret it. I hope you know that."

She seemed riveted by his words. And to his horror, he could see tears glistening in those beautiful eyes. But luckily the tough exterior, with which he'd become so well acquainted, kicked in and she blinked the moisture away. Once she'd composed herself, she told him in a sassy voice, "You'll probably still go to hell for all that, but maybe the devil will give you time off for good behavior."

The next thing Ash knew, Rhett had thrown up his hand and called out, "High five, sis, you sure told him. If I'd known we had an awesome new sister, I'd have visited sooner. Ash never tells me the good stuff. Hey, Dana, have you ever thought of relocating to Miami? Just think, you'd be closer to the most charming brother and away from the jerks of the family. Something to consider, right?"

"She is best friends with Zoe," Ash snapped. "I

think it's highly unlikely she's going to leave her for you. Plus, last time I checked, you were in a relationship with that yoga instructor."

Rhett shook his head. "Nope, that's over. I think I was infatuated with all of those bendy moves she could do. But when the smoke cleared, she wasn't the one for me. She was also a bit too territorial. I took a class she taught and she tossed another girl out for offering to show me how to do one of the poses. I thought there was going to be a catfight right there. It was freaking hot in a scary kind of way."

"Ah, that's too bad." Dana smiled sympathetically. "I'm in between people as well. Oh, unless you count Ash. But we're seeing other people, aren't we, baby?"

Rhett looked between them, clearly intrigued. "Wait, so you're dating?"

Ash sat forward in his seat and did his best impersonation of a besotted fool. "Absolutely. Right, sweet cheeks? It's a fairly new thing, but we're happy. She does love to bust my balls like with that little scene you walked in on. Our waitress was a former—"

"One-night stand?" Dana supplied helpfully. "Wait, she isn't the one who peed on your towels, is she? But she did mention there being a friend who joined you, so probably not. I can't believe Rosa hasn't told me about them. Surely, there's a story there."

"Damn." Rhett whistled through his teeth. "Clearly your life is much more interesting than mine. And you live in Pensacola, where everyone goes to bed before the sun sets. How do you manage all this?"

Before Ash could answer, Dana chimed in, "I'd say it has something to do with the company he keeps. When you troll for chicks at fast-food restaurants, you're bound to have a few problems along the way. Of course, Brittany was a prime example of that. Do you know that she calls your brother 'Ashey'? And sucks on his armpits in public? I had to pry her off him a few weeks ago. I was afraid she'd get some kind of deodorant poisoning if I didn't remove her tongue from his body. Everyone in the place had their phones out recording it."

Rhett shook his head in disgust. "Dude, that's nasty. I don't think I envy you after all. I can't believe what these people around here are into. Unless you're gonna suggest Dana, I'll pass on you setting me up with anyone."

"Well, it appears that you're out of luck then." Ash forced the words out through gritted teeth. "To start with, Dana is her own person and makes decisions for herself. And secondly, there's no way I'll be walking away so you should look elsewhere." Rhett stared at him in surprise. Ash was afraid he'd revealed more than he'd intended, but the words had come out before he'd been able to push them back. He might not do relationships, but he did feel territorial where she was concerned. They had slept together, which admittedly usually wouldn't mean much to him, but she was different. She always had been. Hell, he didn't even know what to do or how to deal with how different he felt around her. The only thing he was certain of was that he wanted to spend more time with her. And do crazy things like find out about everything he didn't know. Where did her family live? Did she have any brothers or sisters? This kind of thing was so out of character for him that he felt a cold sweat form on his brow.

"That sounds oddly like a back-off warning," Rhett

mused. "I can't remember getting one of those from you since . . . Well, it's been a hell of a long time."

Dana had her face propped in her hand as she studied Ash. He was beginning to feel like a science experiment. When Rhett got up to go to the restroom, Dana shifted her chair closer. "Is there another game at play here that I'm not aware of? Am I supposed to pretend to be your girlfriend around your family as well?"

"What're you talking about?" Ash asked impatiently. "If this is cramping your style because you're trying to hit on my brother, then that's too damned bad."

"You're so juvenile," she said with a scathing eye roll. "I'm not doing anything with him. He's a flirt in case you haven't noticed. He's also very likable, so it's all in fun. Are you playing the part of the jealous boyfriend now? If so, it needs a little bit of work. But you've got the cranky aspect of it down."

Ash reached for his wallet and pulled some bills out before tossing them onto the table. "You know, it occurs to me that the only time we communicate well is when we're naked. So let's get out of here. We'll go back to my place and I'll bend you over the nearest surface and fuck the attitude right out of you."

He could have probably timed that declaration better, he thought as she spewed water at him. He hadn't noticed she was taking a drink until it was too late. He calmly picked up his napkin and began mopping himself up. "I'm going to assume you didn't do that on purpose," he murmured. His face and neck were now dry, but his shirt was uncomfortably damp. It was amazing how far a little liquid could go.

Instead of being embarrassed, she smirked at him. "You deserved that. Too bad I don't have some contagious illness. Although you've probably got plenty of germs already."

Ash shook his head before getting to his feet. He extended a hand to her, saying curtly, "Let's go, baby."

She looked momentarily nonplussed. Obviously, she hadn't expected him to back up his earlier words, but she should have known better by now. "I— What about Rhett?" she asked as she glanced around the crowded bar. "I'm sure he was planning to spend the evening with you."

Without taking his eyes from hers, he pulled his cell phone from his pocket and sent a quick text to his brother. "There, problem solved. He has a room reserved at the hotel and a rental car, so he's all set." He could literally see her inner struggle as she remained seated. She wanted to go with him, yet her need to resist on principle was making it hard to give in. She needed a little nudge and he was happy to give it to her. Leaning over, he placed his lips against her ear, letting the tip of his tongue drag across the outer shell before saying, "I'd love a reason to spank that ass. It's your call, honey."

Dana popped up so fast they almost collided. Her eyes were wide and her cheeks were flushed. Her voice came out unusually high when she said, "You're a bully. It must run in your family. No wonder your sister is such a sweetheart."

He planted one hand on her ass as she attempted to stalk past him. "You'll leave your car here. I know better than to let you out of my sight. You'd take off just to spite me."

She turned, leveling a frown at him. "What if some-one steals it?"

He chuckled, remembering that she was playing the part of his pretend girlfriend because her car was basically falling apart. "How likely is that? I feel confident it'll be safe. If by some chance it's not, I'll take care of it."

"I hate you," she grumbled. "I'm only going because you're decent in bed. It's really your only redeeming quality. The other ninety-nine percent of the time, you're just a jerk. I guess it is true that you can get away with anything as long as you have a big dick."

Ash wanted to take it as a compliment, but he was afraid if she noticed, she'd put a knee to that part of his body. She was a little spitfire and he fucking got off on it. He was forced to put his hands in his pockets and try to hide the fact that she had him hard as a rock. The self-control he'd always prided himself on was nonexistent when she was around him. A few insults from those luscious lips and he wanted her in a desperate way that he never had another woman. That alone gave her a power over him that scared the hell out of him. He felt absurdly vulnerable where she was concerned. The fact that he was even using that word was insane. He made an effort to keep his voice level and his face carefully blank as he put a possessive hand on her lower back and steered her toward the exit. "Luckily for you, I know what to do with it."

"Oh goodie," she said sarcastically, but he caught the slight quiver in her voice. He might be freaking out over how she affected him, but the same could be said for her. Dana hardly seemed immune to his presence. He suspected that they were both in unchartered territory. Two people who didn't do relationships or many repeat liaisons with the same partner. Yet here they were rushing for the nearest exit before they tore each other's clothes off in a public place. And he knew with a certainty that this wouldn't be the last time. He couldn't seem to get her out of his system. He not only wanted her in his bed, but enjoyed spending time with her. He'd laughed more since they'd begun their pretend relationship than he had in ages, and he wasn't ready to let that feeling go.

But he didn't have a clue as to what to do about it. Sex was the easy part. He could do a bang-up job—pun intended—without even having to think about it. How did he go beyond that though and did he really want to? It was risky as hell. Dana might well laugh at him if he even suggested such a thing. Of course, why was it necessary to verbalize it? Only pussies talked about their feelings. No, better to ease into it and see where it took them. That way he wasn't committing to something that would likely end in disaster. He knew better than to give someone else that kind of ammunition. And Dana more than most people certainly owed him a lot of payback. If he were her, he'd be tempted to do exactly that.

He rubbed the back of his neck as they made their way toward his car. This shit was already giving him a migraine. How in the world did people cope with things like complicated feelings day in and out? Dylan must be secretly taking Prozac by now. Maybe they could get a group rate for family therapy. He had a feeling they'd all need it if the women in their life had anything to do with it.

Eleven

They were moving well past the complicated point, Dana thought to herself uneasily as she lay sprawled across Ash's chest. True to his words, they'd barely closed the door to his apartment before the clothes had once again been flying in all directions. Her thong had been ripped from her body and replaced with his mouth and oh so talented tongue. The things that man could do with no hands were mind blowing. He'd nipped, sucked, and literally driven her out of her mind. She'd come three times before he'd finally heeded her cries for mercy. She knew she should have probably returned the oral favor, but she'd been limp by that time and barely coherent. That had quickly changed when he'd held her up with one arm, sheathed himself in a condom with the other, and then arranged her facedown over the arm of his leather sofa before going balls deep inside her. She'd screamed his name loud enough for the restaurant patrons many floors below to hear her. He'd shown no mercy though. She could only brace herself for the ride of her life as he'd positioned himself to rub against her clit with each hard thrust. She hadn't been lying earlier. He did have a big dick, and sweet Jesus, did he know how to use it. She was grateful he couldn't see her face because she knew her eyes were rolling back in her head as the friction drove her insane. She came around him, screaming his name. But that wasn't enough for him. He put an arm around her and pulled her back against his chest. She was surprised when he turned her head sideways and lowered his mouth to hers. His tongue mimicked the action of his hips as he claimed her in both ways. When she reached another orgasm, he shuddered against her back and gave a hoarse shout before stiffening. She felt him jerk as he found his release, then his body rested against hers.

They'd showered together afterward and he'd washed her almost tenderly before tucking her into bed. She knew she should at least make some token protest, but obviously he expected her to stay once again. Maybe this was the norm for him. She'd heard enough stories from Rosa to know that women did spend the night at his apartment on occasion. So she wouldn't make the mistake of believing that she was special to him. That could be another reason he was so popular. Ash might very well be a cuddler. And hadn't she had a relationship of sorts with Paul? She'd never been in love with him, but they had spent many nights together. An overnight didn't have to have any significance; she knew that. But God, Ash made her long for things that she'd never given much thought to before. No doubt he'd laugh his ass off if he knew. He certainly wasn't thinking in terms of being her boyfriend or whatever you called it when you were over the age of thirty.

His hand rubbed soothingly up and down her spine almost as if he was unaware of the movement. Then his fingers ran through her short hair, caressing her scalp. Tingles shot through her nerve endings as she bit back her moan of pleasure. What was he doing to her? If she didn't know better, she'd think he was trying to woo her. Shit, that sounded like something straight out of a romance novel. Nobody really talked like that. She couldn't read anything into this. That would be a huge mistake on her part. It was simply sex. The best of her life, but sex just the same.

She was so deep into her thoughts that she almost jumped out of bed when he said, "I have another family dinner on Sunday. Do you feel brave enough to go with me? I would imagine that Claudia will be on good behavior for the most part. Bart has no doubt warned her about it. I'll keep an eye on her as well."

"You really do like to stir shit up, don't you?" She laughed softly. "I didn't think you'd ever take me back there again after the whole chair exploding backwards thing."

"Are you kidding?" He chuckled. "That was the highlight of my year. It was like watching the wicked witch in *The Wizard of Oz* get the house dropped on her. I swear, I wouldn't have been surprised to hear her crying, 'I'm meltinggg.'"

Dana's body shook in hysterics as he did a perfect imitation of the witch's voice. The movie had always creeped her out, but he'd definitely put a comedic spin on it. "Stop," she cried, while trying to catch her breath. "I'll never be able to keep a straight face when I see her now."

"So you're saying you'll go?" He sounded surprised.

"I wouldn't have held it against you if you'd said no. After all, she did spit coffee on you."

Dana shrugged. "Sundays are pretty slow so I could use the entertainment. And Zoe will be there, right?"

"Unless Dylan can manage to get out of it, which isn't likely," Ash confirmed. "Rhett will probably join us as well. As I remember, you two hit it off quite well earlier."

"You sound jealous," Dana teased, then instantly regretted it.

Such emotions would indicate that feelings were involved. She was trying to figure out how to do some damage control when Ash shocked her by admitting, "I am, which is new for me, especially where my brother is concerned." He appeared puzzled by his own behavior, and she didn't quite know what to make of that fact.

She wasn't sure how to respond, but sensed that she should tread carefully. Ash was no more used to this type of thing than she was. What could she say to keep from sending them both into a panic? Finally, she settled on changing the subject altogether. "What time is dinner on Sunday?"

"Oh, it's at six," he replied right before a yawn escaped him. "I'll pick you up on the way. If you need a new outfit, you know the drill. It should be casual so wear whatever you'd like."

Dana didn't intend to bother dressing up this time. It wasn't as if it had worked that well before. Plus, she'd rather be comfortable. Claudia had already seen her in her work uniform, so really, what was the use? She wasn't intimidated by the brat. She could hold her own regardless of what she wore.

As she drifted off to sleep nestled securely within the circle of Ash's arms, Dana was hit by one last fleeting thought: that this couldn't possibly end well for her.

Twelve

I think we've landed in some alternate reality setting," Zoe murmured softly as Claudia beamed at them from across the room. The younger woman had indeed been on her best behavior, even going so far as to toss out a few compliments. Dana didn't believe a single kind word she said, but it had been a relief not to be slugging it out on the expensive dining room table.

"Look at her eye twitching," Dana whispered back. "This is killing her. I'll bet you twenty bucks that Bart threatened to cut off her allowance if she didn't kiss our asses. That must royally suck for her."

"She's certainly never been this pleasant to me," Zoe agreed. "Whatever Ash said must have really made an impression. Even Bart has been like a different person. Meanwhile Charlotte looks as amused as Dylan and Ash do."

"I think she gets off on a little smackdown." Dana nodded. "She puts up with a load of crap from him for some reason and you know she can't stand Claudia. I bet she's been looking forward to this show all week.

For the life of me, I can't figure that woman out. I'd rather be alone than with such a pompous man. How much entertainment could he possibly provide? Surely it's not a bedroom thing because that would be just gross."

Zoe shuddered. "Yuck, no way. I bet she has to do all the work there as well. He's too self-centered to care about anyone other than himself. They probably don't even do anything like that. For her sake, I hope she has someone else on the side. That would explain her being able to stomach his terrible attitude."

"That does make more sense," Dana mused. "But if that's the case, then why doesn't she boot his ass out the door? According to what I've heard, he brings absolutely nothing to the table. She provides everything. I mean, sure, she said he was always there for her, but how long does she have to show her gratitude? You would think that debt has been paid by now many times over. Maybe he's blackmailing her?"

"Wow, I never thought of that," Zoe said, looking intrigued. "I should ask Dylan and see what he thinks. Oh crap," Zoe hissed, "she's coming over here. Quick, what do we do? I've never had to hold a conversation with her before."

Dana forced herself to relax as Claudia glided across the floor toward them. She saw Ash frown and knew he was wondering what was going on as well. "Hey, girls." Claudia smiled as she reached them. "I hope you don't mind me joining you. I simply had to escape from my dad for a while. I swear, the man is constantly worrying about me. I've already told him I was fine in three different languages, but still he says I look pale." Flipping a well-manicured hand toward her face, she added, "It's probably this cheap makeup I was forced to buy since he cut back on my allowance."

"Yeah, I hate it when that happens," Dana deadpanned. She doubted that the younger woman had ever lowered herself to buy products from the local pharmacy or chain store. That reminded her of one of the things she loved about Zoe. Even though she was technically wealthy now that she was married to Dylan, she still got excited about sales and bragged about finding bargains.

"So how's school going?" Zoe asked, her voice sounding a bit strained. "Any idea what you want to do when you graduate?"

Claudia made a dismissive gesture with her hand before saying, "Oh, you know, I'll probably do something at the resort. No use finding employment elsewhere when there's a perfectly good family business. I'm sure Dylan and Ash would be happy to have me."

The younger woman was giving them an innocent smile, but Dana was almost certain there was a double meaning behind her words. She could tell by the way Zoe's frame went tense that she was of the same mindset. Refusing to let the little hussy get to her, Dana reached out and patted her shoulder. "Don't sell yourself short. I bet there are plenty of opportunities out there for someone with your—talents. You don't want to be forced to rely on the charity of family forever, do you? After all, you'll have a perfectly good college degree soon. What's your major?"

The cracks in the younger woman's demeanor were beginning to show. Obviously it was a challenge to remain pleasant for an extended length of time. Although to be fair, Dana was making it difficult by baiting her. But dammit, it was so much fun she couldn't resist. "It's a general degree," she said defensively. "Meaning I can do a lot of different things. I didn't want to be stuck in only one area."

"Oh sure, that's smart." Zoe nodded, clearly trying to hold back her laughter.

"What about you, Dana?" Claudia asked. "Did you always want to serve coffee or did you dream of bigger and better things?"

Her particular fantasy right then involved sticking her foot up the insolent troublemaker's ass, but she managed to restrain herself. Instead, she smiled broadly, which appeared to confuse the hell out of Claudia. You really had to love the young, dumb crowd. Dana tossed her arm around the bimbo's shoulders and lowered her voice. "Well, my passion has always been to make those little hearts and smiley faces in the foam of a cappuccino. But then I met your brother and now all of my goals have changed. I want to be his wife and the mother to five children. You see, when other girls I knew coveted sports cars, I was drooling over minivans. And don't even get me started on those McDonald's playdates with the other mothers and summer vacations to Disney World. I figure that Zoe and I can time things right and end up pregnant at the same time. Then this house will be filled with little Jacksons running around. And hey, we'll have a built-in babysitter. I bet you were born to change diapers. You'll have to come along to a few of those mommy and me classes with us just to get the hang of everything."

"Oh, absolutely," Zoe chimed in. "You could even be in the delivery room. You know it's common to include the whole family now. How do you feel about cutting the cord? Dylan has a sensitive stomach, so I might need you to fill in."

"That's a great idea." Dana clapped. "Ash would gladly step aside and let you do mine as well. Plus, don't even get me started on all the barfing. Those little things can spew puke ten feet in the air. We'll probably all have it in our hair and on our clothes. Hey, have you ever thought of being a nanny? Zoe and I could share you! We'd even throw in some hazard pay when you were dealing with stuff like potty training."

"Ugh, no kidding. Picking up stray turds would certainly be worth more money." Zoe shuddered. "I'm so glad we're figuring this all out now. By the time our first kids arrive, we'll have a plan of action firmly in place. You could even fill in at the coffee shop while we're on maternity leave."

Dana was hard pressed to hold in her laughter. She didn't think she'd ever seen anyone look as repulsed as Claudia did at that moment. Ash gave Dana a questioning look from across the room and she made a discreet thumbs-up sign. She could tell by his expression that he knew she was torturing his stepsister, but fortunately he didn't seem to care. Claudia shook her head slowly before backing away. "You're both insane," she choked out. "There's no way I'm taking care of your brats. I hate kids. Ugh, I've gotta get out of here." She gave them a look of total distaste before hurrying off.

"That was awesome." Zoe giggled as she leaned a shoulder against Dana's. "I thought her eyes were going to pop out of her head. I swear, that was a stroke of genius on your part. Where do you come up with this stuff?" Then her mouth fell open and she groaned, "Please don't tell me that you actually think Ash is going to settle down and be a family man. I know you're getting along better now, but that's a far-fetched idea. I don't even see Dylan wanting children for a while."

Wrinkling her nose, Dana said, "Definitely not. It's just all I had on such short notice."

"Do I even want to know what you did to make my dear sister run like the hounds of hell were nipping at her heels?" Ash asked as he and Dylan joined them.

Dana batted her eyes up at him. "Oh, I was asking her to be our nanny, sweetheart. We don't need to wait to start our family, do we? Zoe and I want to get knocked up as soon as possible, so you need to send a call to arms out to your swimmers. Wait, have you ever been tested? What if you have a low sperm count or lazy boys?" Clicking her tongue, she added, "This could cause all kinds of delays. I can't believe this didn't occur to me sooner. As much as you've been spreading it around town, you've probably depleted your stockpiles. We need to get you in for a physical as soon as possible. I know you said you have regular STD checks, but how about other things? Most men don't realize that their counts are off until it's too late."

"What is she talking about?" Dylan whispered loudly to Zoe. "Did you tell her we were having a baby or something? I mean, I'm not saying no outright, but don't you think this is something we should maybe discuss privately before you go hiring a staff? And Claudia, really? I wouldn't let her watch my dog, much less my kid."

Ash put his hands on his hips as he glared down at

Dana. "Yeah, where is your head? There's no way in hell that nut would be responsible for little Ash Junior. Have you taken leave of your senses? When we decide to procreate, we'll hire someone who's actually qualified and doesn't eat the young for breakfast. Have you forgotten that we might want a live-in nanny? Do you want to see Claudia sitting at our dinner table for the next eighteen years? I'm all for helping out family, but that seems a little extreme. Maybe she could be our cleaning lady instead. I'd rather hire someone hot to babysit."

"Oh, you would, huh?" Dana snapped. "Well, guess what, slick? The only thing in your future is a Mrs. Doubtfire lookalike. And sadly I don't think even that would stop you. We all know that you're an equal opportunity man-whore. Of course, look on the bright side—you're used to carrying on conversations with the simpleminded, so doing baby talk should be a breeze for you."

"You're pregnant?" a shocked voice from behind them asked in astonishment.

Dana swung around to see Ash's mom gawking as if she'd just witnessed the second coming. "Not yet," Ash answered smoothly. "We're just trying to work out the logistics so we'll be prepared. By the way, I bet you can't wait to have someone call you 'Granny.' Doesn't that have a nice ring to it?"

"What in the hell did I miss?" Rhett demanded as he walked over with a beer in his hand. "I got stuck chatting with the landscaper and apparently missed the show of the century."

"Well, let's see," Dylan began. "Dana and Zoe have decided to have kids, and Ash is going to hit on all the nannies. Oh wait, Dana asked Claudia to work for them in that capacity. Although I can't imagine where that idea came from."

"We were actually going to share her," Zoe added helpfully. "But in giving that some thought, I'm fine with Dana having sole custody of your sister."

Rhett scratched his chin as he stared at Ash. "I wasn't aware things had progressed this far. You might want to think about giving her a ring first. I know that's not a requirement, but it's still a nice touch."

Charlotte rubbed her forehead. "Why have these dinners gotten even more bizarre? It almost makes me wish for the tense, silent affairs we used to suffer through. At least they were predictable. I never know what's coming anymore. Dana, dear, you've certainly livened things up around here."

Dana wasn't sure if that comment was actually intended as a compliment, but she murmured her thanks anyway. Ash put one arm around her, then patted her stomach with his hand. "We need to go ahead and feed you, sweet cheeks. You may already be with child."

Dylan burst out laughing, while Rhett made a gagging noise. "I have no idea why I've stayed away this long," he mused. "This is far more entertaining than I remembered. Is there any chance you'll name the first brat after me?"

"Um—no." Dana shook her head. "But if you're nice, I'll let you drive our new minivan."

Rhett wrinkled his nose as if smelling something foul. "Dude, say it ain't so. You can never come back from something like that. You're aware that even

Porsche makes an SUV now, aren't you? There's no reason at all to go with the ultimate manhood killer."

"But it's got that third-row seat," Ash whined, "and the entertainment system. Dana and I could watch porn and make out while the kid was sleeping."

"Asher Jackson." Charlotte coughed. "You're not supposed to say stuff like that in front of your mother. I'd rather remain ignorant to your heathen ways."

"You must be deaf and blind if you've managed to do that." Dylan smirked. "There are practically billboards all over the state about your son's exploits. Be glad that it isn't possible for Ash to get pregnant because no one would ever know who the other party involved was."

"As if you were a saint before you married Zoe," Ash mocked. "I seem to recall you doing your share of entertaining the masses. Out of respect for your lovely wife, I won't go into the details, but we both know I can easily call bullshit here. And don't even think of adding anything of your own, Rhett. I know all about those flight attendants and how you accumulated all the frequent flyer miles you've got. Hell, you could take a trip to China every other day for the next five years and still have plenty left over."

"This is such a proud moment for me as a parent." Charlotte sighed. "I swear, you got this from your father."

Ash looked at his brothers in wry amusement. It wasn't as if they could dispute her claim. Their father had always loved women, and he'd instilled a similar sort of appreciation for the opposite sex in his boys. "Where'd Bart go?" he asked once he noticed that the other man wasn't in the room.

"There is a board meeting at the country club," Charlotte said, before pointing toward the table. "He'll eat at the club, so there's no need for us to wait to sit down to dinner."

Rhett kissed their mother's cheek. "This is an unexpected treat. Both the brat and the bastard have left the building. Was it my presence, do you think?"

"If it is, how about moving here?" Ash joked. "I can't remember the last time we've been rid of them. Oh, no offense, Mom."

"Naturally," Charlotte replied, not looking in the least offended. Ash had a feeling that she shared his sentiments.

He held out a chair for Dana, then took a seat next to her. He absently leaned over and brushed a kiss onto her lips, then froze. *What in the hell just happened?* She had paused with her glass of water halfway to her lips as if she was as stunned by his actions as he was. He needed to play this off carefully because that had clearly been an act of affection on his part. Something he never did. He winked at her, trying to look like he wasn't freaking out inside and said, "Can I get my baby mama anything else?"

Across from them, Rhett made yet another gagging noise. "How about a case of condoms and some birth control pills? The last thing the world needs is an Ash Junior running around."

Ash raised his middle finger and flipped his brother off, effectively ending the heightened scrutiny his unusual gesture had put him under. He'd need to be more careful in the future because Dana brought out a side of him that had been tucked safely away for years—and for both their sakes, it needed to remain that way.

He could have a casual relationship with her without losing his heart and his head so long as he was careful. It just needed to be based on sex rather than affection and connection. Except the problem was that somewhere along the way, even he'd stopped believing his own bullshit.

⁓

"Tonight was fun," Dana mused out loud as Ash shut the door to his apartment behind them. He hadn't even bothered to ask her if she was going home. Instead, he'd driven them to his place like it was the most natural thing in the world. "It's amazing how much more relaxed things are when Bart and Claudia are gone. Your mother is a lot of fun."

Ash seemed to consider her words for a moment before nodding slowly. "Tonight she was. I can't get over the difference in her since our talk the other evening. She reminds me of the woman I vaguely remember from when we were kids. Whereas all these years a part of me thought I had imagined that whole side of her."

Dana perched on the sofa and removed her shoes. She'd worn heels with her jeans tonight for the added height and her feet were killing her. Ash dropped down next to her, and without thinking, she lifted her legs and placed them in his lap. "I'll let you do almost anything to me if you rub my tootsies."

He raised an amused brow and promptly got to work on her arches. "I don't know a man alive who would turn that kind of offer down."

"My ass is off limits," Dana quickly added.

Ash rolled his eyes before huffing. "Why do you

immediately have to assign restrictions to your offer? You know I'd make it good for you. After the first time, you'd never want it any other way again. You'd be all about the anal."

Dana picked up a nearby pillow and tossed it at his head. "In your dreams, baby. You'll just have to make do with the front area. I don't know you well enough to let you explore my no fly zone."

Ash paused and wiggled his brows. "So what you're saying is that after we're better acquainted, I'll be granted back-door privileges. About how long does this 'getting to know you' phase generally last? I mean, are we talking in terms of days, weeks, or months? Do you have a specific time frame? I can set an alert on my watch so we don't forget it."

"I have no idea." She giggled. "I've never done that before."

Ash looked over at her in surprise. "Really? I thought that was pretty common now. I never figured you for a prude. You certainly haven't been so far."

Dana stuck out her tongue at him. "Listen, to me that requires considerable trust in a partner. A woman could easily be hurt by someone who doesn't have any regard for her. And considering I've never been in a relationship other than Paul, it just hasn't happened."

"So why not with him?" Ash asked, sounding tense. "Clearly he's still hung up on you."

"Er—what does that have to do with it? And to answer your question, sex was never a big thing to him. He was more involved with his business and he enjoyed the companionship of having a girlfriend. He wasn't one to push any sexual boundaries."

"Well, he was certainly ready to sign on for that threesome, so I find that hard to believe," Ash scoffed.

"Yeah, I'm still confused over that," Dana admitted. "Paul's kind of a straight arrow." Shrugging, she added, "Maybe he's wanting to get out there more."

"He probably used too many steroids to do much of anything," Ash muttered. "Come on, you can't get muscles like that otherwise. There's no way he's not using. I bet he couldn't get it up most of the time."

Dana looked quickly away, hoping he couldn't see how his words had hit the mark. She let out a loud yawn. "I'm kind of tired. These family dinners really wear you out."

"I'm right, aren't I?" Ash smirked. "He couldn't fly the flag up the pole, could he? Damn, that must have sucked. I bet you got a lot of reading done though. No wonder you stayed with him for so long. It was like hanging out with Zoe."

"You're so mean," Dana snapped. "I didn't agree with you, by the way. I'll have you know he rocked my world multiple times a day. He was a sex god. You could only hope to be that good."

Ash used her foot to slide her down farther on the sofa until she was lying across his lap. "Is that right?" he asked idly. "I'm sorry to hear I haven't been performing up to his standards. I'll have to see what I can do about that right now."

"Um—you're fine," Dana said quickly before trying to roll away from his reach. But he reacted faster, clamping his hands around her hips, holding her still.

"Oh no, I wouldn't dream of leaving you unsatisfied." He unbuttoned her jeans before lowering the zipper. Then he slid his hand inside and cupped her through her panties. She had no idea how he managed to stroke her engorged clit in such a tight space, but within moments he had her squirming at the edge of orgasm, moaning and begging for release. He seemed to know the exact moment that she was on the cusp of her orgasm and he'd change his rhythm just enough to delay her release. He did it so many times she thought she'd lose her mind.

"Dammit, Ash!" she hissed. "If you can't finish the job, then let me do it myself."

Instead of being insulted, he clucked his tongue and chuckled. "So impatient, baby." He pushed one thick finger into her wet heat and that was it. She came so intensely that it almost hurt. Ash slowed his movements, bringing her back down gently until she was capable of rational thought again. Then he removed his hand from between her legs and her eyes widened as he licked each digit clean. "You taste fucking amazing," he groaned as if she were truly the best flavor on earth. He then put his arms under her and got to his feet, moving them toward the bedroom. After his patience in satisfying her, she figured he'd want it hard and fast, which was fine with her. But as usual, he managed to do exactly what she least expected. He laid her down on the bed and slowly undressed her, peppering her body with kisses as he removed each piece of clothing. "You're stunning," he praised, and she knew that he was being sincere. It was there in the near reverence on his face as he stroked her quivering skin.

"I bet you say that to all the girls," she teased, attempting to lighten the moment. She'd never seen this side of him before, and as much as she loved it, she was also terrified by the intimacy.

But he refused to reciprocate her humor. Instead, he murmured, "You know better than that. You're different; you always have been." He seemed almost confused as he added, "I have no idea what I'm to do with you. If I had half a brain, I'd run, but I can't seem to stay away."

"Ash," she whispered uncertainly, then went silent as his eyes locked on hers. Finally she asked, "What're we doing here?"

"I think we're making love," he replied huskily. "Beyond that, I haven't a clue. For once, let's not overthink this tonight."

She should flee. This was far too intense to manage. But for the life of her, she couldn't leave. She knew with a certainty that if she did, something between them would be lost forever. Ash was displaying a vulnerability that she hadn't thought him capable of and he'd shut down on her if she rebuffed him. She didn't know what she wanted or needed from him, except that she had to stay and see this through. In the light of day, things would probably return to normal and this magical moment would be nothing but a fond memory, but what if . . . So she took a leap of faith and hoped she survived it. "Take me, I'm yours," she whispered.

Dana had always been uncomfortable in the missionary position because it was so intimate, but she found that with Ash, it was her favorite. She loved having their tongues tangled together while he moved slowly in and out of her. She locked her legs around his waist, pulling him even deeper as he took one of her nipples into his mouth and laved the tip before biting it gently. "You feel so good, baby," he moaned as his pace increased. "You drive me crazy." He licked his way up to her neck and dropped a string of kisses there before reaching her ear. The feel of his teeth on the sensitive outer shell had her shivering.

She dug her heels into his back, impatient to reach the release that was oh so close. "Ash, please," she begged.

In a move that nearly stopped her heart, he flipped them over until she was astride him. She stared down at him in shock. He flexed his hips upward as he murmured, "If you want it, take it." That was all the encouragement she needed. She rose upward until just his tip remained inside her, then lowered herself back down. He put his hands on her hips, guiding her movements as they reached their orgasm together.

"Oh my God." She sobbed as she collapsed against his chest. "That was unbelievable." She was barely aware of him disposing of the condom. She wanted to protest when he returned with a wet washcloth and gently cleaned between her legs, but she was too tired to care. Then she was snuggling into a position that had quickly become second nature for her. Sleeping within the circle of his arms was an addiction that she was afraid she'd find no cure for. And even scarier was the realization that she had no desire to try.

Thirteen

Dana clicked to end the call, then looked at Ash suspiciously. "Your stepsister just called and invited me to spend the day at the beach with her." When he stared at her in obvious surprise, she sighed. "You didn't know anything about it, did you?"

"Hell no," he muttered. "And I don't think it's a good idea. Just because she's been forced to play nice for the past few weeks doesn't change the fact that she's a Class A bitch. She's not my buddy and certainly not yours."

"Gee, thanks," Dana remarked dryly. "I'm glad to hear how likable you think I am."

Ash pulled her onto his lap and held her as if he'd been doing it for years. It had been hard to adjust to at first, but she'd become accustomed to his easy affection and his almost constant need to touch her when they were together. As much as she'd tried to deny it at first, it had become clear they were in some sort of romantic relationship. They spent most of their free time together, and she slept at his place more often than she went home to hers. Instead of being his pretend girlfriend for hire, at some point she had transitioned into the real thing. There had never been any kind of official discussion; it had just happened. "Baby, I didn't mean any offense. It's simply that I know Claudia. I realize that it makes family events easier when everyone gets along, but you don't have to subject yourself to any of her shit on my behalf. I couldn't care less if you never speak to her."

Dana reclined against his chest as she processed his words. "I know all that." She shrugged. "But she has been making an effort, even though I've rebuffed her at every turn. What if she is trying to turn over a new leaf? Don't I at least owe her one more chance? Remember, I did kick her chair over backwards and I have been rather rude to her from the very beginning. So it's not as if she's the only one at fault."

"I think she evened the score by spitting her coffee on you," Ash pointed out. "Don't feel guilty about anything. She's far from a victim. Underestimating her would be a dangerous mistake. If you're determined to see this through, then you should arrange for her to meet you here. You can use the resort facilities."

"Um . . . I believe security was instructed to bar her from the Oceanix after the coffee shop incident," Dana said dryly. "I can just see them calling in the SWAT team and handcuffing both of us."

"Mmm, I wouldn't mind seeing you like that," Ash purred. "But please don't include Claudia; that ruins the picture in my head." When she elbowed him, he sighed. "I'll have them allow her entrance. If she behaves, her privileges will be restored. If not, she's banned for freaking life."

Dana pushed against his hold, attempting to get to

her feet. "I need to call her back. Plus, I'll have to run to my apartment and get my swimsuit."

"You've got one in my bureau," Ash grumbled as he reluctantly released her. "I swear, I'm not shocked that Claudia's a cockblocker. I had plans for today and they had nothing to do with her."

Dana stuck her lip out at him, imitating his pout. "Poor baby. I promise I'll make it up to you later." Just before she left the room, she tossed over her shoulder, "I'll even let you spank me. You know how you love seeing my ass jiggle."

Ash glared at her as he adjusted himself. "You're evil. A man shouldn't be forced to resort to a hand job on Sunday morning. The Lord frowns on that type of behavior."

"I'm pretty sure he wouldn't approve of anything you had in mind today." Dana giggled as she went to change clothes. A part of her still had trouble believing she actually had her own drawer in Asher Jackson's bedroom. Even Rosa had been impressed when she discovered it. Dana had been careful not to make a big deal out of it in front of Ash though, since men panicked over small stuff. Heck, she always had as well. Paul had tried to get her to leave things at his place, but she never had unless it was by accident. That had seemed like too much of a commitment. But with Ash, she was breaking all the rules.

"You look so fucking sexy in that," Ash groaned as he placed a hand on her lower back. The sleek, black one-piece did look good on her. It had sexy cutouts at the waist and dipped down almost indecently low between her breasts. "I think if we hurry, we can multi-task before she shows up."

"What'd you have in mind?" Dana whispered as she reached out to cup his hard length through his faded jeans. The things that man did for a pair of Levi's should be illegal. Her other hand was sliding down his happy trail on the way to the Holy Grail when the doorbell sounded. "No!" she cried out. "How could she have possibly gotten here so fast?"

"Maybe she rode your old broomstick," Ash joked, referring to the long running insult from Dylan about her being a witch.

"Too bad"—she squeezed his dick one more time— "because I was just about to ride yours." She grinned as a volley of profanity followed her down the hallway. God, how she loved that man. *Wait a minute! Love? No, no, that's not right. I meant lust. It's a simple mistake. They both start with the same letter. Anyone could mix them up.* Dana's pulse was hammering and her heart felt as if it would jump out of her chest. She took a couple of deep breaths, trying to regain her self-control. It was silly to react like that to something so simple. No harm was done, right? At least she hadn't blurted the words out to Ash. That would have been a disaster. She needed to be more careful with her word choices; that was all. *Get it together. You're okay.* She plastered on what she hoped was a carefree expression, but probably appeared more like she was constipated, as she greeted Claudia. Naturally the other woman was wearing a pair of formfitting jean shorts and a bikini top. Oh, to have that kind of confidence. She doubted that Claudia even appreciated the gift that she had been given. Only someone who'd struggled with their weight could ever truly understand that type of thing.

"That asshole security guard totally glared at me

when I came in downstairs," she grumbled. "Like he's wielding some type of almighty power. He probably only makes minimum wage and lives with his mommy," Claudia mocked.

Ash cleared his throat as he joined them. Dana could tell by his tense expression that he'd overheard his sister's insulting tirade. "I'll have you know," he began too pleasantly, "that we pay our associates extremely well. And Jeff is a valued member of the team. If not for him keeping the hoodlums at bay, we'd have far more problems than we do. So I'd appreciate you checking your attitude before I have you escorted off the premises again."

"Asher," Claudia whined, "why must you defend everyone but your own family? I didn't do anything to upset your precious employee. Aren't you in the least concerned about him offending me?"

"You've gotta be kidding." Ash laughed. "You're so thick-skinned that he wouldn't stand a chance of actually getting to you." Then he turned to Dana and lowered his voice to mutter, "Are you sure you want to go through with this? Say the word and we will pick up where we left off. I promise it'll be far more enjoyable than what you're likely to endure otherwise."

Dana hurriedly moved to shut him down before Claudia could overhear. "Take one for the team, baby. We're going to check out the beach now. I'll let you know when we're finished."

Dana had been so distracted that she'd forgotten to put on a cover-up. A fact that Ash brought to her attention by saying, "Are you forgetting something? I don't want you on display for everyone in the hotel to see."

She couldn't help rolling her eyes at his caveman statement. He was a possessive boyfriend; she already knew that. He didn't mind her dressing sexy when he was with her, but he was less than thrilled otherwise. He'd never tried to do anything crazy like forbid it, because he knew that wouldn't fly, but he certainly made his feelings known. This time she had to agree with him. The Oceanix was an upscale resort and she wasn't comfortable sauntering around basically naked, even though plenty of other women there did. Before she could return to the bedroom for the pullover, he produced it from his side. "You're so thoughtful." She smirked as she put it on.

He dropped a kiss onto her upturned lips. "Have fun," he said in a voice that clearly indicated he expected her plans to prove otherwise.

Dana followed Claudia to the elevator and tried to keep up with the conversation as the younger woman jumped from one subject to the next. Within a few moments they were settling in the lounge chairs that Ash had called ahead to reserve for them. The Florida sun was already causing Dana's skin to flush as she slathered on a thick layer on sunscreen. Beside her, Claudia opted for tanning oil, which offered no protection. Dana had to bite her lip to keep from lecturing her about the dangers of skin cancer. She'd been too naive to listen when she was that age as well.

"So how are things going with you and my brother? Are you living together now or what? Charlotte says you're always there."

"I spend a lot of time with him, yes," Dana replied. She didn't care to be the subject of the family gossip.

"You know he'll never marry you, right? I'm not

saying that to be rude, because I like you and he seems to as well. It's just that Fiona messed him up bad. You're the first real girlfriend he's had since things ended with her."

Dana really hated herself for it, but she couldn't resist asking, "Who's Fiona?" She'd heard from Zoe that Ash had been seriously involved several years ago, but Dylan didn't seem to know what had happened. He'd said that Fiona and Ash were an item and then they weren't. Ash had never been very forthcoming about his relationships, so she'd respected his privacy and hadn't pushed the issue.

Claudia lowered her sunglasses and turned toward Dana. "She's a total mystery to us. All we really know is they were serious about each other for years, then she disappeared. He didn't come around for months after that. He was drinking heavily at the time and our brother Seth, who runs the Oceanix in Myrtle Beach, had to cover for Ash in Charleston for a while. Even he didn't have a clue what went on. I heard him telling Charlotte that Ash was off the rails and he was worried about leaving him alone."

Dana was stunned. That sounded nothing like the confident man she'd come to know. What could have rattled him so badly? Was it also the reason he had opted for casuals one-night stands with women like Brittany for so long? "Wow," she murmured, still trying to take it all in. She was on dangerous ground here. If Ash found out she was participating in this type of personal conversation about his past, he would be justifiably pissed off. She certainly would be if the roles were reversed. But it was damned hard not to take advantage of the information Claudia was all but dangling over her head. "I bet that was a difficult time for everyone involved."

Claudia shrugged. "I don't remember that much about it and you already know that Ash and I aren't close. I'm surprised he hasn't clued you in though. That's the kind of thing you should be aware of."

"Ash and I are keeping it casual." Dana felt compelled to mention that he hadn't promised her anything serious. "We haven't exactly shared all of our secrets. What's the purpose of that kind of interrogation anyway? It's better to live in the now than get bogged down in the past."

"If you say so," Claudia said doubtfully. "But as long as you're not expecting him to put a ring on it, I guess it's not a big deal."

Dana nodded and changed the subject. But her mind was whirling. She hated that she'd fallen neatly into the needy girlfriend trap. She was clearly more attached than she'd thought. Otherwise, why would she care if Ash had lost his shit over some other woman at one time? Hadn't most everyone gone through a bad relationship or two? What rattled her was his reaction to whatever had happened. He must have been in love; that much was certain. But which one of them had ended things and why? *This is why I've always steered clear of emotional involvements. A few months with Asher Jackson and I'm in danger of turning into a clingy basket case.* But regardless of how much she tried to convince herself that what she'd learned about Ash's past failed relationship didn't matter, she knew it would drive her insane until she had some answers. Which meant that maybe what she felt for him was more than lust after all. And that was downright terrifying.

For a while Ash wandered around his apartment, at loose ends as to how to spend the day with Dana away. He'd certainly gone and done it. He was in a relationship with the woman he'd tried to hate for the better part of a year. He had no idea when things had taken a more serious turn, but they practically lived together now and he felt happier and more content than he'd been in quite some time. Everything was more enjoyable with her in his life. The sex was phenomenal, her offbeat sense of humor kept him laughing, and dammit, actually carrying on a coherent conversation was amazing.

When he heard the door open and slam closed, a grin tugged at his lips. "You didn't last long, baby. I'd have figured you'd tough it out for at least another hour," he called out before rounding the corner and coming to an abrupt stop.

"Well, the fact that you're this happy to see me warms my old heart right up." Rosa smirked as she tossed her huge pocketbook down on the sofa behind him.

"What are you doing here on a Sunday?" he asked as he tried to hide his disappointment.

"Remember I told you I had an appointment on Monday so I'd swing by today and see what kind of mess you'd made of the place?"

"Oh, that's right." He nodded. "Must be time for Ted to get the old marijuana refill from the doctor, right? You don't want to let that stuff run out."

Rosa grinned without confirming his assumption.

"So where's your other half? She get wise and dump you?"

"She's at the beach with Claudia. I have to give her credit for putting up with her company for this long."

Rosa stared at him incredulously. "Well, she may very well not come back. Why in the world would you let that happen? You know that girl is evil. No telling what kind of stuff she's filling Dana's head with. I thought you were smarter than that."

"I tried," he sighed. "But Claudia has been behaving herself lately and Dana wants to give her the benefit of the doubt. You and I both know it's bullshit, but short of tying her up, I couldn't stop her from going."

"Are you decent?" a voice called out seconds before Rhett joined them in the living room.

"Does anyone knock anymore?" Ash asked sarcastically. "And how did you get in?"

Rhett flashed his keycard briefly before pocketing it. "You know I have a master in case of emergencies."

"How did this qualify as one?" Ash asked.

Rhett ignored his question as he pulled a blushing Rosa into his arms and dipped her backward. "My beauty. When are you going to leave that husband of yours and run away with me? You know you've always wanted a younger man and here I am. We could be out of the country by tonight. I've always wanted to live on love with the girl of my dreams."

Ash watched in amazement as Rosa's face flushed like a schoolgirl's. She'd met Rhett only a few times, but it was plain to see who her favorite Jackson brother was. She patted the other man's arm affectionately before asking, "Can I fix you some lunch, handsome?"

"What about me?" Ash pouted. "I'm hungry."

"There's sandwich stuff in the refrigerator," she remarked dismissively. "Last time I checked, your arms were in perfect working order." She graced Rhett with one more big grin, then leveled a frown at Ash before going to the kitchen.

"You really know how to keep the ladies happy," Rhett remarked as he flopped down into a nearby chair. "Where's your lady? I was hoping to catch her naked with my unannounced arrival."

Ash tossed a pillow at his head, then took a seat on the sofa. "She's with Claudia. Yes, it horrifies me as well."

"If you actually want this one to hang around, you should keep her away from evil influences," Rhett advised him, pointing out the obvious. "I like Dana. I think she's good for you. I'm glad to see you putting yourself out there again. It's been a long time coming."

"Jesus, you sound like Dr. Phil," Ash mocked.

"You know what I mean," Rhett said in a voice devoid of humor. "Whatever happened to end things with Fiona has been behind you for years. None of us ever really understood since you wouldn't talk about it. But it certainly changed you. With Dana, you're more like the Ash I remember."

"Don't make this relationship into more than it is," he warned. "We're having fun. It's nothing serious and never will be." Ash was intent on throwing his brother off the fact that he had developed feelings for Dana that he didn't understand. "She's Miss Right Now, not my future bride. She isn't even my type."

"Whatever you say, bro." Rhett shrugged, clearly unconvinced. How could he be when even Ash wasn't buying into his own denials? The real question was how deep did his feelings run and was he brave enough to find out?

૭

Dana froze as she listened to the man she'd come to count on and cared deeply for discount her value to him so easily. He might as well be telling his brother that she was his fuck buddy because that's what she took away from his offhand comments. Any illusions about being special to him came crashing down around her. She knew that she didn't have any real reason to be upset. He'd never made any promises and she hadn't wanted any from him. He was simply stating what she'd said about every guy she'd been with. So why did it hurt coming from his lips?

The only thing she knew for certain was that she didn't want to face him right now. She needed time to regroup and gather her composure. So she quietly retraced her steps and exited the hotel without Ash being aware that she'd left Claudia on the beach with some guys she knew from college.

She drove home on autopilot. She was blessedly numb as she took a shower and pulled on a long T-shirt before lying across her bed and staring at the ceiling. She had two options where Ash was concerned and she needed to figure which one she wanted. She could either continue to enjoy whatever they were doing together, or she could end it before things got any more emotionally complicated. In a way, overhearing his true feelings had done her a favor. Any sappy notions she'd been harboring toward him had dissipated. It had been infatuation, nothing more. What woman wouldn't lose her head a little over him when he focused all of his attention on her?

Dana knew she should walk away, but somehow that felt to her like the coward's way. After all, the sex was amazing and she enjoyed his company. Now that she knew where they stood, it would be crazy to run off in a sulk over something that boiled down to the fact that he didn't do serious relationships and neither did she. He'd simply reaffirmed that for both of them. A text sounded on her phone a few minutes later and she saw a message from Ash wanting to know when she'd be back. Her first instinct was to say that she was on her way, then she thought better of it. She hadn't spent the night at her apartment in quite some time, and maybe that's what she needed to reinforce her resolve to stay strong. One evening away from Ash would surely do her good. So she typed out a response and hit Send. Then tried not to think about how lonely she felt at the prospect of sleeping alone. *This is so not good.*

Fourteen

"Has Zoe mentioned anything to you about Dana?" Ash asked casually while he, Dylan, and Rhett sat at a popular sports bar in Pensacola enjoying a rare guys' night out. Zoe and Dana were attending a bachelorette party for one of the ladies who worked at the coffee shop. Ash figured they were probably at some male strip club by now shoving dollar bills into a beefed-up dude's underwear.

"Oh, for fuck's sake," Rhett groaned before Dylan could answer. "Is this the portion of the evening where we act like pussies and talk about our feelings? I finally get you two out and we're going to chat about the chicks in your life?"

"You're jealous because your blowup doll doesn't have any friends," Dylan commented. "What is your rubber lady's name this time? I remember the last one sprang a leak so loud that I thought you were being attacked by a freaking animal. Who knew those could make so much noise."

"Hey, that was years ago," Rhett mumbled. "If someone had bought you one as a gag gift, you'd have tried it out too. I'll have you know that Fluffy Muffy was a hell of a lot of fun before she popped. She even did this thing with her mouth; it was—"

"Damn scary, that's what it was." Ash shook his head. "Dylan called me in a panic, sure the place was being shot up. Imagine our surprise when we burst into your room with a baseball bat and found you wrestling your plastic lover. And even worse, she appeared to be solidly kicking your ass."

"In hindsight, we should have gotten you the help you needed back then," Dylan added sadly. "It would have saved years of therapy for the rest of us. You just can't get shit like that out of your head."

Ash tossed a peanut from the bowl in the middle of the table at Rhett. "Thanks for telling us about the oral thing. It was traumatic enough without that detail."

"Don't try to distract us from your issues, Romeo," Rhett taunted. "I believe you were the one begging Dylan to betray his wife's trust. You're so whipped now that you couldn't even get through one beer before bringing up Dana. What's the matter, are you afraid she's about to kick you to the curb?"

Ash glared at his brother, who had hit uncomfortably close to the truth. He almost laughed it off, but dammit, he needed to figure out what was going on with his woman. So he swallowed his pride and turned to Dylan. "Dana has been acting weird for the last few weeks." Actually since her visit with Claudia. But when he'd asked her if something had happened then, she'd shrugged him off as if it had been an absurd question. "On the surface nothing has changed, but there's a distance between us that wasn't there before." Ash fully expected Rhett to heckle him, but instead, he remained quiet as they both waited to see what Dylan had to say.

Unfortunately, he didn't have much to offer. His brother shrugged his shoulders, appearing clueless. "I don't know what to tell you, bro, I haven't heard anything. Maybe it's PMS. That stuff can be downright evil."

"It's not that." Ash shook his head. "This has been going on too long. It's not that she's in a bad mood; it's different. Things aren't as spontaneous as they used to be."

"That's called a relationship," Rhett sighed. "It's like going to the grocery store and buying one thing, only to figure out after you get it home it's completely something else. I call it false advertising. Like those damn stuffed bras. That should be illegal. You're anticipating motorboating those big ones, then she takes the padding off and it's a real mind-fuck. I seriously thought I brought the wrong woman home the last time. I actually argued with her for ten minutes over it. She finally showed me her driver's license to prove it. Not that it really helped since I didn't remember her name to start with."

"You're a total pig," Dylan deadpanned. "Please tell me I was never that bad."

"Let's not even pretend that we weren't," Ash interjected. "It would be a tough call to figure out which one of us was the bigger prick. You're trying to bury the memory before Zoe can quiz you in your sleep one night."

Rhett took a sip of beer from the bottle in front of him before saying, "You and Zoe were best friends, so she already knows most of that and she married you anyway. Maybe she's been sharing some of our greatest hits with Dana. That would be enough to make anyone run for the hills."

"Dana's not like that." Ash rubbed at the knot in his neck. "She's even bailed me out before with a crazy chick. She also doesn't have a history of serious relationships. I swear, things were perfectly uncomplicated until recently. Now weirdly enough, I'd be happier if she was acting clingy because this aloofness is bizarre."

"You think she wants to break things off?" Dylan sounded concerned. "She's not the kind to mince words so she would walk if she wanted out. It must be something else. Have you offended her? You remember all of the shit you used to say. I'm surprised she didn't cut your dick off the first opportunity she got."

"Dude, yeah, that was downright mean. You never call a woman fat, and from what I hear, you tossed some version of that at her every day for months. She's sure more forgiving than most. I'm with Dylan—I'd have been afraid to go to sleep with the family jewels exposed. What if she went all Lorena Bobbitt on your ass?" Rhett shuddered. "I once dated this chick that accused me of doing her sister. She threw every knife in my kitchen at me. I almost pissed my pants before she ran out of silverware."

Dylan studied Rhett in amazement. "The question I want to ask is, why did you stand there while she tossed sharp objects? Also, were you guilty?"

"I couldn't move because her sister was blocking the doorway, and yes, I had perhaps shared my love with her family. But in my defense, the sister was way hotter and she came on to me. I turned her down twice before I couldn't hold out any longer."

"I feel better about myself now," Ash remarked dryly. "To think, it only took a few stories from you to accomplish it. You should teach self-help classes. Or more accurately, what-in-the-hell-to-never-do courses."

"You have no right to get all high and mighty." Rhett leveled him with a stare. "I know all about that one who sucked your armpit in public. It's on YouTube, isn't it? Oh, and the lovely young lady who pissed on your towels. Dude, where in the hell did you find them because I need to avoid those places."

Dylan crossed his arms over his chest as he stared at Rhett. "Didn't you date someone who wrote her name all over your new BMW with pink paint? Seth bought you that personalized tag for Christmas that said 'PINKCAR.' What was it again that you did to flip her switch?"

"Slept with her mother," Rhett mumbled. "But she looked really young for her age and she knew stuff that you guys wouldn't believe. I swear, nothing was off limits with her, but when she shoved a finger up my ass, I had to end things."

"Wait . . . what?" Ash gaped at him. "You let her do that to you? Like, voluntarily?"

"Hell no!" Rhett snapped. "She was going down on me, then before I knew what was happening, she'd invaded my sacred land. Doesn't everyone with half a brain know there's a strict no trespassing order in effect there? I had no idea that it needed to be spelled out or put in writing. I still can't enjoy a blowjob without being paranoid."

Dylan dropped his head in his hand. "I feel certain this is too much sharing even for brothers."

"So what's your shameful secret, bro?" Rhett asked. "Don't even act like there's not one because we're Jacksons. We come by it naturally. I think it's the main trait our father passed on to us."

Dylan looked conflicted before he finally sighed. "If either of you mention this to my wife, I'll kick your ass." He lowered his voice and looked around before continuing. "I once let the girl I was dating talk me into a threesome with her best friend."

Ash frowned at his brother. "That's it? We've all done that. Big deal."

"Her best friend's name was Jack," Dylan whispered.

"Holy shit," Rhett yelled before yelping when Dylan punched his arm. "Can you keep your big mouth shut? I'd rather it not make the news tonight."

"Bro, are you saying . . ." Ash wrinkled his nose up.

Dylan flushed. "No, I didn't do that with him. We just did her at the same time. Still it was far more up close and personal than I've ever been with another penis."

"So which end did you get?" Rhett joked, but appeared intrigued.

"None of your business," Dylan mumbled. "This ends the sharing portion of the evening. Let's save this for the next time Seth and Luke are in town."

"Now that Seth's married, he'll be all prim and proper like you are," Rhett pointed out. "But Luke is a different story. He says the women in St. Croix are up for anything. I've been meaning to get down there for a nice, long visit."

"How's he doing?" Ash asked, thinking of the rough time their brother had been through. He'd been in a bad car accident a few years back and had endured months of physical therapy to walk again. The wreck hadn't been his fault, but Ash knew he'd had a hard time dealing with the fact that the other driver had died at the scene.

Rhett ran a hand through his hair as he studied Ash. "You know Luke. He's pretty closed off about it. I believe he's still struggling, but he won't admit it. He also refuses to have surgery to minimize the scars on his face. I think he sees that as a punishment for being the one who walked away from the accident."

"We should go see him soon," Dylan added thoughtfully. "He's down there all by himself. Whereas the rest of us see each other on a regular basis, he has no one. And what concerns me is that he wants it that way. Remember the last time we were all there for the renovations on the luxury suites and he made sure he was out of town the entire visit? For some reason, he only wants to deal with us via phone or Skype if he's forced."

"I'm worried too," Ash admitted. "I've pondered showing up without warning to see what in the hell is going on. The resort is running well and turning a great profit, so he's got it in hand. But I'm not sure the same can be said for him."

"Let's talk to Seth and get something in the works," Dylan agreed. "This has gone on for long enough."

"While we're talking about family," Rhett began, "what's going on with Mom? Things are weird as hell. She's actually talking back to Bart. Don't get me wrong, I think it's fucking awesome, but when did she grow a pair? She told Claudia the other day to stop with the whining, that it was getting on her last nerve. Can you remember her ever telling the princess that?"

Ash raised a brow, impressed despite himself. He'd told Rhett all about their mother's revelations concerning her marriage with their father and the reason she'd gone on to tie the knot with Bart. Things had been a little different at each family dinner since then. "The dynamic has shifted, I've noticed. Bart appears almost nervous around her now and tries to please her, which has always been her role with him. I can only hope that she's finally come to her senses and is laying down the law. Hell, she hasn't hit us up for money in a while either."

Dylan raised his beer and drained it. "I, for one, hope it lasts. Family dinners might be tolerable if Bart and his horrible daughter were living elsewhere. Like another country." It was almost midnight when they stood to leave. Rhett walked ahead while Ash followed Dylan. They were almost at the door before Dylan stopped and looked back. "I'll see if I can find out anything about Dana from Zoe. It's probably nothing though. Most of the time we never know what we did to piss them off, but luckily they eventually get over it."

"Thanks, man," Ash said gratefully.

Rhett was waiting for them in the back of a cab. They'd known they'd be drinking so they had opted for an alternate means of transportation. As his brothers picked on each other, Ash thought of the woman he'd come to care for so deeply. What Dylan didn't know was that Ash was terrified that history could be repeating itself. Had he fallen in love once again only to find out that the person who had his heart didn't want it?

Ash was very much afraid that Dana would shatter him into a million pieces if that was the case. Because regardless of his intentions, he'd gone and given her the ultimate power to wound him. He could only hope that she'd use it for good and not to destroy him.

⁓

"Where'd everyone go? I used all of my ones already; how 'bout you?" Dana squinted at Zoe to try to see her more clearly.

"Me too," Zoe pouted. "I gave the last of mine to that guy who was dressed like a cowboy."

"Mmm, that was money well spent," Dana agreed. "Did you see the outline of his big gun? No way was that all stuffing."

"Heck no," Zoe agreed. "I saw it moving and everything. He was almost as big as my boo."

"Ahhh, that's so sweet," Dana cooed. "I'd call Ash a pet name if he wasn't such an asshole."

Zoe blinked as if attempting to bring her into focus. "I thought you two were getting along now. What's he done to mess it up? He better not have called you fat 'cause I'll kick his butt, or I'll make Dylan do it. My man would totally take care of it if I asked."

Dana leaned forward and whispered loudly, "I heard him telling Rhett that I was nothing but Miss Right Now and he'd never been serious about me. Not that I wanted that, but come on. How freaking insulting. It was like he was doing me a favor by being with me. He said something about me not even being his type."

"What?" Zoe shouted. "How dare he! You're way too good for him. You're beautiful and you have a brain. He's not used to women who can count past ten or have more than three words in their vocabulary. I bet you intimidate the hell out of him."

"You're damn right I do." Dana fist-pumped the air. "He's my bitch in this relationship. When I come home, he should be kissing my feet and begging to know how he can make me happy enough to stay. After all, a big dick will only get you so far. So what if he totally knows how to work it? Oh, and his oral skills are unparalleled. He can stay down there for days. I've never been with a guy who had that much self-control. I swear, he enjoys getting me off more than he likes it being done to him."

"Dylan's the same way," Zoe sighed. "Those Jacksons were raised right. There have even been times that he didn't get his either. He told me that it was all about me. Can you imagine? At first, it made me feel kind of guilty, but I got over it. Multiple orgasms scramble my brain."

"Ash is the best I've ever been with by far," Dana murmured. "And to think I was falling in love with the big jerk. But since I heard how he really felt about me, I've been working extra hard to keep things casual. There's no way I'll give him the satisfaction of me following him around like the rest of his bimbos always have. If he's expecting that to happen, he's in for a major disappointment. The funny thing is that I didn't figure he'd even notice the change in my behavior, but he has. He's even asked me several times if something was wrong. I acted like I hadn't a clue what he was talking about, which I could tell only made him feel more paranoid."

"Serves him right." Zoe sniffed. "Just when I thought there might be hope for him, he goes and disappoints both of us."

"No kidding." Dana frowned. "The only positive thing that has come out of this is he seems to be trying even harder in bed. I come so many times when we're together that I can barely stand it. I swear, he's trying to lick me into liking him again."

Zoe giggled. "I bet that's tough to take. Maybe his tongue will fall off before it's over with. Oh wait, that would be a damn shame. Just lay back and let him do all the work. He owes you that much."

"Has Dylan mentioned anything about Ash? Like maybe him wondering why I'm acting different?"

Zoe shook her head. "You know I'd have mentioned it if he had. As far as I know, Dylan thinks you and Ash are doing great together."

"Do men not discuss this stuff like we do?" Dana wondered out loud. "Oh, and by the way, you better not tell Dylan anything that I've told you. I refuse to give Ash the opportunity to lie to me. I know what I heard. He might not have told Dylan anything, but he sure didn't have a problem dishing to Rhett that day."

"You never got brave enough to ask him about Fiona, did you?" Zoe asked as she swayed unsteadily in her chair.

Propping her face in her hands, Dana said, "Why bother? He's not going to confess his darkest secrets to his bed buddy. It would have been difficult to have asked him before, but after hearing where I stand with him, I certainly couldn't do it."

"I don't care what he says," Zoe said firmly, "he has it bad for you. I'd even go so far as to say he's in love. Even Dylan thinks so. You know how men are. They get the worst case of denial when things get too intense for them to handle. I think that's what happened to Ash. Otherwise, he'd have bolted by now and he hasn't."

"He's a complicated man," Dana said wistfully. "I'm not sure anyone ever truly understands him, even his own brothers."

Before Zoe could respond, the driver that Dylan had arranged for them showed up at their table. "If you ladies are ready, I have the car waiting out front."

Dana got to her feet and linked arms with Zoe as they weaved their way through the crowd. "I don't suppose you have any extra dollar bills on you?" Dana asked Marcus, the driver.

His lips twitched before he said, "I'm sorry, Miss Dana, but the boss might fire me if he found out."

"That figures." Zoe hiccupped. Marcus ushered them into the back of the limo before getting behind the wheel.

Dylan was waiting outside for his wife when they pulled into the driveway of their home. "Baby!" Zoe squealed as he laughed softly and all but carried her in the door.

"Mr. Jackson says that I'm to drop you at the hotel," Marcus stated, although Dana could hear the question in his voice. It was on the tip of her tongue to instruct him to take her to her apartment instead, but she didn't really want to be alone tonight. She might be pissed at him, but shouldn't she enjoy their time together while she was able? Because sooner or later he'd end things and she'd be left to pick up the pieces. She only hoped when that happened that Ash had no clue that she'd gone and fallen in love with him just like all the women who had come before her.

Fifteen

Someone was groaning and Dana had no idea if it was her or the warm body behind her. *Wait . . . what?* She turned her head so quickly that immediately afterward she was afraid she'd toss her cookies right there in bed. But luckily a few deep breaths helped calm her stomach from the alarming rolling it was doing. She'd also managed to make out Ash's features in the dim light of the room. Thank God she hadn't lost her mind and gone home with some stranger last night. She didn't even remember coming to Ash's apartment, but apparently she had. The pained sound filled the air once again and Dana saw Ash rub the side of his head. "Are you all right?" she asked, then immediately winced. Why was her voice so loud?

"Shhh," Ash attempted to quiet her. "Make the voices stop, baby. There are like a dozen of them banging shovels inside my skull."

"Poor thing," she whispered. "I'll do it for you if you'll do it for me."

"Deal," he muttered as he rolled over on his back. "I think I had too much to drink. Rhett kept buying shots and calling us pussies if we didn't toss them back. I hope he's dying a slow, painful death somewhere this morning."

"I stuffed my salary for the week down some guy's underwear before doing body shots off some chick at the next table."

"That's my girl." Ash grinned weakly. "Although I'd rather you keep your hands off another dude's junk. Maybe next time you could toss the bills at his feet instead."

"Where's the fun in that?" Dana asked seriously. "Plus, it was a bachelorette thingie, so it's a rite of passage. I'm sure you've been to a few strip joints in your time. Half of the girls there probably have your name tattooed on their ass."

"I'm glad to see you have such a high opinion of me, honey," he mocked before letting out a groan. "I swear, I'll give you anything you want if you'll go to the kitchen and get me a bottle of water. I'd do it myself, but I'm deathly afraid I'll embarrass myself by throwing up if I make any sudden movements." He peered over at her with the one eye he had open. "Are you in any better shape than I am? If not, I can call down for reinforcements. I'd personally rather beg the concierge for help than have Rosa find out we're too hungover to get out of bed."

Dana sat up gingerly next to him, giving her body time to adjust before she slowly inched toward the side and swung her feet over. "Here goes nothing," she murmured.

"You've got this, baby," Ash called out his encouragement. "Get us the whole bottle of Advil while you're in there."

Dana was proud when she managed to get to her feet. She waited for a moment until she felt steady enough to move, then inched forward. It took what seemed like an hour to make the trip into the other room and back, but she did it. When she handed Ash his drink, she thought he'd weep in gratitude. Instead, he thanked her profusely before washing down three Advil with a huge gulp of liquid. When Dana had done the same, they both flopped backward, worn out by the small amount of activity. "I'm off alcohol." She shuddered. "My mouth feels like it's stuffed with cotton and my whole body hurts. Did I fall at any point?"

"I have no idea," Ash muttered. "We probably both wiped out at least a few times. I even think I remember one of the security guards putting me to bed. I hope like hell that didn't actually happen. Especially since I'm only wearing boxers."

"If we were both that out of it, how did I end up wearing your shirt? I seem to recall Marcus picking us up at some point. Surely he wouldn't have changed my clothes for me."

"I'd kick his ass," Ash snapped. "I'm guessing that one of us managed to do it because I can assure you that Marcus knows better."

"That's good." Dana yawned and moved over to rest her head against Ash's chest. They were both dozing when the sound of a door slamming shut had them grabbing their heads and cursing.

"Who in the hell is that?" Ash hissed. "Too damn many people come and go from my apartment. No one knocks anymore. I need to change my fucking locks."

"Well, lookie what the cat dragged in," drawled an

amused voice. "You two look like shit and you don't smell much better. I thought I was coming to clean the apartment today, but it appears you need to get hosed down first. I swear, I'm getting drunk from inhaling the fumes in this room."

Dana peeked over to see Rosa outright laughing at them. "Where were you five minutes ago when I had to crawl to the kitchen?" Dana choked out. "And why would you put the Advil in such a high cabinet? I had to stand on a chair to reach it. I almost broke my neck."

"Take that up with your boyfriend," the older lady advised. "He needs to make the area height accessible for his lady love."

"Sorry 'bout that, baby." Ash patted her back. "I'll take care of it as soon as I'm off my death bed. That could be a few days though."

Rosa put her hands on her hips as she surveyed the room. "I'm not going to find any other people here in various stages of undress, am I? If this was some kind of swingers event, I'd appreciate a warning. I'm no prude and I got nothing against a little nudity, especially if it's a male. But if there's any crazy fornicating going on, then that's different."

Dana couldn't help it; she started to giggle at the same time that Ash's chest began to shake. "I'm not running a sex club," he managed to say. "If you see that going on, then you should call the cops because I might have accidentally invited someone in last night."

"Or it could be my stripper," Dana added. "At one point I may have asked the cowboy if he wanted to come back to my place while I wrote him a check."

"I can't wait to share all of this with Dylan." Ash grinned. "Knowing his sweet wife was being bad will drive him crazy. This may be your last girls' night for a while. I hope you made the most of it."

"Don't you worry about it, sweetie," Rosa huffed out. "I'll be happy to fill in for Zoe if it comes to that. Ted wouldn't mind me having a little fun."

Dana dug a finger into Ash's side until she heard him groan before she smiled brightly at Rosa. "I'm sure we'd have a blast. Let's definitely plan that soon. Hey, maybe Ash could invite Ted over and keep him company that evening. Then no one gets left out."

"That's a brilliant idea," Rosa said excitedly. "Ted would love watching a movie on that big-screen television you've got."

When Rosa stepped out of the bedroom, Dana turned to smirk at Ash, but he'd beaten her to it. "Oh, baby, you tried to screw me over, but this round goes to me. Good old Ted has quite the stash of medical marijuana. So while I'm over here burning one with him, you'll be watching Rosa slap some stripper's ass. You rolled the dice, my love, but you lost the game. Too bad, I was really rooting for you."

Dana rolled over and put her back to him before tossing out over her shoulder, "When I'm feeling human again, you will not be getting sex. So you should become well acquainted with your hand now. You set me up for the fall, and it's either blue balls for you, or barbequing alone."

"You realize that to make me suffer, you'll also be depriving yourself."

"I hate you," Dana hissed. "You always have the last word."

"Oh, pookie," Ash cooed as he pulled her against his chest. "There's no need to sulk. You and I both know I can't hold out. And Rosa will likely never take the bonding experience that far, so I figure you're home free."

Dana wrinkled her nose. "You reek of cigarette smoke. Maybe you could crawl to the shower and hose off."

"You've smelled better as well, baby," he replied, not sounding in the least offended. "At this point, we're going to have to hope we cancel each other out until we're able to do something about it."

Dana snuggled farther into the covers and promptly began drifting off. She had no idea how much time had passed when she jerked awake to find Ash's side of the bed empty. She rolled to her back and listened for a moment. The water was running in the shower so he'd obviously made it out of bed. She felt much more human herself, even though she was still a bit tired. There was no way she could be the smelly one if he was clean, so she decided to join him. The thick layer of steam in the bathroom indicated that he'd been in there for a while. "Room for one more?" she asked as she opened the glass door to find him leaning against the wall with his eyes closed and water cascading over his hard body. Her mouth went dry as she stood there admiring the intensely hot picture that he made.

"Stop objectifying me." He smirked without looking at her. *Dammit, how did he know?*

"Then put that thing away," she retorted as she pointed toward his rapidly hardening dick.

"Oh, I'd love to," he purred. "If you'll be so kind as to get on your knees and open wide." She wanted to make a smart comment; truly she did. But almost as if she had no control over her movements, she found herself doing exactly as he'd suggested. She was at his feet, with her hands braced on his thighs, waiting to see what he'd do. His eyes were heavy lidded as he reached out to cup her cheek. "Take me in," he murmured, then hissed when she licked her lips before licking the tip of his cock. She teased him, making small circles around the head until he was gritting his teeth in frustration. Then without warning, she sucked him fully inside until he hit the back of her throat. "Fuck yeah," he moaned as she used her hand and mouth to cover every inch of his hard length. It gave her a heady sense of power as his body shook with the force of his desire. As she relaxed her throat, taking him deeper, he shouted out his release as he came on her tongue.

Dana leaned back onto her heels, marveling at how beautiful he looked with his face flushed and his body trembling. *Mine*, she thought to herself and didn't bother to remind herself that it was impossible. Because in that moment, he did belong to her and she was certain that they both knew it. The question now was, where did things go from here? She was so far in over her head that she hadn't a clue how to handle the situation. The only thing she did know was that she was in love with Asher Jackson, and regardless of what he'd told Rhett, he had feelings for her as well. Was she brave enough to put herself out there in the face of the possibility that he'd never be able to admit that they meant more to each other than just sex? She needed to make a decision once and for all because this emotional roller coaster was driving her mad. He may well panic and run, but what if he didn't?

Was there any chance at all of having the fairy-tale romance that she'd always scoffed at and pretended she didn't want? Or would their relationship go down in flames as he moved on to another no-strings fling like Brittany?

Sixteen

Ash couldn't remember ever feeling this nervous before. He was taking Dana out on an official date tonight. It was not as if they didn't do couple things, but he'd never actually asked her out on a date. A fact that he'd changed that afternoon when he'd walked down to the coffee shop with sweating palms and a wildly beating heart to extend the invitation. It wasn't the planned meal that made him nervous though. It was the declaration that he planned to make at some point. For he, Asher Jackson, was once again going to say those three little words to a woman and hope like hell he fared better the second time than he had the first time.

To say that Dana had been surprised when he'd made a bumbling mess of his carefully planned speech earlier would be an understatement. Zoe had been forced to elbow her to bring her out of the stupor she'd been in. But she'd nodded yes to his date invitation, which was good enough for him. He'd kissed her quickly and all but ran before she backed out.

The plan was that she'd go home after work to get

ready and Ash would pick her up from there. He probably shouldn't have let her out of his sight, but he had to trust her at some point. He'd come home early to shower and change. So now he had time to kill as he paced his apartment in a suit. "You look like hell," Rosa declared as she clucked her tongue. "Are you going to pop the question?"

"What? No!" Ash assured her quickly. "We're simply having an evening out. And I might possibly tell her that I love her, and God willing, she'll say it back to me."

Rosa perched on the arm of a nearby chair. "Any idea if that's gonna happen? I mean, she seems to like you well enough. But you've been a little lazy in the romance department, so it's hard to say."

He couldn't even argue with her. He hadn't exactly been wining and dining Dana. Beer, pizza, and Netflix were about as close as they'd come to that. Oh, and dinners at his mother's house. He didn't think that counted as a positive though. He did buy her a bag of those Cadbury eggs that she loved for Easter. *I suck at this. I'm a failure.* All this time he'd been blaming Fiona for their relationship falling apart, when it was more than likely him. If he'd been this lazy and unimaginative back then, no wonder she tried to hedge her bets and have the best of both worlds. Ash looked at Rosa in a panic. "I'm screwed," he whispered. "How could you have let me mess this up so badly? You're a woman; shouldn't you have been making suggestions?"

"Hey, don't blame it on me," Rosa muttered. "I'm married to a man who doesn't write any message in my birthday and anniversary cards because he thinks

I won't notice that he recycles them every five years or so. Plus, let's don't forget that I make sure she eats. If I left that up to you, she'd be trying to choke down dry cereal for every meal."

"You've got a small point," he reluctantly agreed. "You're definitely an added bonus. It's probably why she's still with me. I should cancel this whole thing and retreat. We've got a good thing going. What if this makes her reconsider?"

He was already tugging at his tie when Rosa got to her feet and held a hand up. "When did you turn into such a wimp? Where's that swagger that I'm used to seeing? Hell, if you go out there looking like a whipped dog, you're doomed to failure. You need to grow a pair and try to act confident. Don't go all chicken shit now or you will lose her."

Staring at the floor for a moment, he said, "There's no going back, is there? If I love her, then I need to take this to the next level. She deserves that."

"Indeed she does," Rosa agreed. "Now get out of here before you freak out again. I swear, you don't pay me enough to hold your hand like this. I'm your maid, not your mommy."

Ash chuckled, knowing her words held no malice. She was attempting to lighten the mood in the only way she knew how. Picking on each other had always been the main dynamic of their relationship, and he took comfort in the familiarity of it now. "You're overpaid and you know it," he scoffed. "Your last batch of lasagna was dry and tasteless. I could save a lot of money and eat better if I stocked a bunch of frozen meals. It would be nice to have someone who was actually familiar with a mop and a broom as well. There are cobwebs the size of a Buick rolling around under my bed."

She snorted, putting her hands on her hips. "Those are old condom wrappers from your man-whore days with those bargain-basement floozies. I hope you've kept up to date on those STD checks. That would be one sure way to scare Dana off."

Ash grinned as he moved past her, then stopped at the last moment and pulled her into a hug. She froze, unused to displays of affection from him, before she briefly patted his back. She cleared her throat, then pushed him away. He didn't say anything else because he figured they were both embarrassingly tongue-tied. But his world felt centered once again, and the panic he'd been experiencing had settled. Even if things didn't go as he'd planned tonight, at least he could say that he'd put himself out there again . . . and in the end, wasn't that all anyone could do?

⁓

Dana stood before Zoe in yet another dress, waiting to see if her friend thought this one was better than the last dozen or so she'd tried on. After Ash had stopped by the shop and asked her out on their first official date, she'd almost passed out. Zoe had called in one of the other girls to cover for them and they'd rushed to Dana's apartment for an emergency planning session. When Zoe wrinkled her nose once again, Dana groaned. "I knew we should have gone shopping on the way home. Or I could have borrowed something from you if you weren't so freakishly tall."

"That one looks fine," Zoe said, shrugging, "but it's still not what I had in mind. It's boring and black. We need a pop of color here. He's already seen you in that one as well. Don't you have anything else?"

Dana shook her head before it hit her. "Oh my God, I bought a green Michael Kors dress on clearance last year and I've never worn it because it was too dressy. Crap, where is it?" she muttered as she ran back into her closet and began pulling hangers frantically out of the way in her haste for what she hoped was buried treasure. She was almost ready to admit defeat when she felt the slinky material brush against her finger-tips. She held it up in the air, waving it around as she bounced on her feet in excitement. "Here it is! Please let this be it because otherwise we have just enough time left to make a Walmart run."

"I love the color," Zoe said in excitement. "Oh my God, this is going to be perfect. Why in the world didn't we start with this one?"

Dana rolled her eyes, but her friend's enthusiasm was contagious. She discarded the last outfit and stepped into the dress. It slithered down the length of her body, fitting her like a second skin. She knew be-fore Zoe opened her mouth that they'd found the win-ner. "Please say this looks as good as it feels," she begged.

Zoe jumped up and down, doing some strange cheer. "Heck yeah. You look like a sexy fairy princess. There's no way we could have picked anything better suited to you. Ash is going to swallow his tongue and probably yours as well before the evening is over."

"What if he breaks up with me?" Dana asked, fidgeting nervously.

Zoe shook her head. "There's no way he'd go to all of this trouble to dump you. Men don't operate that way. He'd send you a text or start avoiding you. I think this is it. He's going to tell you how he feels."

"But I was supposed to do that first," Dana mumbled as she began applying makeup. "You know I'd already decided to take the leap. But nooo, he had to go and beat me to it. He's so competitive."

Zoe giggled. "Are you actually sulking about the possibility of the man saying that he loves you? You both deserve each other in that case because you're completely irrational when it comes to affairs of the heart."

"Well, it's not like I know what I'm doing here," Dana snapped. "I've never felt like this before. Is there some book you're supposed to read or steps that have to be followed? Crap, do I lose points if I say the wrong thing when the time comes? What if I have food stuck between my teeth, and for the rest of our lives, that's all he remembers?"

"Oh brother," Zoe groaned. "He screwed up by giving you advance notice. Was I this bad when Dylan and I were first together?"

"Honey, you were a virgin," Dana pointed out. "That's in a league all of its own. You did do and say a lot of whacked things though. And Dylan wasn't much better. You'd still be dressing like his golf buddy if not for me stepping in and showing you the error of your ways. It was all over for him the first time he saw you in a dress and figured out that you had legs and tits."

"That was fun." Zoe smiled softly. "He was eating antacids like candy that night. I was afraid he was having a heart attack."

"Ash already knows I have the right body parts, so there's not going to be any surprises there."

Zoe put a hand on her arm, looking suddenly serious. "I know you're scared, but let him talk, okay? He'll be feeling the same things that you are; remember that. But he took a big step today by setting all this up, which means he's making himself vulnerable to you. The male ego is extremely fragile, so no jokes until you're both relaxed enough to handle them."

"All right," Dana agreed. She knew that her friend was right. This was potentially the most important night of her life. Hiding behind sarcasm as she normally would wasn't an option. Even though things hadn't started off on the best foot for them last year, she knew now that Ash wouldn't hurt her. She could let her guard down and trust him to take care of her heart. If she was wrong, then she'd unleash the worst volley of male bashing that he'd ever endured—and considering the amount of women he'd pissed off, that was saying something.

Seventeen

This had been one of the most awkward evenings of his life, Ash thought miserably. Since the moment he'd picked Dana up at her apartment, things had been tense and so unlike them. He'd done everything a man in love was supposed to. He'd complimented her outfit, which wasn't hard because she looked beautiful. He'd also been so nervous that he'd not only knocked over his water glass, but had flung his fork clear across the room, almost stabbing some poor kid in the forehead. His usual finesse had completely deserted him. He had no idea how Dana had kept from laughing when he'd dribbled soup all over the front of his expensive dress shirt. Why wasn't she giving him hell as she normally would? He'd feel better if she'd insult him. But, instead, she kept hiding her face behind her napkin. "Sorry," he muttered when he attempted to hand her a dinner roll and instead lobbed it into her lap.

She put her elbows on the table and lowered her head into her hands. Her shoulders were shaking so hard he knew she must be sobbing. He wanted to reach out and comfort her, but he was afraid he'd knock the candle in the middle of the table over and set her on fire. He was seriously considering crying right along with her when she exclaimed, "What in the hell is wrong with you? You'd better tell Zoe that I tried to be good, but dear God, you're a mess, baby. If I don't do something, we'll be thrown out of here in another few minutes and probably banned as well."

He froze. Was that . . . a giggle? She had tears on her face all right, but they appeared to be from laughing so hard. "You think this is funny?" He wanted to clarify her reaction in case he was reading it wrong.

"Absolutely." She smirked. "Honey, we suck at this. My underwear is on backwards, I have a piece of steak in my lap, and for the last hour I've been biting my tongue to keep from teasing you. Oh, and when your silverware went sailing past my head, I snorted wine up my nose and damn near drowned. You didn't notice because you were too busy apologizing to the kid you almost killed."

"Fuck." Ash sagged back into his seat. "I thought you'd turned into a Stepford wife or something. It's been making me so nervous I keep doing all of this stupid shit. I wanted to make things special so that you'd remember the first time I told you that I loved you, but instead, I've lost so many cool points I'm surprised you're still sitting there. Heck, you're probably just afraid to get up for fear that I'll pin you beneath the table or something."

"I love you too," she said softly.

"Now I've made a total mess out of everything. I bet you're planning to call Paul and beg him to take you back as soon as you can get away from me. I wouldn't blame . . . Wait, what did you say?" He stuttered to a stop as her words finally penetrated his pity party.

"I'm in love with you, Asher Jackson. I have been for a while, but after what you told Rhett, I was afraid to admit it."

Confused, he asked, "What does my brother have to do with this?"

She took a big gulp of her wine, then her gaze locked on his. "I overheard you telling him that what we had wasn't serious and never would be. That I wasn't your type."

He shook his head. "Baby, I have no idea what you're talking about. When did this happen? You know how crazy things get at those family dinners. I think you must have misunderstood something."

Ash could see the hurt that she was trying hard to hide from him and it hit him like a punch to the gut. "It was the day I went to the beach with Claudia. I came back to your apartment and used my key to get in. You and Rhett were in the living room. I couldn't see him, but I recognized his voice. He was saying he was glad you were getting out there and dating again and you said that I was Miss Right Now."

"Oh shit." Ash felt his face go white. He'd been trying to keep Rhett from seeing how he felt about Dana because he'd been firmly in denial at that point. "That's why you started acting differently," he guessed. He carefully reached across the table and put his hand on hers. "I'm so sorry, sweetheart. I was freaked out about what you were making me feel, and I said some stupid stuff to throw my brother off the scent. I didn't mean it. I realize that with my track record where you're concerned, you have no reason to believe me. But I was already in love with you, and not handling it very well."

"It's all right." She smiled softly. "I said some similar things to Zoe for the same reason. I'm not going to pretend that I wasn't hurt, because I was. But I do understand. What I would like for you to explain though is why you despised me at first sight for so long. I know it has something to do with Fiona. If we're going to make a go of this, I need to know about her."

He was stunned. "How did you find out about my ex-girlfriend?"

She shrugged. "Zoe mentioned it, although she really didn't have any details to share. Then Claudia brought her up that day at the beach. Apparently your family knows you were involved with this woman, but none have been privy to what happened."

Ash studied her for a moment before saying, "I'll tell you whatever you want to know. But can we finish talking at home? For one, I think they'd like us to leave now, and I could also use a drink. With the way my luck is going, hard liquor would be a disaster."

"Of course, honey," she agreed. He paid the bill, adding a big tip since their table looked like a group of toddlers had eaten there. He helped Dana out of her chair and placed a hand on her lower back as they left the restaurant and waited for his car to be brought around. He'd cleared one hurdle. She loved him even after he'd made an ass of himself. Now the only thing left was to share his past, something he'd never done before. Only two other people knew what had happened because Ash had never wanted to admit to anyone, not even his family, how much of a fool Fiona had revealed him to be.

He'd only recently come to realize that it was his ego that had taken a hit more than anything else because he now knew that he'd never really felt for Fiona what he did for Dana. But a blow to a man's pride was sometimes just as damaging as the pain from a broken heart. Both were hell to recover from and move past.

⌒〜⌒

Ash had held Dana's hand almost the entire way home except for the few times he'd needed both hands on the wheel to navigate through traffic. He'd been so adorably nervous during dinner that she could hardly believe it. What a pair they made. She had stains all over her dress and his clothing hadn't fared much better. For two people who were normally cool under pressure, they'd certainly lost it tonight. When he'd blurted out that he loved her, she'd returned the sentiment without a moment's hesitation. She'd also taken the opportunity to bring up the conversation with Rhett and the subject of Fiona. She could tell that he didn't want to talk about his past, but he was willing to do it for her.

He pulled her against his chest on the ride up in the elevator, dropping a kiss onto the top of her head as they exited on his floor. He opened the door for her, then shrugged off his coat and tie before crossing to the bar in the corner and holding up a bottle of scotch. "Want one?" She shook her head no. She'd have a glass of wine later, but for now she wanted to keep a clear head for the impending conversation.

Dana kicked off her shoes, then settled onto the couch. Ash joined her a moment later, putting his arm around her shoulders. "I love you," she whispered reassuringly, sensing that he needed that from her before he started.

Ash blew out a breath before saying, "I love you too." He gulped down the contents of his glass, then put it on the coffee table. "It's been five years since things ended with me and Fiona. Her brother Hunter actually runs the Oceanix in Charleston now. He introduced us. A fact that he's apologized for repeatedly. But you always want to see the best in your family, until they prove you wrong. I've never held what happened against him. Hell, look at Claudia. I certainly can't throw stones."

He paused to gather his thoughts. He wasn't used to this level of honesty with a woman. Dana, of course, read him perfectly. "Take your time, honey," she murmured. "If it's too much tonight, then we can try it again tomorrow."

In that moment, he loved her so much that he could barely stand it. His heart ached as if he missed her even though she was sitting right there next to him. "Fiona was different than my usual crowd. She was a petite, dark-haired spitfire who didn't take shit from anyone. I know this sounds bad, but I was used to women catering to my every whim. I didn't chase them; it wasn't necessary. So when I meet Fiona, I expected her to—"

"Fall on her back with her legs in the air?" Dana asked dryly.

"More or less," he admitted sheepishly. In hindsight, he probably should have left some of the details out. He didn't want Dana to think he was an even bigger asshole than she had accused him of being more than once. "Anyway, she literally laughed in my face when I mentioned her coming to my place. From that moment on, I was intrigued. We dated for months before we ever slept together. I'd never waited that long before. I thought I was in love. We'd been together for close to a year when she came to me in tears. She said she was pregnant and she was afraid I'd break up with her over it. At first I was offended that she had such a low opinion of me. I reassured her that we'd get married and I'd take care of her and the baby. Instead of being nervous, I was thrilled. She wanted to wait for a while to tell everyone, so I went along with it. Hunter and I had already gotten pretty close by that point, so after a month or so, I confided in him, then swore him to secrecy. I remember thinking that he acted really funny about the whole thing. I put it down to Fiona being his sister and him not liking the idea of her having sex. Kind of the way you feel when you imagine your parents doing it."

"Ugh," Dana groaned. "Luckily my parents divorced years ago, so I don't have to dwell on that."

Ash wanted to quiz her further. This was one of the few times she'd voluntarily shared information about her family. But he knew now wasn't the time. Although if he was sharing confidences, then he'd want the same from her soon. "Anyway, another few months passed by, and she was beginning to show. I wanted to tell my brothers since I'd always been pretty close to them, but she insisted on waiting until we were married first. She said she didn't want them to have a bad opinion of her for getting pregnant. So I agreed. Most of our relationship had been shrouded in secrecy anyway. Whenever my family was visiting, she was always conveniently out of town or couldn't get off work. I'd never been in a serious relationship, so I was fine with her running the show for the most part. I wanted her to be happy. We decided on a simple wedding at the courthouse. Her mother had passed away when she was little, and neither she nor Hunter was close to their father. She promised we'd do something bigger after the baby was born. She was self-conscious about the weight she'd gained even though I tried to reassure her that she was beautiful."

Ash didn't realize that his hands were shaking until Dana got up and fixed him another drink. She handed it to him carefully, then resumed her position on the couch. "Do you need to stop for now?"

He took a few grateful sips before shaking his head. "I'm fine, baby, thanks. So, anyway, the day before we were to get married, Hunter and I were having an unofficial bachelor party since Fiona had to work. Hunter had never been much of a drinker, but that night he got pretty hammered. I'd only had one beer so I drove him home. When we got to his place, he asked me to come in. I was impatient because I wanted to get home, but he was my best friend, so I agreed. We'd barely been there more than a few minutes and I remember being surprised that in that short time he'd gone from being wasted to appearing stone-cold sober. He told me to have a seat, that he had something to tell me. Then he said that he'd found out that Fiona and her boyfriend were running a scam on me. The baby she was carrying wasn't mine; it was some other guy's."

"Oh my God," Dana whispered, putting a hand over her mouth.

"My first reaction was to laugh. I thought he was bullshitting me. He got a piece of paper and wrote something on it before handing it to me. "She's not at work tonight. That's his address. You're not going alone though because I don't want you ruining your life further by lashing out. You can drive us both there. You'll never believe it unless you see it with your own eyes. You're like a brother to me. There's no way I can let them do this to you. I don't care if she's my sister or not. It makes me fucking sick. I don't even know who she is anymore. I've made excuses for her for years because she grew up without a mother, but I have to face the fact that she's not a good person. She had both of us convinced there for a while, but I heard her on the phone with him a few days ago. Then I followed her this morning."

Ash glanced at Dana and was surprised to see tears trickling down her cheeks. "I'm sorry," she choked out as she wiped her face with the back of her hand.

He hugged her against him, kissing the top of her head. "I was weirdly calm. I didn't protest as we re-traced our steps and I followed his directions to one of the worst areas of the city. He instructed me to park a few spaces down from a run-down white house. He wanted me to stand out of sight while he went to the door and talked to his sister. None of it made any sense to me, so I simply followed his instructions. It was Fiona that answered the door. She sounded shocked to see him there. Then when he told her that he knew what she was up to, she got angry. She'd always been feisty, but that night she sounded like something straight from the gutter. She cussed, threatened, and then laughed at Hunter. She told him to go ahead and tell me. That I was so hung up on her that I'd never believe him. She slammed the door in his face and I could hear her talking to someone inside. Hunter motioned for me to join him and look in the window. And my world tilted. There was the woman I thought I loved, passionately kissing some other guy. I have no idea how long I stood there until Hunter ushered me into the passenger seat and managed to get us both back to his place in one piece. I got drunk off my ass that night, then the next day I told her there would be no wedding until the baby was born and I got a paternity test. She knew at that point that Hunter had told me."

"I'd so love to kick her ass right now," Dana hissed, looking murderous on his behalf. It felt oddly right for her to be protective of him.

"It was a long time ago," he reassured her. "She didn't bother to deny it that day. Oddly enough, she tried to explain it away by saying she was tired of struggling to make ends meet and felt that she deserved something more from life than she'd always gotten. She agreed to take a paternity test, even though she assured me that there was very little chance that the baby was mine. I think she was still holding on to the outside chance that she might be carrying a meal ticket. So I paid her medical bills until the baby was born and then a few days later it was officially confirmed that I wasn't the father. I was relieved, but also strangely disappointed. I didn't want anything to do with Fiona, but I had been excited about being a father."

"What happened after that?" Dana asked softly.

Ash winced, hating to share the last part. "I went off the deep end for a while," he admitted. "I'd held it together after I found out about her because there was still an outside chance that the baby was mine. But when that was over, I lost it. I stayed drunk for weeks. I was literally tripping over liquor bottles in my apartment. Hell, I didn't shower or shave for longer than I'd care to admit. I lost weight thanks to my liquid diet and looked like someone with a terminal illness. Hunter threatened to tell my family, but I wouldn't listen. Finally he called my brother Seth and told him he'd better get down there before I did something stupid. By that point, I'd been like that for a few months. Hunter didn't tell Seth the whole story, but he did give him a condensed version of it. Imagine my brother's surprise since none of them really knew I was seriously involved with anyone, much less that it was serious enough to cause that kind of damage when it ended. It took Seth another month to get me halfway cleaned up. By that time, my brothers were covering for both of us without really knowing the whole truth. I'll never forget that. We bust each other's balls, but when the chips are down, we're there. I don't know what would have happened without them. And the shitty part of it is that, to this day, they still don't know the full story and they've never pressed me for it."

"Oh, honey," Dana sighed. "It breaks my heart to think of what you must have gone through. No wonder you stuck with women who only wanted a good time with you. It makes perfect sense to me now." Then she froze, staring up at him. "Did you hate me because I reminded you of her?"

Ash swallowed, feeling a lump the size of a basket-

ball in his throat. He wanted to deny it, but if they were
to have a future together, it couldn't be built on a foun-
dation of lies. Even though she might never know the
truth, he would and that was enough. "I was confused
when we met. Your coloring is completely different
from hers, but you both have a similar build and there
was just something about you. That first day, it was
like a punch to the gut. Even as I tried to rationalize it
afterwards, I couldn't stop comparing you to her. Then
I'd tell myself that I was crazy. You didn't even look
like her and you'd never done anything to me. But the
next time I was around you, I was punishing you for
her sins once again. It made me sick, but I couldn't
seem to stop. Add in the fact that I was wildly attracted
to you and it was an explosive combination of denial,
desire, and downright confusion. It took me months
to figure out that it wasn't so much that you reminded
me of her, but more the fact that you made me want
things again that scared the hell out of me. I was looking for any reason to put distance between us and that
was a convenient excuse. It was easier for me to handle than the fact that I was terrified of getting hurt
again." He could feel the moment that she stiffened in
his hold. He was making a mess of this last part. Why
had he been such a jerk to her in the beginning? And
then he'd continued doing it for a freaking year. He'd
barely been able to believe she'd forgiven him for it the
first time. But now that she knew that it had all been
over another woman, all bets were likely off. He could
easily put himself in her shoes and he knew he'd have
a hard time moving past it. Did he really expect her to
laugh it off and say something trite like "these things
happen"?

He was seriously considering throwing himself off a cliff somewhere when she finally said, "You should have told me sooner. I deserved to know what I was guilty of."

This is bad, he thought as he struggled for the words to control the damage that his actions had wrought. "Baby, I'm so sorry. I was confused over the whole thing for so long. Then I began falling in love with you, which was a huge mind-fuck." *Oh hell, why did I say that? I might as well go ahead and insult her one last time and end it before I say something else worse.*

She wanted to blast him; he could see it in her tense expression. He had to give her credit for keeping it together. She turned sideways on the sofa, loosening the hold that he had on her. "I'm honestly not sure what to do here. On the other hand, it means so much to me that you shared your story. Trust me when I say that I know it wasn't easy. I'm also aware of how past traumas can color your perception of others. Am I upset that I remind you of the woman who broke your heart? Absolutely. Crushed is probably more accurate. It also frightens me that you'll continue to struggle with that very thing." When he opened his mouth to protest, she gave him a look that had him closing it once more. "I know you think that you're over it now. And maybe this was the first step. But I believe that we also need to give ourselves some time to make certain that we can move forward without this cloud hanging over us. I tried my best not to let you see it, but you put me through absolute hell with your insults. You had no way of knowing it at the time, but I was bullied by some kids in high school and it did a real number on me. You brought all of that back and

252 · SYDNEY LANDON

I was once again living the nightmare that it took me ages to get past the first time."

"Dear God," Ash choked out as he dropped his head forward. He'd felt like a big enough dick before, but now he was devastated that he'd hurt this beautiful woman whom he'd come to love so much. No one deserved what he'd put her through. He'd been the worst kind of bully, and it made him physically ill to imagine what she must have felt day after day as he chipped away at her insecurities with his cruel taunts. "I have no justification for the things I said to you," he admitted. "I can blame it on Fiona and what she did to me, but I'm a big boy. In the end, I'm responsible for my own actions. The fact that I'd never dealt with what happened is no excuse. I should have talked to someone a long time ago. But, instead, I remained in denial, pretending it didn't matter and that I'd moved on. Then I met you and still couldn't accept that I had a problem. Hell, Dylan was on my ass constantly about it. I'm surprised Zoe is even speaking to me at this point. Everyone could see that I had a problem but me. Even Lisa, Dylan's assistant, attempted to have a conversation with me, but I blew her off. If I had listened to any of them, I'd have been forced to pull my head out of my ass, and I wasn't ready for that. It made me sick when I said those things to you, but then I'd go and do it again. I had no control where you were concerned. It took you coming to my rescue with Brittany that night for me to admit that I'd been so wrong about you."

"I wanted to hate you," she confessed. "I even told Zoe that I did. But I was also attracted to you, which

I hoped you'd never find out about because I was convinced you'd use it against me. That day I brought lunch to your office, I was determined to wage a war against you. I'd had it with the verbal battles because you always won those. So I wanted to throw you off by being nice and it worked. You were visibly rattled. I left there feeling the best I had in months. I'd planned to continue doing something along those lines every day until you cracked. But I ran into you and Brittany at the bar that night and you were so embarrassed at what she was doing. My first inclination was to break out my cell phone and record the whole spectacle like everyone else was doing. I figured I could leak it and have some much-needed revenge. Then it hit me that I would have become the bully that I'd always despised. So I opted for the high road instead and saved you. Then we made the agreement for me to be your pretend girlfriend, and as we started spending time together, I was finally seeing the charming Asher Jackson that you showed to other women. I'd begun to think that man was a myth until that point. I fought against falling in love with you, but you barreled through my defenses and managed to do something that no other man ever had before. Even with the disaster we both made of dinner, this was still the happiest night of my life. I know that you truly love me; it's there in your eyes. But I also see the fear that you're trying to hide. Like me, there's the tiniest bit of uncertainty as to whether you can look at me and only see Dana Anders. Or whether your ex will rear her head from time to time to bring back a past that has haunted you for five years."

"What're you saying?" he asked, not sure he wanted to hear the answer. He couldn't lose her; that wasn't an option. He'd do whatever necessary to prove himself to her.

"Simply that we don't need to rush into any decisions. I'm incapable of rational thought when I'm with you due to my feelings, and you probably are as well. What we need right now is some space. Let's take a few weeks to ourselves and think everything through. Maybe you could talk to one of your brothers and gain some perspective as well. I'd also like to confide in Zoe if that's okay with you?"

"Of course," he muttered numbly. This night had completely derailed. Instead of making love as he'd expected, he may have very well lost her. He wanted to plead his case further, but he could tell by the expression on her face that he needed to stop. Pushing her would get him nowhere. He'd spent a year being the bully she'd accused him of. Now was the time for patience and understanding even if it killed him. So with that in mind, he reluctantly got to his feet and extended a hand to her. "Let me take you home. I'll do whatever you want. Please just know that I love you more than anything in the world and I'm so very sorry for what I put you through. If I could take it all back, I would. But I can only promise that if you give me the chance, I'll never give you another reason to doubt my love for you. I'll spend the rest of my life making it up to you in every way that I can."

She gave him a sad smile that nearly ripped his heart from his chest before linking her fingers through his. That small gesture gave him hope that all wasn't lost. They might not have the answers yet, but if love could build bridges, then surely it could bring her back into his arms for their forever to begin. Until then, he'd never stop trying to show her that when he looked at her, he saw only Dana and not the ghost of the woman who might have cost him everything.

Eighteen

Ash looked questioningly over at Dylan the moment they walked through their mother's door. She'd summoned them both earlier, but had given no indication of the reason behind their visit. It was unusual for her to demand to see them. Ash really didn't feel like being there, but curiosity alone had made the decision for him.

Dylan had already left the office when their mother had called, so Ash had driven himself. Truthfully, that suited him fine since he wasn't in the mood for conversation. He hadn't heard from Dana at all and he'd respected her wishes for time to figure things out. He remembered Dylan going through a similar torture before he and Zoe had worked things out. At the time Ash had encouraged his brother to go to the coffee shop and force Zoe to talk to him. But now that he was in the same position, he found that he was hesitant to take his own advice. What if she told him outright that it was over? In a strange way, there was some comfort in her silence. At least he still had hope that everything would be okay. "Any idea why we're here?" he asked his brother.

Dylan shook his head. "Your guess is as good as mine. At least Rhett got out of coming since he flew out this morning. I think I'll kick his ass the next time I see him."

"I swear, he's so lucky," Ash grumbled. "Naturally our mother would decide to stay in Pensacola even though I've suggested a dozen times that she visit Seth in South Carolina."

"We owe the thanks to Bart and Claudia," Dylan pointed out. "Apparently Claudia and her buddies wanted to attend school near here for their last year. Probably because it's some kind of college where wet T-shirt contests are considered fashion merchandising."

Before Ash could knock, his mother was standing there waiting in the open doorway. She must have been watching for them to arrive. Then he did a double take. Was she wearing jeans? He couldn't remember the last time he'd seen her dressed so casually. "Boys—finally." She smiled in greeting.

"Boys"? What in the hell is going on? he wondered as she pulled each of them into a hug. For her, this was downright affectionate. Maybe she had her own stash of medical marijuana. If Charlotte was willing to share, Ash wanted first dibs. He decided to test the waters by saying something that would normally annoy her. "Hey, Mommy, what's up?" Dylan laughed, then turned the sound into a cough.

She didn't even flinch at his words. *Yep, she's either drunk or stoned. It was bound to happen eventually, living with Bart and Claudia.* "Can't I spend some time with my handsome sons without a reason?"

"You could," Ash agreed, "but you normally wouldn't. So let's get down to the numbers and the details. How much does Bart want this time and what's the brilliant business idea?"

Dylan sighed in resignation. "I hope it's better than the last few schemes. Does he realize that he'd need to leave the golf course and actually work in order to turn a profit? Most things don't run themselves."

Their mother waved them into the living room. Ash flopped down on the sofa and promptly put his feet on the coffee table. He knew it was childish, but getting a rise out of her would make this ass-chapping a little more bearable. But again, she didn't take the bait. She simply took a seat beside of him, then dropped a bomb. "I've asked Bart and Claudia to leave. They moved out this morning. Granted, it wasn't pretty, but your uncle Judd was a big help. I believe I would have been forced to call the police without him. Those two can be so difficult."

"Wait—what?" Dylan sputtered. "You finally kicked them to the curb? Really? And why in the hell didn't you call me to witness that? I don't suppose you taped it. Was there crying?"

Their mother rolled her eyes. "You know how Claudia is. Do you really think she shed actual tears?"

"I was talking about Bart." Dylan smirked. "I'm surprised his little princess didn't throw a punch at you."

"Did you say 'Judd'?" Ash asked in confusion. "As in Uncle Judson?"

His mother began fidgeting and he could have sworn she was blushing. "Yes, that's right. He and I have remained friends over the years and he offered his assistance when I told him what I planned to do." Ash wasn't aware that she'd even stayed in touch with their dad's brother, but she must have if he was there. He certainly hadn't mentioned a visit to Florida when they'd had their weekly conference call just days earlier. Judson and his daughter ran the Oceanix Resort in Bermuda, so they were in communication on a regular basis. Despite that, his uncle never mentioned their mother, so this was a bit of a surprise.

When Dylan began humming the theme from *The Twilight Zone*, Ash struggled to keep from laughing. He decided not to comment on Judson's visit right then. Instead, he asked, "So what brought this on? I thought you were happy with the arrangement you had with Bart. That's what you led us to believe at dinner that night."

Ash was shocked when she laid her head back on the sofa and said softly, "I'm tired of living this way. I did feel that I owed him for his support through the years, but I'm getting older and I'd like to be happy for once in my life. In the long run, I think it will be the best thing for Bart as well. We've never been in love, not even close to that. We filled a mutual need for companionship for a time, but life feels different now. I want to begin a new chapter and I'm hoping I'll have your support."

Here comes the money request. Ash had been waiting for it, so it wasn't unexpected. Truthfully he'd rather give his mother financial assistance than continue throwing money at Bart and his daughter. "How much do you need?" he asked, only half listening at that point.

She gave him a blank look, before realization dawned. "Asher, your father left a trust that provides me with a monthly income." Her mouth tightened as she added, "But Bart will probably go after alimony, so he'll get a chunk of it. That's why I've decided to get a job to cover my own expenses."

"You're going to work?" Dylan exclaimed loudly. "Er—I mean, really? Wouldn't this be a first for you?"

"There was that library gig where she met Dad," Ash supplied helpfully.

"It's true that I've been out of the workforce for many years," she agreed. "And normally that might make things difficult, but Judd has agreed to show me the ropes. He and I have always got along well, so I see no reason why there would be a problem."

"Except that Judson lives in Bermuda, right?" Dylan asked. "What exactly would you be doing?"

"I'll be his assistant," she replied primly. "His current assistant is leaving in a few months on maternity leave and doesn't plan to come back. So I'll have time to train with her. We've already spoken on the phone and she's a perfectly lovely young woman."

"I need a drink," Ash muttered. "Maybe the entire bottle. First of all, congratulations on finally making the break with Bart and his evil spawn. That was a long time coming for sure. We'll have our lawyers hammer out a financial agreement so that he doesn't take you to the cleaners. I'd also recommend some kind of restraining order so that Claudia doesn't mug you in a parking lot somewhere. As for this whatever the hell it is with our uncle, I'm not sure what to say to that. I had no idea you were bosom buddies, so this will take some getting used to. I'm not sure it's the best idea, but leaving Pensacola until the dust settles might be your smartest bet at the moment."

Dylan cleared his throat as he shifted around in his chair. "I'm just going to go ahead and ask, is there something going on with you and Judson? You blushed like a schoolgirl when his name came up."

Ash had his answer when she artfully evaded his brother's question. "Judd and I aren't related. If there was anything romantic there, it would be socially acceptable."

"Um, yeah." Ash rolled his eyes. "I've never much cared about what society thought. I'm speaking more of the family dynamic here. We all work together and have always been close to him. It's rather strange that he wouldn't have mentioned this to us. Heck, your name never entered any of our conversations. I wasn't sure he knew you were still alive, much less anything else."

"Due to my situation as a married woman, I felt that it was best that our association be kept confidential and he reluctantly agreed. He wasn't happy about it though because you boys are like sons to him."

Dylan grimaced. "Now might not be the best time for that analogy. So I assume that none of our brothers have heard this bit of news?"

"No, you two are the first people I've told," she agreed. "I'll call the rest of them tomorrow. I'll be moving in a few weeks, so it's going to be hectic for a while. Judd is having my things shipped and the house will need to be put on the market. I had thought to let Bart remain here, but it's absurd for him to have such an expensive place. It's time that all of us learned to live within our means."

Who is this woman and where did our mother go? This was the most rational conversation they'd ever had with her. Well, except for the mention of the secret affair that she may have been carrying on with Uncle Judson. Strangely enough, Ash felt the urge to give her a fist bump over that. It was rather comforting to discover that she hadn't been happy all these years with Bart.

Ash and Dylan stayed for a while longer as they went over the details of what was to come. When they were leaving, Ash took a deep breath and put a hand on Dylan's arm. "Do you have time to grab a beer? I'd like to talk to you about something, and if I don't do it now, I probably never will." Dylan looked wary, but immediately agreed. Telling yet another person about Fiona was the last thing in the world he wanted to do, but to win Dana back, he needed to continue the process of healing and moving on from that painful period in his past.

He only hoped Dana would be there in the end to see that he'd taken her advice and was ready to make a life with her, free from the past.

⤫

"Dylan's going to get a drink with Ash before he comes home. They probably both need it after answering that summons from Charlotte. I can't wait to hear what it was all about." Zoe shook her head ruefully. "Do you want to go have dinner somewhere? I'm starving."

Dana's first inclination was to turn the invitation down and go home to throw another epic pity party, but that wasn't healthy. She needed her friend's advice and this seemed like a perfect opportunity. The shop had been unusually busy for the last few weeks with several conventions being held at the hotel. There'd been no time or privacy for anything other than casual chitchat and truthfully Dana had been too depressed to attempt it. So she forced a smile and said brightly, "That sounds great. How about the Mexican place next door? I could use a margarita. We can always call a taxi if we need to."

"I was thinking exactly the same thing." Zoe grinned at her and they quickly finished cleaning up, then locked the shop before walking the short distance to the popular oceanfront restaurant.

Within a few moments they were snacking on chips and salsa and enjoying a delicious, frosty drink that was going straight to Dana's head. "This is exactly what I needed," she sighed. After taking another sip, she added, "This has been the week from hell."

Zoe eyed her carefully. "You've been avoiding talking about Ash since your dinner that night. I could tell that you were upset and I didn't want to pry. Are you ready to talk about it now? Did it not go as you thought? I was so sure he was going to say he loved you."

"Oh, he did," Dana said glumly. "We both made a total disaster of it, but the end result was that we feel the same about each other. I had exactly a car ride home to bask in the moment, before he told me all about Fiona. I shouldn't have forced the issue. If I hadn't, then I might be happy instead of freaked out over being her clone."

"Say what?" Zoe asked with her glass suspended

halfway to her mouth. She set it back on the table before adding, "Could you maybe word that a little differently? I think I missed something along the way."

Dana started at the beginning of the story, telling her friend about Ash's romance with the other woman and how she'd tried to trap him into marriage by pretending the baby she was carrying was Ash's. "So that's what sent him into the downward spiral that his brothers know about, but they're not aware of the exact cause. They think it's only a failed relationship."

"And you're upset that he was in love with her?" Zoe asked carefully. "It was a long time ago, right?"

"It's not that," Dana muttered. "Although no woman likes to think of her man with someone else. The real issue is—I guessed and he confirmed—that the reason he was so ugly to me last year is that when we first met, I reminded him of Fiona."

Zoe stared at her in shock. "You look like his ex?"

Dana shrugged. "Apparently there's some resemblance and our personalities are similar. He confessed that when we met, he was freaked out by it. Then every time he was around me, it made him angry because it brought all those memories back. He claims that he has realized it was that he was attracted to me, and as he developed stronger feelings, it was the fear more than any resemblance between us that had him acting like such an ass."

"Holy shit," Zoe groaned. "Why am I not surprised? Nothing has been easy for you two, has it? So what happened afterwards? Obviously you're not happy, and according to Dylan, Ash hasn't been acting like a man in bliss either."

"I told him that we needed to take a few weeks and

think things over. I wanted him to talk to his brothers about everything that had happened with Fiona and I asked if I could tell you. I need to make sure that he's able to move forward free of any associations between the two of us. I can't go through that. I'm in love with him and it already hurts like hell to be separated. I can't let myself get in even further, only for him to discover that when he looks at me, he still sees her."

"Oh, honey," Zoe whispered. "No wonder you've been out of sorts. I understand where you're coming from, but I also know that he's crazy about you. How long has it been since your last relationship, other than Paul?"

Dana put her arms on the table and decided it wasn't only Ash who needed to come clean about his past. He was having a drink with Dylan tonight, hopefully doing as she suggested. Now maybe it was time to take her own advice. "Well, you see, I've never been seriously involved with anyone before. And here's the reason why . . ."

Nineteen

Dana opened the door to her apartment several hours later and felt pounds lighter, even after a ton of chips and a heavy meal. She'd left her emotional burden behind her for the first time in fifteen years and it felt amazing. She'd lived her entire adult life carrying around her past baggage and even she hadn't realized how it had defined her. When the doorbell rang, she smiled, hoping it was Ash. Maybe he'd had the same kind of epiphany after talking to Dylan. Without checking the peephole, she threw the door open and blinked in surprise. Claudia stood there with a sullen expression on her face. "Um, hey," Dana said uncertainly. "What are you doing here?"

Claudia shoved past her, which left Dana with no choice but to shut the door and follow her into the hallway. "Oh, don't pretend you haven't heard. I'm sure your asshole of a boyfriend has been laughing all evening after his mother tossed me and my dad out on our ear."

Shit! I guess I know why Charlotte called her sons over tonight. She decided to reply honestly. "I really haven't spoken to Ash in a few days, so I had no idea. I'm sorry that happened, Claudia. Maybe there was some kind of misunderstanding." That last part was doubtful, but she thought it sounded nice to add.

"Oh, give me a fucking break," Claudia snarled. "None of them give a damn about what happens to us. We've been the outcasts of the mighty Jackson family since the beginning. You're deluded if you think you're any different. Even if by some miracle you get Ash to marry you, all you'll have is his last name. You'll be a second-class citizen to them."

Dana had opened her mouth to give the insulting bitch the verbal slap she deserved, when she saw it. At first she thought it was a trick of the lighting, but no, it was so clear in her expression now. The younger woman's anger was a front for her deeper issues. She was hurting . . . badly. Dana sighed, not really feeling up to this kind of scene, but she realized that Claudia likely had no one else and never had. Bart might dote on his daughter, but he'd obviously missed a few important things along the way. "Why don't we talk?" Dana suggested gently as she gestured toward the sofa.

"I have nothing to say," Claudia huffed, crossing her hands defensively over her chest.

"Sit down now, Claudia," Dana said firmly. A command seemed to be all that she understood or responded to.

Dana followed her and took a seat as well. She decided to wait it out, wanting Claudia to start the conversation. After a few minutes she said, "They never cared about me. I was always some kind of joke to them. Dumb Claudia who can't even make it through high school without her daddy paying off the principal, much less college. And Dad just made it worse by constantly bragging about how smart I was, even though he knew it wasn't true. I wanted to quit, but he wouldn't hear of it. Yet he refused to listen to my teacher in elementary school when she told him I was dyslexic. To him that was like admitting to some horrible disease. Instead of getting me the help I needed, he shelled out Charlotte's money every time it was necessary."

"Oh, sweetie," Dana murmured softly. The pieces were clicking into place, and even though it wasn't an excuse for Claudia's behavior, she could understand what had driven her to act out so often. Hadn't Dana acted similarly in school when faced with bullying and ridicule? Going on the attack was easier than waiting for someone to knock you down first. *Oh God, was that what I did with Ash when faced with the prospect of losing him? Did I push him away because I was scared or I wanted to get in the first blow?*

Before she could examine the motivation behind her actions any further, Claudia huffed out defiantly, "Don't you dare feel sorry for me. I'm no one's victim. I can take care of myself. I allow my dad to treat me like a baby because that's what he needs. It's all for show though. The minute we're out of sight, he pushes me away. He says it's the roles we were both given to play, and I have to do my part unless I want him to starve to death."

Dana shook her head in disgust. Bart had done quite a number on his daughter. The man was nothing more than a con artist. Thank God his wife had apparently reached her limit. "Listen, Claudia, you can stay with me for the night. We'll figure something out."

Claudia turned her head away but not before Dana saw the tears she was trying to blink away. When she'd gotten herself under control, she said hoarsely, "I want to get out of here. I have a friend in Miami who's offered to get me a job where she works. I just need some money to get by for a few weeks until I get my first check." She looked down, studying her hands before adding, "I asked my dad, but he told me that I was on my own unless he got a big settlement from Charlotte. He said I couldn't expect him to change his style of living because I couldn't support myself."

Father of the year right there, folks. And I thought I had a terrible role model for a father. Dana didn't have a lot of extra money, but she hadn't spent what Ash had paid her for the pretend girlfriend gig. She'd been planning to give it back to him since it felt wrong to keep it. But now it was clear to her that Claudia needed it the most, and she thought that Ash would agree when she explained everything to him. So she got up and picked up her purse. She wrote a check to Claudia for two thousand dollars, which was everything that she'd received, and handed it over without hesitation. "This is all that I can afford. I hope it helps. If you get there and run into trouble, please call me and I'll figure out a way to help." Claudia's mouth dropped as she looked at the amount. "I know it's probably not much to you," Dana began, "but—"

The younger woman launched herself into Dana's arms, nearly stealing the breath from her body. "Thank you, Dana. I've been perfectly horrible to you, yet you're the only one who's willing to help me. I'm so sorry for everything. The coffee, my attitude, all of it."

"Shhh, it's forgiven." She patted the younger woman's heaving shoulders. "I want you to promise to call me when you get there so I'll know that you're safe, all right?"

Claudia nodded. "I will. And good luck with Ash. All that I said earlier was a load of crap. We deserved how they treated us. My dad made sure of that. You're the only woman he ever brought home or looked at the way he does with you. Just take it from someone who knows—if there's a chance to be happy, grab it. I wish I had years ago instead of letting my dad fill my head with a bunch of bullshit."

Dana walked out with her, hugging her once again, then standing in the parking lot until her taillights were out of sight. Strangely enough, Claudia thought that Dana had saved her tonight, but in reality, she may have very well saved Dana because she'd given her the strength and clarity that she needed to break free of her own daddy issues. And the only way to begin that process was to tell Ash exactly why he was the first and only man she'd ever allowed herself to love. Then she hoped they could start over and learn to trust again as two imperfect people who were perfect for each other.

✎

Ash wasn't proud of the fact that he was lying in bed watching bad reality television when he heard a door shut in the distance. He froze before glancing at the bedside clock. It was almost midnight. That was late even for the odd hours that Rosa kept. Which left only his brothers . . . or Dana. No one else had a key, and security on the property was too tight for any kind of mix-up to happen. So he waited to see who would appear. If it was Rhett, he might actually cry in disappointment, which would give the twerp years of material to taunt him with. He saw a shadow seconds before someone's presence filled the doorway. His heart skidded to a stop, then galloped. "Hey, baby," he murmured softly. He held open the sheet he was lying under, silently inviting her to join him. *Please.* She hesitated only a few seconds, but it felt like an hour. Then she was kicking her shoes off and sliding in next to him. Her scent filled the air and he inhaled it greedily as he pulled her close.

"I was fifteen when my dad left me and my mom. They were never really happy, so it wasn't a surprise. She was constantly raging about his girlfriends or his drinking. And how she had to work two jobs to support us. When he took off, she became so bitter. Night after night she'd come home and spend hours telling me how he'd ruined her life and that men could never be trusted. I was overweight, which she thought was a good thing. She said I'd never have to worry about a man messing with me because they didn't like fat girls."

"Oh, baby," Ash sighed. "How that must have hurt. I know you were as beautiful then as you are now regardless of what your mother thought of your size."

She snuggled closer and continued, "Then in high school I was the target of these mean girls. They taunted me mercilessly for months about my weight and the fact that I didn't have nice clothes. Everything that I owned was old and too tight, which they pointed out constantly. They'd say things like why didn't I sew some sheets together to make a shirt that fit. It was horrible. I hid in the bathroom through half of my classes, trying to avoid them, but they always found me. Finally I couldn't take it anymore and my mom was more than happy to let me drop out and go to work. So for the next few years I waited tables in a restaurant. The owner gave me a lot of extra hours and staying on my feet so much slowly helped me lose some of the excess weight. However, instead of being happier about me getting healthy, my mom seemed to hate me for it. We fought constantly. And eventually I couldn't take it anymore. So I took my last check and left. I moved around a lot, but never formed attachments to people or places. I believed what she said about people always letting you down. I was determined that I wouldn't end up like her. When I moved here and went to work at the coffee shop, Zoe was the first real friend that I'd had since I was a child. And it took me a long time to trust her. I kept waiting for her to do something to show me that she was like the rest. But she did the exact opposite. She believed in me, which made me feel like I mattered. I'd never had that before from anyone."

"And I took that security away from you when I began attacking you without any justification. You had one place where you'd found what you needed and I ruined it. Baby, you must have hated me for it. You wanted to run, didn't you?"

He felt her nod where she lay next to him, and it crushed him. In an attempt to save himself from his demons, he'd unleashed hers. "What stopped you?"

She was quiet for a minute before she admitted in

a surprised tone, "My family. Zoe, the girls at the shop, and even Dylan are the only consistent presences I've ever had. I might not have known it at the time, but I had been in a relationship from the moment I let Zoe in. No matter how I felt about you, I couldn't start over again. It would kill me to lose them."

"Baby, you don't ever have to do that. If you aren't able to forgive me, then I'll move to another location. This is your home and I'd never take that away from you. I love you enough to let you go if that's what you need from me. I'll pack up tomorrow and be out of here. The choice is yours."

It was the most selfless thing he'd ever offered to do, and he meant every word. As hard as it would be, she needed the stability of the friendships that she'd formed. He'd never be able to live with himself if he ruined that for her. She turned until they were lying face-to-face. He could hardly dare to believe his ears when she said, "Then I choose you. They're my family, but you're my future. My life truly began the day that we met. It might not have been an easy road, but how can I regret it when it led me to you? As crazy as it sounds, maybe we needed to experience that in order to be free of what had haunted us for so long. I don't think I'd have been open to a relationship with you otherwise. I'd been too traumatized by my past to accept anything that resembled a normal relationship. Your taunts forced me to look inside myself and it did the same for you. We might not have a fairy-tale kind of romance, but we have love that will go the distance because it's raw and honest."

"I love you so much, Dana," he professed to her. "You opened my eyes and showed me that I had only

274 · SYDNEY LANDON

been going through the motions of living until I met you. Now I'm more alive than I've ever felt before. There's a hope inside of me that I didn't dare dream existed. Finally I have a woman who truly loves me for who I am, flaws and all. You are the most beautiful and amazing gift I've ever received and I'm never letting you go."

She wrapped her arms tightly around his waist and kissed his lips before saying, "You'd better not, Jackson, or I'll have Brittany hunt you down. Trust me, you don't want that." He laughed as he returned her embrace.

That night they made love truly for the first time, and as they fell asleep in each other's arms, Asher said a silent prayer of thanks to his horrible ex. For if she hadn't done what she had, then he'd have missed out on finding the one woman who was meant for him. After all, how many women would rescue a guy from a bar while another girl was licking his armpit? He looked down at Dana, smiling softly. Yeah, she was truly one of a kind.

Epilogue

The wedding was the talk of Pensacola, Florida. Dana didn't think there had been a single day in recent memory when one of the coffee shop customers wasn't asking her for all the details. Finally, the big day had arrived, and as she stood in the church holding Ash's hand, she had to agree that it was indeed worth the wait.

They might have been surrounded by their friends and family, but Judson and Charlotte only had eyes for each other as they took their vows. No one else had been privy to the information, but these two had been in love for many years. Only now were they finally free at the same time to be together.

"She looks so happy," Claudia whispered from Dana's other side. "She barely even smiled when she was with my father. Not that I'm surprised."

Dana squeezed the younger woman's hand before laying her head on Ash's shoulder. These last six months had been the most amazing of her life. She had moved in with Ash the day after she'd gone to see him that night, and neither of them had ever looked back.

She was completely secure in her love for him and knew that he was in hers. Instead of being bogged down by their emotional baggage, they'd been set free. And true to her word, Claudia had contacted her from Miami and they had stayed in touch. She was a different person away from Bart's influence, and Dana had come to consider her the little sister that she'd never had. Oh, the attitude was still there from time to time, but so was a shared affection. She was very much a part of this family that Dana had built for herself. "I love you," Dana murmured in Ash's ear, smiling as he turned his head to kiss her forehead.

"I love you too, baby. I can't wait 'til the day that you finally decide to marry me and I get to see you standing up there."

She smirked up at him. "We're not church wedding kind of people. Meet me on the beach one evening at sunset. I'll be the one wearing a dress . . . well, unless I opt for shorts. Depends on the mood."

Zoe peeked over her shoulder from the pew in front of them. "That sounds like a yes to me, Ash. You've got a witness, so make this happen. But if we don't stop talking, Charlotte is going to kill us."

Dana grinned as she always did when she was surrounded by the people who meant everything to her. She looked around the church as the ceremony came to an end, and she noticed something that took her by surprise. Claudia was positively riveted by something or someone in the next row. Rhett? *He does live in Miami. No . . . surely not.*

"What has your attention?" Ash asked in amusement. "I've been calling your name, but you were zoned out. I hope you were at least thinking of your future husband."

"Always," Dana purred. She pondered mentioning her suspicions, but then decided that they could wait. After all, she had plans to make an honest man out of Asher Jackson. But for now . . . she'd let him make a naughty future wife out of her.

Acknowledgments

As always, to my editor at Penguin, Kerry Donovan, and my agent, Jane Dystel. These two ladies work tirelessly behind the scenes to make each new book possible.

Don't miss

KEEPING IT HOT

Available now in the Breakfast in Bed series
by Sydney Landon.
Continue reading for a preview.

One

Zoe Hart walked through the familiar lobby of the Oceanix Resort in Pensacola, Florida, but she saw none of its usual elegance and grandeur. She'd woken in a bad mood that morning, which was unusual since she normally loved her birthday. She was twenty-nine today, and despite her best attempts, she was no closer to seducing Dylan Jackson, her best friend and landlord, than she had been last year.

She owned and operated the coffee shop in the Oceanix, Zoe's Place. Even though she worked her ass off to make it a success, she was also grateful to Dylan for giving her a chance when she was trying to get her business off the ground. All the big coffee chains had vied to open a location in the ultra-high-end resort, but Dylan had believed in her business plan and had celebrated her success every step of the way.

Her close friend and shop manager, Dana Anders, was busy loading the pastry display cases for another busy breakfast rush when Zoe arrived. The comforting smell of freshly brewed coffee filled the air, and her stomach growled in response. For the first time that morning, she took a moment to appreciate her surroundings. She'd designed the interior layout with comfort in mind but had also wanted a place that appealed to a variety of customers. There were tables for her business customers who wanted to work while they drank their espressos, there were sofas for those who were truly enjoying their vacations and wanted to relax while they sipped frappes, and there were overstuffed chairs arranged in cozy seating areas for the groups who were recharging with a latte after a long day at the office or relishing a morning away from the kids. Of course, with their location inside the hotel, they had many customers who visited once and never returned, but she was particularly proud of the loyal local customers who had become like her friends and family.

"Well, well," Dana murmured as she noticed Zoe's dejected expression. "The birthday girl doesn't seem to be in the mood to celebrate this morning." Her friend patted the counter and sat down on a stool behind it. "Park it right there and tell me all about it."

Zoe shook her head in disgust. "I'm twenty-nine, still carrying around my big V-card, and I've been friend-zoned by the man I've secretly lusted after for years. So yeah, not exactly in the mood to celebrate another year of my love life going nowhere."

"Finally! I can't believe you're admitting this. I've been waiting forever for you to ask me for help. Whenever I brought it up, you always acted like you had no idea what I was talking about. Oh, and by the way, friend-zoned would be easier to deal with. Some friends have sex together all the time. You've been sister-zoned, and that's the kiss of death if you're hoping for a fling."

Zoe planted her hands on the counter and shook her head vehemently. "I haven't been sister-zoned. I'm still completely and totally in the friend area. Dylan and I are buddies. We talk about all kinds of things you wouldn't discuss with your sibling."

Dana clucked her tongue before taking a big drink of the coffee she had sitting nearby. Finally, as if she were talking to a toddler, she said, "Sweetie, when he hangs out with you, does he take calls and texts from other women?"

"Of course." Zoe ground her teeth, thinking of how much she hated overhearing him employing his sexy laugh on some bimbo of the month.

Putting a hand under her chin, Dana studied her for a moment before asking, "Does he ever tell you anything about his dates? As in bedroom stuff or kink level?"

"Yes, all the time," Zoe growled. "I guess that proves that he doesn't see me as his sister, though, right?"

"It's worse than I thought," Dana said dramatically. "You're officially one of the guys. You've ceased to have a vagina where he's concerned."

"*What?* No way!" Zoe sputtered. Pointing to her ample chest, she argued, "How could he miss these babies?"

Refusing to back down, Dana fired off, "Does he ever bump you on the shoulder with his fist? Or high-five you?"

Zoe's mouth went dry and she stared at Dana in growing horror before dropping her head onto the counter. "Oh God, I'm just like one of his guy friends," Zoe mumbled in despair. "You're absolutely right. I might as well have a penis."

Dana patted the top of her head consolingly. "I don't know about the whole having-a-dick thing. I'd say you're more gender neutral where he's concerned."

"Wow, that's so much better," she snapped. Dana was silent for so long, Zoe finally lifted her head, thinking maybe they'd had a customer wander in before the shop officially opened. Instead, her friend was giving her a calculating look that immediately made her nervous. "What?" she asked warily, not even sure she wanted to know what was running through the other woman's mind. She and Dana were about as opposite as two people could be, but regardless of that, their friendship worked. Dana loved men in all shapes and sizes and seemed to be dating a new guy every week. She was adventurous, outgoing, and the customers absolutely adored her. She stood just over five feet tall with short blond hair and a personality that made everyone feel special. A few years back, not long after Zoe had hired her, Dana had convinced her to come out for a drink. Zoe had ended up having several past her limit and had drunkenly admitted to Dana that she'd had a crush on Dylan for years. She'd also confessed to being a virgin, something that had blown the other woman away. After that, Dana had tried her best to set Zoe up on blind dates, but none of them compared to the infatuation she carried where Dylan was concerned. The heart wanted what it wanted—and Zoe's appeared to be particularly stubborn.

Dana folded her arms and leaned forward. "You can come back from this. As long as you haven't entered the death zone where he looks at you like his little sister, there's always hope. We can turn this around . . . *if* you'll really apply yourself. Starting with that." Dana pointed to Zoe's white polo shirt as she spoke.

Zoe frowned, looking down in confusion. "What's wrong with my clothes?"

"Sweetie, if you want Dylan to stop seeing you as a member of his dude squad, then you can't continue to dress like one of the guys." When Zoe opened her mouth to protest, Dana held her hand up. "What are they wearing when they come in here for coffee before hitting the golf course?"

"I've never noticed—" Zoe began before Dana interrupted her.

"Cut the crap," Dana huffed. "You know they dress just like that. Polo shirts and khaki shorts. Dylan sees you as one of the guys because you blend in so well with them. It's time for that to stop. You have so much going for you. Big tits, small waist, and plenty of butt. You need to dress to showcase your assets." As Zoe gulped, Dana pointed to her hair. "And that spinster ponytail has got to go. Your hair is gorgeous, but I've only seen you wear it down a few times and that was when I hid those freaking bands that you seem to have a million of. Men go crazy over long, wavy hair, which you naturally possess. You don't need a lot of makeup because you look great without it. Let's just start with the things that I've mentioned and I guarantee that Dylan will be tripping over his tongue in no time. Let me give you a makeover for your birthday. Whether you realize it or not, it'll help you with your self-confidence. And that is something that will benefit you in every aspect of your life. Getting the guy is just an added bonus."

"I don't know . . ." Zoe murmured. "Clothes really

don't change anything. I'm still the same person that he's known for years. I could probably parade around naked in front of him and it wouldn't make a difference. It seems silly to pretend to be someone I'm not."

Dana walked around the counter and put an arm around her. "Honey, men are visual creatures. You and Dylan have been friends since you were children. He's grown up thinking of you in a certain way. We're just attempting to show him that there is another side he's never seen before. He's overlooking the fact that you're a beautiful woman who is flipping perfect for him. Right or wrong, sometimes a new set of curtains makes the room look completely different."

A giggle burst from her lips and Zoe grinned at Dana. "Are you comparing me to draperies now?"

"Hey, I'm just trying to give you something to work with. Now go ahead and tell me you're on board. No, let's go one better than that." Dana pulled far enough away to extend a hand to her. "Zoe. Do you agree to do whatever it takes to finally land the man of your dreams this year? Are you prepared to surrender that V-card to Dylan before your thirtieth birthday? If so, let's shake on it. No wimping out, though. We're declaring war on the friend zone with Dylan. Are you ready to trade in your polos for plunging necklines and rising hemlines? Once you agree, there's no going back."

As Dana wiggled her hand impatiently, Zoe thought back over the revelations her friend had just placed at her feet. Could it really be that simple? Had Dylan overlooked the fact that she was a potential romantic partner because she'd never made the effort to show off her femininity? And truthfully, she knew that she dressed for comfort most days. Her mother, who'd been the executive chef at the Oceanix for years, rarely wore makeup or fancy outfits, so Zoe hadn't grown up wearing dresses or bows in her hair. She'd been a tomboy and possibly she'd never stopped seeing herself that way.

But now she was almost thirty and she couldn't keep pining away for a man who didn't want her. She would let Dana help her and spend this next year giving it everything she had. If at the end she and Dylan were still only friends, then she'd have to accept that and move on with her life. As much as she cared for him, she wanted a husband and children of her own at some point in the future.

So, straightening her spine, Zoe took Dana's hand and gave it an enthusiastic shake. "Let's do this," she said bravely. *Please let Dylan be the one*, she thought to herself as she listened to Dana's plans for their first steps. The next twelve months might not go as Zoe wanted, but they certainly wouldn't be boring.

Two

It had been a hell of a long week and Dylan Jackson was looking forward to kicking back and relaxing. He usually had dinner with Zoe at least one evening a week, but thanks to a business trip to one of the other Oceanix Resorts, it had been closer to two weeks since he'd seen her last and he missed her. He'd even missed her birthday, which he tried never to do. He'd texted her earlier and she'd suggested they meet in one of the resort restaurants since neither of them had felt like cooking. Dylan lived in the penthouse, so it was a simple matter for him to take the elevator back downstairs at seven. He'd figured Zoe was working late at the coffee shop as she usually did, but when she responded to his text, she'd already been at her condo a short distance from the hotel.

He walked into the restaurant and automatically headed for his usual reserved table in the corner. It was private and had an amazing view of the Gulf. He'd been so busy looking around that he was abruptly brought up short when he realized that his table was occupied. A woman with long, dark hair cascading down her back sat in one of the chairs sipping a glass of wine. Dylan stifled a surge of irritation. Even though the woman looked stunning from behind, now he'd have to deal with the aggravation of finding somewhere else to sit himself, which would be no small feat, as the restaurant was packed.

As he stood uncertainly pondering his options, the woman turned, seemingly sensing him behind her, and he froze. He blinked a few times, thinking he was imagining things. Then she smiled and it hit him with the force of a sledgehammer. "What are you waiting for, an engraved invitation?" She laughed as she motioned him closer.

Dear God, what is going on here? The woman with the short, clingy dress, amazing legs, and plump breasts sounded like his best friend. If he looked closely, her features were the same. But everything else was wrong—very wrong. Zoe wore her hair in a ponytail and dressed in sensible clothing. Half the time she had a coffee stain on her white polo. She didn't make his mouth go dry—or his cock go hard. She was his buddy, the one constant in his life that never changed.

"Did someone die?" he finally asked, thinking maybe she'd been to a funeral or something. Why else would she be wearing a dress?

She wrinkled her nose, as she was prone to do when she was thinking, before shaking her head. "Er . . . no." Giving him a look of concern, she reached out and put a hand on his arm. "Are you all right? You look pale. Would you rather we just go upstairs to your place and order in? I'm fine with that if you're tired."

"*No!*" he protested loudly, causing people at nearby tables to look over at him. Great, he was making an ass out of himself. But there was no way he was going somewhere more private with Zoe looking like . . . that. He needed to get to the bottom of this, preferably in public with lots of people around. So he took a breath and made an effort to collect himself. He stepped forward and took his seat. He was saved from making conversation while they placed their orders, but after the waiter had gone, an unusually awkward silence settled between them.

This type of thing never happened with them, and he found he wasn't sure how to handle it. Should he go ahead and ask her why she looked the way she did? Or ignore it and hope it never happened again?

She moved closer to him, putting her new and improved breasts only inches from his hand. "You seem a little stressed out," she said softly. "Are you sure you're okay?"

To his utter horror, he heard himself blurting out, "What's happened to you?" He pointed to her outfit, and then quickly gulped down a mouthful of his water. Maybe he was getting sick. His throat was so parched.

"What are you talking about?" she asked, looking at him as if he'd lost his mind. Hell, he was beginning to think she was right. He needed to check into his family's health history a little closer.

He knew he sounded nuts, but he couldn't stop himself from saying, "The dress, and the hair. You're even wearing high heels. You know those make your feet hurt."

"Oh, I've got a date later." Zoe shrugged. She gave him a bright smile, and then began filling him in on what he'd missed at the resort while he was away. She appeared to have no clue that he wasn't an active participant in the conversation. Making small talk seemed impossible for him right now; because all he wanted to do was demand to know who she was going out with. He had figured they'd watch a movie after dinner, as they normally did, but apparently that wasn't going to happen. Dylan had never been one for change, and this transformation was almost more than he could wrap his head around. He knew Zoe, though. This was just a one-time thing. She'd go back to looking the way she usually did tomorrow and then his world would be back in balance once again. Otherwise, he was going to have to face the fact that somewhere along the way his best friend had turned into a very desirable woman. And that, he was afraid, could only spell disaster for the relationship that he'd always valued above all others in his life.

Sydney Landon is the *New York Times* and *USA Today* bestselling author of the Danvers series and the Breakfast in Bed series. When she isn't writing, Sydney enjoys reading, swimming, and being a minivan-driving soccer mom. She lives in Greenville, South Carolina, with her family.

CONNECT ONLINE

sydneylandon.com
facebook.com/sydney.landonauthor
twitter.com/sydneylandon1

Ready to find
your next great read?

Let us help.

Visit prh.com/nextread

Penguin
Random
House